THIS BOOK IS DEDICATED TO

BOB BURNS

J.MICHAEL RODDY'S
HAUNTER'S TALE

TABLE OF CONTENTS

FOREWORD

BY TOM SAVINI

Okay, what the hell do I know about haunted attractions? Well, I've built or supervised them all over the east coast of this country. Sometimes they just pay to use my name. Some were lovely, some were scary, but one attraction in particular…Tom Savini's TerrorMania …was the best one I've ever seen.

There is a science to scaring people. Anyone can jump up and yell boo with a mask on, and that scare lasts about two seconds …maybe. And that's what I see in big haunted attractions everywhere. It's just people jumping up and screaming at you. The best scares come from suspense. Show a monster or a psycho or a tentacle creature right off the bat and have it disappear into the house and now the scare has begun. We don 't know when that thing is going to come out and get us.

When someone enters a haunted attraction, they are looking for what they think is going to startle them because they don't want to be scared. Well, we know this... so they might enter what seemed like a padded cell with a body in a bed. We made the body move with a motor in the ceiling and invisible black fishline. When you came in you were like '*Oh yeah, that body is going to do something*.' So you moved away from the bed to the outer part of the room…AND THEN THE WALL GRABBED YOU! Well, you know…someone behind the wall grabbed you, but we misdirected you into their grasp. See? It doesn't have to someone jumping up and screaming at you.

But you have to be careful. You cannot scare a group, and usually, they come through the house in a group of say eight from the front. They won't budge from where they are if you do. You want to keep the group moving, so you scare them just behind the middle. That propels them forward. And you shouldn't have an exhibit that is like a three-act play where the group has to stand there and watch it unfold. It should continuously be happening.

At TerrorMania, we made up a ghost story and gave the group a ten-foot length of rope. We said we couldn't guarantee their safety if they didn't hang onto the rope. This kept them together because sometimes they like to wander on their own, and it ensured their feet would step on the pad that activated the animatronics.

A haunted attraction should also be slightly annoying, and psychologically disturbing. It should bug you… literally. One I remember vividly had me traversing a long dark hallway. Along the walls were the projected images of black bugs. Combined with the sound of crawling, and scraping, were styrofoam peanuts spread all over the floor, so you felt like you were stepping on insects. Hung fishline from the ceiling, completed the illusion, so there was always something touching your face, and it made you feel like you were walking through spider webs. It doesn't always have to be people jumping up and yelling "Boo!" I'll keep repeating that.

We had people walk down a long, dark hallway into a room painted with tiny red, green, and blue dots. Under black light, these dots seemed to fly off the walls in 3-D. Many found this disturbing. They were not ready for the agile guy wearing a black head-to-toe leotard, also painted with the same glowing dots, when he slid out of a corner or crawled along one of the walls. Loud screams from the psychologically disturbed patrons. See? It doesn't have to be someone jumping up and yelling "Boo!" I'll say it over and over again.

We had twenty-seven rooms at TerrorMania. Film companies would come there to shoot because we had a swamp, a cemetery, a subway, caves, and a funeral parlor. We also had "The Spider Room," which a lot of people never made it past. Use your imagination. We had a lot of pants pissers, mostly pregnant women.

One grand illusion I remember from Morris Costumes' Haunted Attraction in Charlotte, North Carolina was entering an elegant Victorian set beautifully decorated with antique furniture and a massive mirror over an ornate fireplace. You walked into this room wondering what was going to happen. Was someone going to jump up and yell "Boo?" No, but what did happen is a ragged, chiffon-blowing-in-the-wind, white-costumed hideous ghost catapulted at you right THROUGH THE MIRROR! It was merely a beautifully framed hole in the wall above the fireplace, and everything on the other side matched the room you were in. You know…what a mirror would do. It was disconcerting and genuinely scared me.

Another one that stands out in my memory is one that J. Michael Roddy had a hand in creating at Universal for their annual Halloween Horror Nights when he worked there. It was traversing a massive hole in the floor many, I mean *many*, stories down below your feet. It gave me weak knees, and it was merely an enormous mirror on the floor reflecting the many levels above it. And then there was the floor of glass you walked over that was many stories below your feet. Again, shaky queasy knees.

We love this stuff. We pay people to scare us. Like a service we seek. We do it at amusement parks, haunted attractions, and at the movie theatres where, yes again, we pay to be scared. We love to be scared, and we will go back as long as there are artists and thinkers out there willing to do it to us.

Pleasant dreams,

Me at TerrorMania

WHAT IS A HAUNTER?

BY J. MICHAEL RODDY

What is a Haunter? The term has come to prevalence in the last few years. When I was designing haunted experiences, we called them haunted houses. Then the terminology transitioned into haunted mazes with the idea that you could potentially get lost within the darkened spaces. The maze was quite the misnomer, though, as it always seemed to be a contradiction to the operations that wanted the maximum throughput, hence why in many cases you have guides with flashlights showing you the way. But, like all things, once awareness of a trend sets in and it becomes part of a culture, we name it. Like Trekkies and Deadheads - the designers/operators of a haunt are called Haunters.

The industry has certainly grown in the twenty-five years that I have been involved, and the benefit is that creativity allows for some genuinely terrifying experiences.

My first experience with a haunted house was when I was a child of probably six. I loved horror and was excited to visit a scary house… until I actually got in line. The more I looked at the structure which in my nostalgic recollection looked exactly like *The Old Dark House*, the more anxious I became. The screams coming from inside seemed to echo in the night. I chickened out. Years later I was part of a haunted woods scenario with future director Erik Hollander. He spent a full month building real structures along a wooded path. His attention to detail and story were only surpassed by his dedication.

Then when I moved to Orlando, I met David Clevinger who brought me on board for Terror on Church Street. This was my first real experience with the business of haunted houses. What a phenomenal experience. I owe a lot to that old haunted Woolworth building on Church Street (yes, it was really haunted). I was able to see how David combined quality theatrics with genuine scares and even given the opportunity to create some of my own.

Then I was cast as Norman Bates for a Halloween event at Universal Studios Florida. What a blast. I met Leonard and Jeanne Pickel who designed the *Psycho Path* maze. To this day they both call me Norman. Long story short, I turned that experience into a future career as a Halloween designer. I was involved in the creation of Halloween Horror Nights shows and experiences from 1995 until 2002 and then again from 2006 until 2009.

I love a good haunted house. I love the anticipation and the clues to what's to come. Within these pages are some of my friends who have been a part of the haunt industry over the years. Our connections vary, but there is one particular, consistent thread: we love to scare. The promise of a scream is our fuel. We have all done it. Remember

Me at the House
of Frankenstein!

back through your life, and at some point, somewhere, you jumped out from a hidden space and yelled Boo. That really is the core. We are all still saying boo, but now we do it much more elaborately. We also have a real love for the genre. We are fans of the things that go bump in the night. We are most closely associated with the films, as most of what we accomplish is a living horror film. We fabricate the story, we prepare the scenes, we rehearse the actors. The difference is a mix of traditional living theatre where we can hear our audience react. We want them to feel every moment that we have been tirelessly creating weeks, sometimes months in advance.

I am a Haunter. I love the experience of creating something in the hopes that it will give you nightmares, or at the very least a sense of foreboding and dread.

So, this book of tales is an opportunity to let our creativity loose on you in a new way. Inside are stories, drawings, photos and a few true encounters that hopefully allow you inside. I hope to make this a yearly anthology, celebrating the kindred spirits and allowing them to roam. Regardless, I hope you like what we have prepared.

MEET THE HAUNTERS

GRANDPA'S HANDS

BY ROB WINN ANDERSON

She looked at the handle of the door; the etchings on the surface reminding her of the crochet squares her Grandmother so meticulously created with her tarnished, blue hook, and gnarled fingers. The smell of fresh polish wafted to her nose. Looking closer, she could see some of its white residue embedded in the deep filigree of the burnished gold and black knob. Even before she touched it, she knew it would weigh heavy in her hands.

"Funny," she thought, "how you notice so many little things at times like this. How everything jumps out at you."

The handle felt cold against her sweaty palm but it turned smoothly. She hesitated as the door swung open, silently, on its hinges. She stood in the frame for a few moments taking in the scene. Everything was as it should be. Slender, white candles sat carefully around him, flickering in a staccato fashion that sent shadows dancing on the now-faded William Morris papered walls. The light darted off the small crystal bobs in the chandelier swinging in the breeze created by the pressure change when the door opened. The dance reminded her of fireflies bobbing frantically in a dark, night sky their flight a canon of well-choreographed, yet seemingly arbitrary movement. The walls of the small room began to melt away as her mind reversed itself to the first memory she had of her Grandpa.

"Girl, you come on out here!"

Her Grandpa had a loud and commanding voice so accustomed was he to calling over the din in the auctioneer's hall as he enticed bleary-eyed antique hounds to purchase "the last known of its kind!"

"Looky there," he said as he nodded his head forward.

It took a second for her eyes to refocus from the bright kitchen glare to the soft summer night. When they did, she gasped at the sight before her. The moon was high and full and the fir trees stood like giants guarding Grandpa's "stretch of land". Licking the dark like the lights she saw at her first carnival were hundreds of fireflies.

"Oh," she sighed as she stared at the twinkling before her.

"Quite a sight for them three-year old eyes to see, ain't it, girl?"

"Qui' a sight, G'anpa," she whispered, afraid to talk too loud in case these wonderful pieces of moonlight might disappear at the sound of her voice.

"Them bugs got lightnin' in their tails, girl," he said bending close to her ear. "At nighttime, they use 'em to scare off the shadow monsters and keep us safe out here."

He started down the weathered back stairs. Just as he neared the bottom, he turned back and offered his hand. She looked down at the roughness of the thick palm reaching out to her and allowed it to close over her tiny fingers. Even as he stood below her, she marveled at her tall and straight hero commanding her silently to walk among the lightning.

"You were my hero, Grandpa," she found herself saying out loud as the parlor walls came back to this time and this memory.

The hand she held now didn't feel as big as it had a moment ago and the rough skin was replaced with the cold veneer that death brings to the flesh. She looked at her Grandpa's fingernails. She could see dirt embedded under the yellowed and chipped nails of the index and middle fingers.

"How careless," she thought. "Yet, how right."

Grandpa was a man of the earth. When she was younger, she could remember watching him on that darn John Deere. How that thing would scare her whenever Grandpa would reach the northeast corner of the field where she and "the old girl", as he called Grandma, sat under a beach umbrella drinking lemonade and watching the rich, black soil roll under the awesome blades of the plow. Grandpa would turn the corner that put that green monster on a path headed straight for them. Panic would come across his face and his eyes would open as wide as Matilda's, the neighboring farm's milk cow. The knuckles on his hands would turn white as he gripped the steering wheel of the tractor, trying to maintain control of its unpredictable power.

She stopped her flashback in mid swerve to chuckle, realizing that the far east furrow of that field was crooked every year for eight years. From the time she was three, the first memory year, until she was eleven and the possessed John Deere bit evoked nothing more than a roll of her eyes, Grandpa had a slanted field.

In his later years, Grandpa's two-acre pride and joy was reluctantly diminished to a thirty by thirty vegetable garden near the back stairs. Long gone was the demonic machine. In its place was a small hoe and shovel, but the dirt was still black and rich and Grandpa's enthusiasm for feeling its cool density never waned.

Still, the dirt on his hands bothered her now. Looking around, she saw a piece of splintered wood. Deciding it would do, she cleaned his nails. When she was satisfied that the remaining speck of dirt was just discoloration in the nail itself, she pulled a handkerchief from her pocket and folded the wood neatly into it.

As she put the hankie away, a fly alit on her inner thigh. She jerked her leg to make it go away, her dress swirling to the left and then back right.

Her dress.

"I hope what I'm wearing is okay, Grandpa," she said, smoothing the pocket flat.

The garment was not black as one might expect; it was a brilliant royal blue that set off her eyes and made her long blonde hair seem shinier than normal. It was of modest fabric but well-tailored and fit to hug the form of her curvaceous, if slightly plump, figure. The neckline was cut in a sweetheart fashion and was echoed in the overstitched waistband. The sleeves came to just below the elbow allowing the porcelain skin of her forearm to peek out and direct the eye to her hands. Here, the fragility of her appearance came to an abrupt end. Here, the inherited strength of her Grandpa's hands was evident.

"You picked it out for me. Do you remember? You took a shine to it right away. I know it was a couple of years ago but it still fits and, even though the styles have changed some, I've left the hem right where you wanted it. My knees aren't showing for all them..."

There was that bug again. It felt like it was out for its daily constitutional. It was making its way toward her knee when she decided it was time for a roadblock. She reached down to brush it off. When she withdrew her hand from under the dress, she saw that there was blood on her fingers.

"Damn," she said, resentful of the crimson smile that mocked her feigned composure.

"Damn. Dammit! Damn!!" she screamed, losing all control.

She dropped Grandpa's hand and clawed the crisp, linen square from her pocket. Stepping back, she hiked her skirt. From beneath her panty hose, she could see blood dripping from her crotch making its way past her knee and on to her calf. She wore no underwear so nothing obscured her view as she glared at the damaged dike between her legs.

"That's just great. You did it again, didn't you? I thought this was over now!"

She plopped down on the floor, her legs open wide, her neatly pressed skirt wrapped tight around her waist. She snapped open the handkerchief and the piece of wood flew across the room and skidded to a stop under a loveseat in the corner.

She looked over at Grandpa's now-limp hand and tears began to stream down her cheeks. She didn't notice that she had torn her hose or that the skin on her thigh was becoming red and raw as she scoured to remove the stain that had turned her unshaven thigh cherry red, and matted. She didn't notice that the dried flow was now being replaced by blood from the wound she was creating. She did notice that the walls were melting away again.

"Ow, Gran'pa."

It was the first and last time she voiced any discomfort from the ritual that began that day, July 4, 1982. As the celebratory fireworks were being set to explode above Addlewood Park, some six miles away, her world was exploding in flashes of pain and humiliation; her tall and straight hero opening wounds that would never close.

"Quiet, girl." Even in hushed tones, he was convincing. "Now, you listen to me. Some day some dope-headed boy's gonna try to mess with this here, you understand?"

She held her eyes shut tight to keep her from crying out as his large fingers probed her.

"This ain't for them, y'hear? It ain't their spoil, 'cause its already done and it's done by one who loves ya, girl. Not by one of them punks who'll throw ya 'way. I know what's good. You trust me. Now, open them eyes and let's get you cleaned up for the rocket show. The old girl'll be here with the car all gassed real soon. Let's go."

And he smiled.

Every summer from her eighth year to her sixteenth she visited Grandpa and Grandma, and one time each summer Grandpa "spoiled her." It's crazy because she could have told someone, anyone, but she didn't. It wasn't like she forgot or had temporary amnesia or any of that crap. Those talk shows with their repressed memory bullshit. How could anyone forget? How could anyone be subjected to that kind of torture and degradation and not throw up twice a day when July neared and not cry out in their sleep from the nightmares and not shirk away from the boys when they got too aggressive? Hell, she couldn't even go through puberty like most girls. Bleeding was nothing new to her. Just as the damage that was done to her during those summer visits might appear to be fading a bit, something stressful would happen. Grandpa's hands would flash in her mind's eye and she would bleed.

And, she didn't tell and it doesn't make sense why but she didn't and it hurt and it made her sick and she loved her Grandpa anyway and that was the worst part of it all. And, even when she was seventeen and Grandma had passed away and the spoiling stopped because she convinced her mother to let her work during the summers, she never forgot. It was over. But it wasn't. It would never be. Because she was spoiled and when she bled, she found that she could hate.

"Damn you! These were new hose!"

She lay back on the floor and covered her face with her hands, sobbing heavily, her legs pulled tightly together. After awhile she regained her composure and sat up. She straightened her skirt and smeared the mascara down her face in her attempt to dry her tears.

"This won't do," she said wadding the handkerchief and stuffing it in her pocket. "This is Grandma's parlor and we're respectful in this house. Besides, it's over."

She looked down at her hands. So strong. The blood now on hers an echo of what once was on his.

Brushing her hair from her face, she made her way back to Grandpa. She smiled as she took his hand in hers and inspected the nails one final time. She laughed even as she placed Grandpa's hand at his side...

...And slid the floorboard back into place.

THE END

a few words from

ROB WINN ANDERSON

What do you love about the genre of horror?

It's the knowing of what you are getting into but not the when or the why of what lies ahead.

What is some of your favorite horror literature?

The writings of Stephen King and Dean Koontz stand out for me. The development of character, place, and time in their work allow you to feel and react to the horror in a much deeper way.

What are some of your influences?

Stephen King, Dean Koontz, Shirley Jackson, and Edgar Allen Poe.

What is your favorite Halloween treat?

Caramel corn balls!

You are hosting the perfect Halloween movie marathon. What are the films you choose and why?

The *Nightmare on Elm Street* franchise. The moving between realities and the threats incurred in each keep me hooked. *The Birds* because it's Hitchcock at his finest and the unanswered questions about the attacks still haunt me to this day. Stephen King's *It* and *Carrie* for their story, characters, and action. They have it all. *Ghost Story* starring Alice Krige and Fred Astaire. The rich backstory makes the horror even stronger.

If you could continue any horror story, what would it be?

The Cask of Amontillado by Poe.

As a designer of horror theatre or experiences, explain your process.

First comes story. Then comes character. The horror is a natural offspring to these parents.

When is the last time you were genuinely scared by something someone created?

I recently saw *The Conjuring* for the first time and there were moments in there that genuinely caught me.

Tell us about your contribution to our book. What was the inspiration?

A discussion I had years ago with a friend about a person's hands and the stories that they tell. So many intriguing ideas can come from the size, thickness, texture of the skin, strength of the grip. The story developed from there.

Describe the perfect Halloween.

Alone. In the darkness. Silence. Reading *The Exorcist*. That's terrifying to me because it creates the perfect environment for imagination to take over. And nothing creates horror better than an active imagination.

SCARE CRED: ROB WINN ANDERSON

Rob's work has been seen onstage, on video, and across the world of theme park entertainment. As an award winning-playwright and director, Rob has written and directed over a hundred projects for Walt Disney World. From live shows to television, Rob has crafted some of the most high-profile projects on Disney property. He holds the distinction of being the only director to create and direct a major project not based on any previous Disney material. This parade, "The March of the Artimals," debuted at Disney's Animal Kingdom and was described by Michael Eisner as "the most creative thing we've done".

Rob majored in Theater, Film/Television, and Radio at Northwestern University. He enjoyed a successful career as a performer and choreographer in national tours and repertory theaters. His move into the world   o f writing and directing was guided by influences like Eric Bogosian and the Lincoln Center's Directors Lab. As a distinguished playwright, Rob's plays have been featured at Edward Albee's Great Plains Theatre Conference as well as the Kennedy Center Playwrighting Intensive and Sewanee Writers' Conference. Rob is a member of the Dramatists Guild of America Inc., Chicago Dramatists, the Lincoln Center Directors Lab, the Playwright's Center, SAG, AEA, AFTRA and AGVA.

BORN AFRAID

BY ROB ARAGON

Dark stage except for a main character (male) sitting in the middle of the stage in a single chair. He speaks to audience.

> MAN
>
> I've always been afraid. If it's possible, I guess, I was born afraid. It's my nature or should I say, it's the result of a man's nature.

Stage blackens on the left there is a bed scene as described. Main character continues to speak in the dark.

> MAN
>
> You see, before my mother was to expect me, she was visited thrice by the devil himself. It was always in the dead of night. Always after the clock struck three. My father would violently grumble in an incohesive and somnambolistic ancient tongue. This would startle my mother, who would then turn onto her back as a means to find comfort and there he stood by her side of the bed. A silhouette of black and his horns concealed by a black fedora.Poised with arms crossed. There he stood. He

uttered not a sound, nor a movement did
he make. She lay there striken in silent
terror as her heart skipped a beat. He
stood there. Without movement. Without sound.

Bed scene is darkened and main character is lit.

                    MAN
          Then, as silently as he had arrived, he
          vanished. My father being the practical
          man, laughed and dismissed the event.
          After ridiculing my mother's fear, he
          returned to his slumber. Unafraid and unmoved.

The second night was like the first. The speaking in tongues,
the heart skipping it's beat, the black suited devil and my
father's dismissal.

The third night was different, for my mother kept silent in
regards to the hellish visit.

A month later, I was conceived. From a drunken marital rape. I
was conceived.

On the day of my birth, My father was nowhere to be found.
He was self consumed by another lost weekend.

                    MAN
          During my arrival and as I breathed
          in the painful reality of this life,
          my mother succumbed to cardiac arrest.

Main character leans forward in his chair...........

                    MAN
          You see, her heart had been weakened
          by nocturnal terrors. Thank God, she
          was resuscitated after I had lost her
          for ninety eternal seconds. The devil
          did return, but not until I was five.

Stage darkens and on the right of stage there is a bed scene as described below is now lit. Main character continues.

(LOUD BANGING SOUND)

> MAN
> I quickly sat up. I listened with eyes
> and ears wide open. It was my parent's
> bedroom window. It slammed open. Through
> that opening and into our home crawled
> forth an unimaginable parade of the damned
> as the howling winds and thunderous roar
> of hell fire lamented their very existence.
> Then silence. An absolute and sheer silence.
> I sat there, terror-striken pale white
> surrounded by the blackest of all nights.
> Then, he laughed. The Devil laughed out
> loud and boastful! He is victorious and
> has made this home his own.

Bed scene is darkened and main character in chair is only lit.

> MAN
> After that night, I would regularly
> see the devil. He would stand in the
> corner of my room or he'd whisper
> softly from within my closet. Regardless
> of the occasion, he would always stand
> before me. Awaiting for me in the distance.
> Awaiting for something unknown to me. My
> mother passed away last year. She can rest
> now. My father passed away six months later.
>
> After my father died, I realized he must
> have taken the devil with him. For I have

not seen the devil since. I still search
for him on occasion. But, he's nowhere to
be found. Perhaps, now, I won't feel this fear.

(walking slowly right up behind him is the silhouetted/fedora
wearing black devilish apparition... arms crossed and silent)

                              MAN
            Perhaps, now, there will be no more fear!

LIGHTS GO OUT ON STAGE.......

FINI

ROB ARAGON

What do you love about the genre of horror?

I'm not truly comfortable with the word "horror." Being an enthusiast of older works, I feel my taste and interests fall more into the gothic or grim fairy tale category. I believe it is in the grim realm of storytelling where we acquire life lessons of the battle between light and dark, good and evil, inclusion and loneliness. It's where we learn to recognize ourselves as being one or the other. That is indeed frightening.

What is some of your favorite horror literature?

The Erl-King by Johann Wolfgang Von Goethe. *Alone* by Edgar Allen Poe. *The Minister's Black Veil* by Nathaniel Hawthorne. *The Demon of the Gibbet* by Fitz-James O'Brien. *The Graveyard Shift* by Richard Mathewson

What are some of your influences?

I don't know if I've been influenced or if what drew me towards a specific artist is their unfolded and creative truth, somehow being recognized as paralleling my own. I simply do not know. Perhaps that is what an influence is: the recognition of a collective and universal truth?

What is your favorite Halloween treat?

Candy corn. I buy bags of it during October which are stored and savored throughout the new year.

You are hosting the perfect Halloween movie marathon. What are the films you choose and why?

The Innocents: Chilling and subconsciously will haunt you during your sleep. *The Last Man on Earth*: The sole survivor inspires me to believe in the fight. *The Bride of Frankenstein*: It's because of this film, I equate Schubert's *Ave Maria* with finding sanctuary. *The Omen '76*: A reminder of the tragic hand of fate falling upon a decent man. *Black Sabbath*: Boris makes me shudder with a simple line: "I am hungry."

If you could continue any horror story, what would it be?

The Tell-Tale Heart by Edgar Allen Poe

As a designer of horror theatre or experiences, explain your process.

I have not forgotten the emotional reactions, both internal and external, caused by childhood experiences. I believe if one wishes to communicate to most, if not all, of one's audience, we need to tap into the audience's inner child's emotional reservoir. Regardless of the uniqueness of the individual childhood experience, the emotional response is a universal one and understood by all. Fear, joy, acceptance, alienation, and so forth. Truth be told, I believe all living creatures share this early developmental emotional reservoir as a common denominator. So, when creating something from the world of fear, I simply recall what has or would frighten me.

When is the last time you were genuinely scared by something someone created?
I recently saw a work of art which disturbed me. Then I became quite scared contemplating the quality of some art in this world.

Tell us about your contribution to our book. What was the inspiration?
I was at a Hollywood gala event and somehow the topic of discussion for the evening turned towards the supernatural. A young lady commented how fun it would have been to have grown up in a haunted home. That was the inspirational moment. I wanted to create a short tale that would discourage the romantic notion that the supernatural is a realm of enjoyment, diversion or disrespect by the curious minded.

Describe the perfect Halloween.
It's a cold and windy autumn moon night as gnarled trees sway in absolute fright. Fright for the ghouls and goblins and ghosts. Fright for the devils and witches with toads. Fright for you and fright for me, as children fade fast with dreams towards sleep. Dreams of a creepy and merry Halloween!

SCARE CRED: ROB ARAGON

Upbeat writer and self-taught artist, Rob Aragon has thrilled countless fans with his award-winning art. One of his more notable admirers was friend and genre legend Vincent Price. Rob's work ranges from museum fine art paintings, film projects, magazines, comic books, trading cards, and everything else in between. When not painting, he enjoys collecting art and film memorabilia and playing classical piano.

CREATIONS FROM A VILE BRAIN

BY TOM BASORE

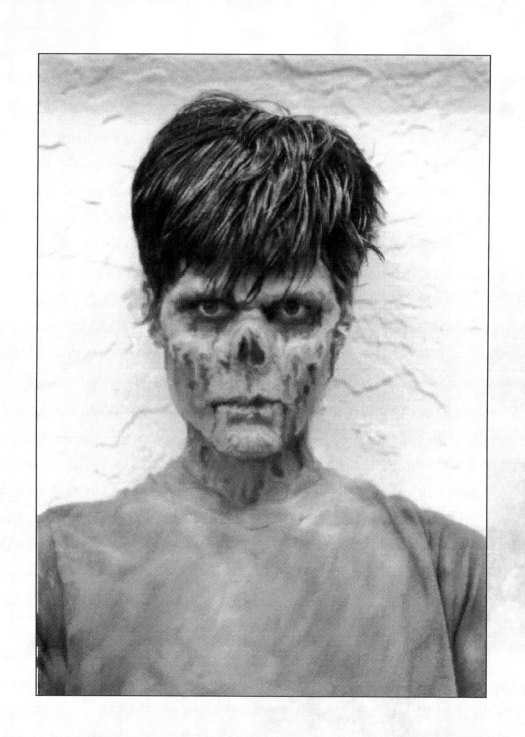

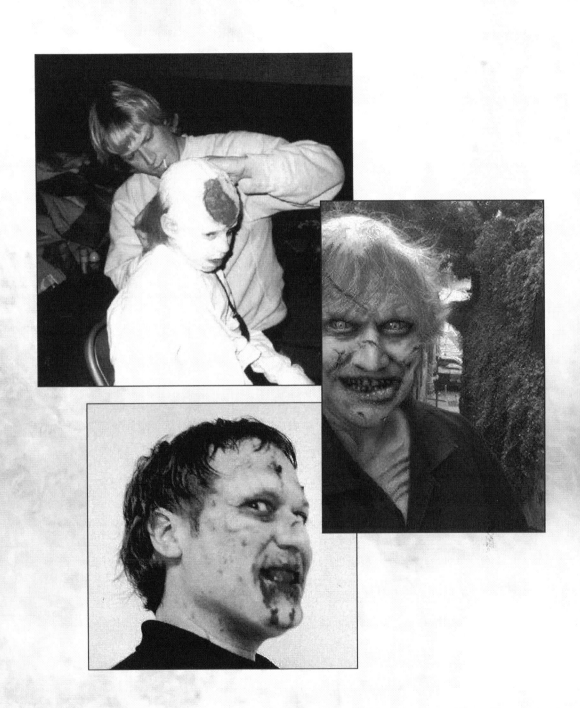

TOM BASORE

What do you love about the genre of horror?

I suppose it's the adrenaline rush you get by being scared to death, I just love it! I have been addicted to horror ever since I was a little feller perched in front of the TV set every Saturday afternoon for the Sir Graves Ghastly double feature. I never missed it! I don't know. Perhaps it was just bad wiring.

What is some of your favorite horror literature?

Anything by Stephen King, Clive Barker, Edgar Allan Poe, Bram Stoker, Mary Shelley, Ramsey Campbell, Dean Koontz, Ray Bradbury, H.P. Lovecraft, Shirley Jackson, Ann Rice, William Peter Blatty, as well as the classic horror comics such as *Tales from the Crypt, Creepy, Eerie, Vault of Horror*, etc. All guaranteed to warp anyone's mind!

What are some of your influences?

As a makeup artist, it would have to be Lon Chaney Sr., Jack Pierce, Dick Smith, John Chambers, Rick Baker, Rob Botin, Tom Savini, and Greg Nicotero. These guys have all blown me away with their genius. They inspired me to become a makeup artist. As a somewhat normal humanoid creature, it would have to be my Grandfather David Monroe Basore who I deeply respected and dearly miss. Also my Art Teacher Ed Ramsdell, my Grandmother Causby Basore, and my Aunt Shirley Basore. They recognized my talent at an early age and fanned the flame.

What is your favorite Halloween treat?

I love creepy cookies and cupcakes but no Halloween would be complete without the beloved candy corn!

You are hosting the perfect Halloween movie marathon. What are the films you choose and why?

I am a sucker for the early classic horror movies. All the Universal Studio movie monsters are a must in my Halloween lineup followed by old cheesy movies - the good, the bad, and the ugly! I love them all! When I watch them, I'm in heaven! To me, the old stuff is just far superior to the newer movies. The black-and-white just takes you to a whole different world. To me they're unforgettable, unlike many of the newer films today.

If you could continue any horror story, what would it be?

I'm not really hot on sequels. I would however love to see a faithful black and white rendition of Mary Shelley's classic *Frankenstein* based on the illustrations of Bernie Wrightson with an amazing musical score. No one has ever done *Frankenstein* right. It is one of my favorite stories and it would be awesome to see someone finally do it justice.

As a designer of horror theater or experiences, explain your process.

I create things that tend to scare people the most and then throw them all into a dark place before bombarding their senses with horrible sights, sounds, smells, and things that brush by them in the darkness. I like the idea of sending people into a house one at a time, it's always scarier when you're alone.

When is the last time you were genuinely scared by something someone created?

That would have been the *Texas Chainsaw Massacre* house from Halloween Horror Nights 26 in Florida. This house scared the bejeezus out of me! Nothing scarier than an enormous maniac flying out of the shadows with a buzzing chainsaw to send you into cardiac arrest! They really nailed this one, I swear I thought I was going to die!

Tell us about your contribution to our book. What was the inspiration?

These pictures are from my days at Universal Studios Florida, all original creations from my twisted vile brain.

Describe the perfect Halloween.

1) A Halloween party in an old creepy house with family and friends. 2) A nice simulated thunderstorm as seen from the inside of the house. 3) Live roaming reproductions of all Universal Studio's classic monsters and other random B-movie faves. 4) Live music by Oingo Boingo, Tito and the Tarantulas, and Dead Man's Bones. 5) A kick-ass haunted hayride. 6) Scare the hell out of the little trick-or-treaters!

SCARE CRED: TOM BASORE

Tom is a farmer extraordinaire, makeup artist, and part-time ghoul. He began his training in 1992 at the Joe Blasco School of Makeup before enrolling in Dick Smith's Advanced Professional Makeup Course. He spent the next fifteen years as a makeup artist and creature fabricator for Universal Studios Florida where he was instrumental in pooling together Orlando's most talented artists to form the park's first makeup department. He also supervised teams of makeup artists during the early years of Halloween Horror Nights. Tom later transferred to an exciting new department - The Universal Studios Creature Shop. He served out his remaining time at Universal working with a new team of incredible artists and techs creating amazing creatures and monsters. Tom left USF in 2007 and moved to South Florida to rejoin his family's business. He still dabbles in makeup from time to time. Tom currently resides in a dark house in Wellington, Florida with a strange old woman and his dead dog Bubba, which he keeps in a box.

BITTEN

BY DIANNA BENNETT

I find it's far easier to write from experience, rather than have to craft something from the aether. So this should come as no surprise when I tell you this is a true story. It happened to me when I was working in Downtown Tampa at an upscale event called "The Vault of Souls".

We weren't a "Haunt" as most people know them. There was no blood, no gore. No one in an absurd costume would jump out from the darkened recesses and shout "BOO!" at you. No, we were an immersive, theatrical experience. One you were invited to participate in, how deep you got was up to your own level of involvement. It was a unique and exciting venue for the market, something that not everyone "got."

The building that our event was held in was the original First National Bank of Tampa, we occupied three floors. The Main floor had you at an elegant soiree with dancers and other entertainment, the upper floor, which is where out Tarot readers and aerialist performed to our guests amazement, and then there was the basement, where the Vault actually was This place was unique and where the story actually happens.

You see, this is a rare thing in Florida, a basement, but it's also the FIRST drive through for banking in the city of Tampa among other things and it's rumored to be haunted. I can honestly say, it's not a rumor but the truth. When they were preparing the building for our arrival, part of the floor in one area suddenly just 'erupted', causing the folks working in that particular area to leave and not come back to working. If I remember my numbers correctly it's over 35 people who started working on the build out and that never came back after being disturbed.

We had many of the usual things happen, and by usual I mean we heard our names called, phantom footsteps and music boxes that would go off on their own, this stuff was creepy, but somewhat explainable. What was NOT explainable was the night I got bitten.

The night I got bitten, it was our 2nd weekend into the run, and I believe a full moon. Our Tarot readers and psychics were all amped for the weekend and one of them went downstairs to do a cleansing since we'd recently found out the name of a prospective spiritual resident. My room seemed to be an area of draw, whether that's due to me or to the building's design is neither here nor there, but Camile was drawn to my room and started her prayers. When she came up, I noticed that the moonstone at her throat was unusually cloudy, and suggested she put it in salt and under the moonlight to clean it, and that's when she told me what she'd been up to. She'd gone through my specific area and done a cleansing, and the spirit (Spirits?) there didn't want to go. She warned me I might be in for a little tumult that evening. She couldn't have been more right.

That evening, our guests were cantankerous, we had a few that needed to speak to security and the feeling in my room was decidedly off. My character was that of a 1920's dominatrix, and in as much, I was wearing a fully steel boned corset, garters, the whole shebang. At one point in the evening, I felt something on my side. A touch? A pinch? I'm not sure, but it was beneath the corset and it was itchy. During the course of the night I could try to scratch it through the fabric of the corset, but I couldn't actually scratch my skin.

During the evening's run, when no one was around, I heard someone call my name, and then felt someone touch my hair. The name thing, I thought was cast mates calling for me, so I asked, and they were just waiting for the next round of guests. The touching of my hair? Nope couldn't explain it. It was just strange.

After the show ended around 1:30 am, and we went up to our dressing room to change back into our day wear, I felt great relief getting undressed; 8 hours in a corset is not bad, but it felt good to be ME again. It was then that one of the other girls asked me "What happened?" I looked at my side in the mirror and there was what looked like a large bite mark on my side, where the odd sensation had been that evening. It was sizable, darker at the bottom than at the top, an angry looking mark on my skin.

My guess is that the work our psychic did in my room riled the spirits up and they took it out on me. That's the first time I was ever "bitten" by a spirit.

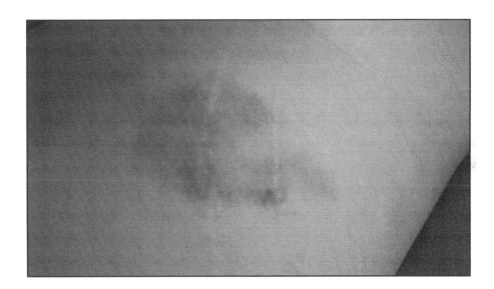

DIANNA BENNETT

What do you love about the genre of horror?

Horror can mean so many different things. It's not just blood, guts, and gore. It can mean trips to the dentist or ants and spiders. It's all about what scares you individually.

What is some of your favorite horror literature?

I love the classics, so Poe, Shelley, and Stoker. I'm also a huge fan of writers like Clive Barker, Anne Rice, Dean Koontz, and Ray Bradbury. When I was younger, my favorite book was *Nathaniel* by Dean Koontz

What are some of your influences?

Real life experiences, people I know, and places I've visited. I love historical events and what has transpired in the past. I like to weave and create them into a tapestry.

What is your favorite Halloween treat?

It is *not* candy corn. I have to say that it's probably triple-chocolate Kit Kats. They don't come out frequently and they're incredibly delicious. Baring finding those, I really do enjoy pumpkin cheesecake, which only begins to come out around Halloween.

You are hosting the perfect Halloween movie marathon. What are the films you choose and why? Hard Question.

I wouldn't because I don't host, but I suppose if I have to, it's going to start with something fun and light like *Hocus Pocus* to set the mood. Really, who doesn't love that movie? After that, we would venture onto a darker path, but I'd have to think about it more

As a designer of horror theatre or experiences, explain your process.

I'm an actor in horror theatre, so my process is simple. I give it my all. My characters are written within parameters and I am allowed to bring them to life. I'm glad those I work with trust me to do this.

When is the last time you were genuinely scared by something someone created?

Probably the first time I saw *Nightmare on Elm Street*. Or the worm vomiting scene in *Poltergeist II*.

Tell us about your contribution to our book. What was the inspiration?

My contribution was a real life experience, something that actually happened when I worked at an event.

Describe the perfect Halloween.

Cool air, dark skies, crisp autumn wind that swirls multicolored leaves into tiny tornadoes at my feet. Somewhere in the North East, like Philly, so I can experience the change of the seasons, and enjoy the plethora of haunts that are up there. Good hay rides, gothic mansions open for tours, ghost hunts, and seances. Anything to get a rise out of the senses.

SCARE CRED: DIANNA BENNETT

Dianna Bennett and her alter ego, Luna Mystique have been in the haunt industry for nearly two decades. She first stepped into haunting as therapy after losing her father in 1999. She worked at Busch Gardens' Howl-O-Scream from 2000 to 2014 bringing many memorable characters to life. Her favorite Howl-o-Scream personas include Mistress Macabre (the bewitching Dominatrix of Darkheart's Fear Fair), GiGi (one of the Killer Klowns), and Researcher Gama of the Experiment who made sure you knew just what level of trouble you were about to get your hands into. She left Howl-O-Scream to follow her mentor, Scott Swenson in a new, unique, hands-on fully immersive theatrical haunt experience as Maria Saavedra the Seductress, a 1920's era dominatrix. She was a favorite character each year. During the off season, she attends several Haunter conventions to keep on the cutting edge of the industry. She is a writer, actress, and massage therapist.

PIRATE

BY MICHAEL BURNETT

Michael Burnett

www.michaelburnett.com

MICHAEL BURNETT

What do you love about the genre of horror?

I guess what I love about horror is that it is a safe way to explore the darker side of the human psyche or experience the adrenaline rush from the danger of a monster that's out to get you. Also, it's just good old fashioned fun!

What is some of your favorite horror literature?

Something Wicked This Way Comes by Ray Bradbury, *Ghost Story* by Peter Straub, and *Pet Sematary* Steven King.

What are some of your influences?

Walt Disney and Disneyland. Love the *Haunted Mansion* and *Pirates of the Caribbean*. Even after hundreds of visits over the past forty-plus years, it still never gets old.

What is your favorite Halloween treat?

As a kid when I would go out for trick-or-treat, my favorite treat was an Almond Joy. Now days my favorite treat on Halloween is continuing my mom's tradition of making a big pot of chili and watching kids react to the decorations and effects we do at our house on Halloween.

You are hosting the perfect Halloween movie marathon. What are the films you choose and why?

The original *Halloween* - do I really need to explain? *Trick 'r Treat* for capturing the feel of an 80's horror film and all that I love about the holiday. *The Exorcist* - the scariest movie ever made! *Fright Night* because it has Roddy McDowall and vampires - what else do you need? *Young Frankenstein* - a perfect mix of humor and classic horror.

If you could continue any horror story, what would it be?

That's a tough one but the first thing that comes to mind is John Carpenter's *The Thing*. I want to know what happened to MacReady and Childs!

As a designer of horror theatre or experiences, explain your process.

Most of the time I am given an outline or basic storyline to work with. I start with rough sketches and/or writing down what first come to mind from what I am given. I then like to refine the concepts and designs based on what I would like to see in an experience. Most projects are usually a collaboration with other creative people so once I feel like I have some pretty solid ideas I like to get feedback from those people before finalizing the designs.

When is the last time you were genuinely scared by something someone created?

Being involved in the horror and creating scary experiences for such a long time I don't find myself really scared visiting events or watching movies but I have experienced some really good startling moments. The last time I remember really feeling scared was when as a kid I saw *The Exorcist* in the theater. I had read and heard about how horrifying the film was. I think I psyched myself up to the point that I wasn't sure if I would make it through the entire thing. I ended up seeing it through to the end. It was one of the experiences that solidified my love of horror.

Tell us about your contribution to our book. What was the inspiration?

As a kid (and still today) *Pirates of the Caribbean* is one of my favorite rides at Disneyland. For this digital photo manipulation I turned myself into one of the pirates!

Describe the perfect Halloween.

For me it would be a cool, crisp autumn day. The changing leaves falling and collecting on the ground where they would crunch under my feet as I walked around the neighborhood all decorated for Halloween night. As darkness falls the sounds of kids trick or treating through the streets would be heard and I would have an elaborate setup of scary decorations and effects the kids could walk through to earn their Halloween treat!

SCARE CRED: MICHAEL BURNETT

Two time Emmy nominated make-up artist Michael Burnett has been creating special makeup effects in the film, television, and the haunt industries for more than thirty years. Michael has worked with academy award-winning make-up artists Rick Baker, Greg Cannom, and Michael Westmore. Some of Michael's film and television credits include *The Ben Stiller Show, Universal Soldier, The Forsaken, Star Trek Enterprise, Passions* and *Mad TV*. From 1997 to 2016 Michael designed and ran the makeup for Universal Studios Halloween Horror Nights seventeen times, more times than any other person. Currently, Michael is the director of design & development for FrightNight Studios, a Florida based company that creates makeup and effects for motion pictures, television and theme parks including Bush Gardens, Universal Studios, and Disney.

The Broken Thing

BY DAN CARRO

Jamie's body was slumped over the couch, his chin dug into his chest as his neck bent into an almost 90 degree angle pressed against the back cushions. His body was limp and splayed out along the seat of the couch, his legs spilling onto the floor like a discarded marinate. His eyes stared out, glassy and red and fixed on his killer.

"Time for bed." Mother shouted from the kitchen.

"I just died." Jamie mumbled. "One more game."

It was hard to tell if Jamie was playing a video game on the television or something on his phone. The game controller from the Xbox was nestled on his lap but his phone was securely in his hand. But he would often switch back and forth between the two while waiting on screens respawns to load. It was his 6th hour of game play and the boy hadn't moved from that spot since he got home from school.

"Get to bed young man!" Mom shouted once more.

It was also difficult to tell if Jamie didn't hear his mother or was simply ignoring her. The television, which had be showing a respawn screen for several minutes suddenly revealed the interior of a large space freighter. Dead bodies and blood spatter marked the futuristic corridors within the game. Several undead creatures in radiation suits roamed the screen.

Jamie paused the game on his phone and snatched up his controller. His body tensed more, showing some signs of life as he began to search the pixelated ship for weapons, ammo and power ups.

"Bed!" Mom insisted.

Jamie never took his eyes from the screen, as he sat up, giving the illusion that he was just about to head to bed, that is until he found the Plasma rake, a powerful weapon that would be very formidable against space Cadavers, each exploding like bloody, sinewy party poppers upon contact with his powered up weapon.

"Dammit, Jamie!" Mom huffed as she stomped into the room. "Did you brush your teeth?"

"I did." He didn't so much as glance in her direction.

"Dammit, Jamie, don't lie to me!"

Mom switched off the TV. The hull of the space freighter suddenly vanished. Jamie quickly hit the pause button on the controller before offering protest to his mother.

"Dammit, mom!"

"Where did you learn to talk like that?" Mom asked, eyes widening in disbelief.

"Nowhere." Jamie shrugged as he stood up and made his way to the bedroom.

"Goodnight." Mom yelled. "I love you. Go the hell to bed!"

Jamie stood up and trudged towards his bedroom, his nose instantly aimed at his phone.

"At 6 years old I would have never disrespected my parents the way you do."

"I love you." Jamie technically said. The sound spilled from his mouth with no sentiment or feeling. More of a groan then an expression of anything.

Despite putting his full attention on killing the Bloxtrolls on his phone, Jamie somehow navigated the turns and obstacles of the living room, the hallway, his bedroom door and the array of clutter, clothes and toys scattered around his room on his blind journey to the bed.

Soon Jamie was plopped into the bed. Clothes and all. He climbed under the covers without taking his eyes off of the phone or his forefinger off of the screen.

"Turn that off and go to sleep." Mother yelled from her room as her bedroom light went out.

That was it. The last light in the house. There were no other glares or lights or sounds to distract from game play. This was when Jamie could get past the most levels. When the house was dark and he was alone.

Jamie thought he heard a noise near the foot of his bed, but he found it easy to dismiss. A slight creaking sound, as if his closet door had slowly slid open. Jamie kept playing.

Within seconds he heard it again, but again decided it wasn't worth investigation.

The third time the sound occurred Jamie had just beaten the level. He supposed it was a good time to see if there was something to be concerned about.

And there, on the far wall of his room, yawning wide like a big, pitch black, cavernous, rectangular mouth on his bedroom wall, lay his closet door. Slowly creaking open on it's own accord. Jamie squinted in the darkness, his night vision lacking from having just taken his eyes from the phone screen.

He thought he could make out a thin, gaunt ashy gray hand, reaching from the darkness of the closet. The long slender fingers wrapping around the door jam. Two tiny, slight glows pierced the deep darkness of the closet. Eyes. Which locked in unison on Jamie.

The closet glared at Jamie and Jamie stared back, phone clutched to his chest.

The hand unlatched itself from the door frame as it's little finger curled, followed by the ring and middle finger until finally the inhuman hand had twisted itself into a pointing gesture, it's long slender, knotted forefinger aimed squarely at Jamie.

Jamie had given himself time to let his eyes adjust to the darkness. He could clearly make out the strange, gaunt ethereal form that peered from the darkness of the closet. Not it's full shape, or details of it's face or boney, hunched over body, but enough to know that something that did not belong was indeed there, in the closet, watching.

"I am the Eternal Dweller" it hissed, in a voice that seeped from it's throat like a thousand whispers. "and I bid you -"

"Lame." Jamie went back to the game on his phone.

The Eternal Dweller paused and continued to watch from the darkness of the closet. It's inhuman face, etched with deep lines and crags was famous amongst the netherworld for being incapable of all expression. That said, if it's face could emote, it would certainly be displaying a look of confusion.

It wondered if it had made itself clear. Perhaps further elaboration was in order.

"I am the nightmare of all nightmares. The shadow cast by the darkest of shadows. I am the…"

"Laaaame." Jamie sighed without looking up from his game.

The Eternal Dweller leaned on the door frame and tapped it's long, slender fingers against the wall thoughtfully.

"Are you touched by madness, little one? Do you feel no fear?"

The boy didn't answer, nor did he look away from the device in his hand.

The Eternal Dweller had haunted closet thresholds since the birth of time, (or in any case, since the creation of closets.) The simple, unnerving fact of it's existence had sown fear and despair in hearts of the countless little ones on whom it had preyed for millennia. And yet it never had to fully reveal itself before in order to inflict terror. Never even had to utter a word. It's prey would sense that it was near, would know in their hearts it was watching. And stirring that icy dread within them, it would feed on their panic, their anxiety as is it wafted from their souls, like smoke from the burning flesh on a sacrificial altar, drawn out of their thumping little hearts and sucked right into the dark, hungry chasm where the Dweller's blighted soul should have been.

And yet, this boy would not give him even a morsel… not even the faintest aroma of fear.

The Dweller felt the consternation rising in it. "What the hell is your problem, kid?"

"Perhapssss I can ssssshed light on the matter, Closet Monster." another hissy voice whispered, this time from beneath the bed.

Under normal circumstances, the Eternal Dweller would never think to associate with a Cot Crawler, the lowliest of bedroom monsters, yet it could not resist learning whatever it could about this strange child.

"Speak," the Dweller commanded with a wave of it's gaunt hand.

"I am the Ssssservant of the Sssskull Lord and I…"

"I did not ask," the Dweller spat, angrily. "Just tell me about this one. I starve."

The Under the Bed monsters licked it's cracked, crusted lips and clicked its rotting teeth together. Maybe he didn't want to help this rude Closet Creature after all. But the Cot Crawler quickly thought back to the night before, where the boy barely noticed having the covers pulled off of him or having toys flung from beneath the bed. Perhaps working with the Closet Dweller could lead to a means to scare the boy.

"The child is indeed, unwell."

"I can hear you- " Jamie sighed.

"The child's body is aged 6 years but his eyessss have sssseen too much by far. He has watched the burned man with the bladed hand kill teensss as they ssslept. The drowned man in the mask and he who stalksss on All Hallowsss Eve as they sssnuffed out lives with their gleaming blades." The monster under the bed pushed aside toys and soiled laundry as he poked his head out from beneath the bedfame.

"Surely seeing what such creatures could do would bolster his fear of us!" the Dweller reasoned.

"No," the servant beneath the bed sighed. "For he has not just witnessssed death, he has caused it."

"The boy has taken lives?" The Dweller could feel his once immovable face attempting to twisting into a legitimately shocked expression. It was a strange feeling for the Dweller, who was now concerned that if his face did indeed show emotion that it might become stuck like that.

"He hasss killed many," the Cot Crawler explained. "Through the window in his handsss he has killed and killed and been killed countlessss times. He has taken many livesss and had his life taken as well. He has also done this through the window on the wall. It is the only window in the home that does not reveal the world outdoors but rather shows them how to live lives that are not their own. It has hardened his heart. It has corrupted his mind."

The Eternal Dweller clutched at its empty stomach.

"Tonight, I have roused from a long slumber," the Dweller lamented, it's own fear and frustration apparent. " I have journeyed room to room to sup upon fear. This is the ninth such child I have encountered this evening. The ninth! I shall starve!"

The Dweller leapt upon the footboard of the bed and howled at the child, with a howl that only the young can hear. He shoved his long slender digits into the void beneath his hood and pulled from beneath the veil handfuls of wet, writhing bloody veins and arteries, sliding and wriggling and pulsating in his hand like a swarm of blood-engorged earthworms.

Jamie glanced for the briefest instant. "Lame."

The Dweller pulled open his robe, revealing razor sharp teeth just below his ribcage in the cavity where his stomach and entrails should have been. The gaping maw stretched wide as the Dweller arched his back, opening the giant mouth in his torso even farther.

"Jamie smirked, but his eyes never left the flashing, beeping device in his hands. "Uh huh."

The Dweller closed his robe and hugged it around himself, equally furious and ashamed by the lowly depths he had sunken to.

"Nothing will work," the Monster under the bed groaned. "He is fearless. Desensitized."

"The Dweller leapt off of the foot board and stomped closer, to linger at the boy's elbow.

"Look at me child!" it rasped, it's voice as loud as ten thousand whispers.

Nothing. The only movement in the child's eyes were the reflection of the light the small window in his hand cast as he flicked and tapped at it mindlessly.

"Look! At! ME!"

The Eternal Dweller raised his hand furiously.

"Remember the rules of both our houses!" the Monster Beneath the Bed cried out. "Never touch. Never harm. Only inspire fear!"

The Dweller's hand flew toward Jamie, but the worlds of the Cot Crawler hit the Closet Monster before he could strike the child. Its hand instead veered and found a new target. The floating window in the child's hand. It flew across the room and landed with a crash somewhere in a far dark corner.

"No!" Jamie screamed, sitting up in bed. He leapt to his feet, scanning the darkness, waiting impatiently for his eyes to adjust so he could find the precious treasure torn from his very hands. "you asshole! You probably broke it! My mom'll kill me!"

Both creatures instantly smelled it. Fear. Savory and sweet.

It seems something did frighten the child.

The Eternal Dweller could not just see in darkness. It was darkness. It watched as Jamie leaped from the bed and hurried to the floor where he heard the strange device land. The boy groped around the corner of the room in the dark, searching, desperate. As he searched, and failed to find his quarry, panic bloomed inside him, filling the air with its sweet aroma.

"Where is it?" Jamie cried. "Dammit, where is it?

The Eternal Dweller opened it's hand, revealing what Jamie sought in his slender digits.

"My phone!" Jamie yelled. "Give it to me!"

A grin would have stretched across the Eternal Dweller's face if it were able to do such things. Instead, it opened up it's bony hand. The tiny object free. Jamie watched the small glowing rectangle as it tumbled to the floor. The boy dove for it but it was too late. The phone landed corner first on the ground. A spider's web of cracked, gray lines scarred the screen.

Before Jamie could reach the broken device, before it had even fallen flat after it's oblique impact, a fat, warty hand from beneath the bed snatched the object and pulled it into the darkness.

"My phone!" Jamie screamed in horror.

Footsteps thumped nearer in the hall outside. The Eternal Dweller fled to the closet as the Cot Crawler sank into shadow. For both knew the octave the boy hit could only be achieved by a child who was truly filled with fear. It was a pitch the creator of mankind hid deep within all children, designed to be heard not just with the ears but the heart of the mother, to signal that this was not just a tantrum but indeed an emergency.

"Baby, what's wrong?" The mother cried as she hurried into the room and rushed to the side of the bed.

"My phone! " Jamie shouted, crouched on the floor, peering into the darkness under his bed." It's gone!"

"Did you drop it?" Mom asked, frisking the covers while scanning the clutter on the floor around the bed.

"No." He sobbed. "Monsters took it."

Mom stared at the boy for a moment, hands on her hips.

"I knew it." She sighed. "Ok. That does it. I knew you were too young for this stuff. When we find the phone I'm keeping it for a while."

"NO!" he yelled.

Cold, crisp fear. Sour, galling anxiety. The salty tang in the promise of tears.

Delicious.

The Eternal Dweller peered from the half-closed closet directly into the darkness beneath the bed. It nodded at the fat, wart-covered hand waving at him from the shadows, holding a small, rectangular talisman, glowing prismatically through a shattered window.

And even though it's face was completely incapable of showing even the faintest of emotion, the Eternal Dweller, if he could, would have smiled at the sight of this little, broken thing.

a few words from

DAN CARRO

What do you love about the genre of horror?

I don't necessarily love horror. I love heroes. I love to see characters overcome adversity against all odds. They say "heroes are judged by their villains." Horror offers the best villains. It really puts protagonists through the ringer sometimes. That's my favorite kind of horror, one with a strong hero who is set against evil and has to overcome, no matter what horrific thing is thrown at them. Sure, often times, the protagonist in horror stories don't win. But then again, sometimes the story gives us characters like Ash Williams from *Evil Dead* or Ellen Ripley from *Alien*. If "what doesn't kill you makes you stronger," then horror heroes are some of the strongest you'll ever see.

What is some of your favorite horror literature?

I love when horror finds its way into other genres. For example, superhero comics. Check out *Arkham Asylum: A Serious House on Serious Earth* by Grant Morrison, chillingly illustrated by Dave McKean. Or *Batman the Cult* by Jim Starlin with illustrations by horror comics legend Bernie Wrightson. Or even *Gotham by Gaslight* by Brian Augustyn with artwork by *Hellboy* creator Mike Mignola.

What are some of your influences?

80's movies. Movies that I'd beg my mother to let me watch, that would instantly scar me for life. The one's that came back to haunt you when it was time to swim at the beach like *Jaws*, or go to sleep by yourself with that creepy tree right outside your window like *Poltergeist*. Ones with characters who looked so cool in *Fangoria*, but would come to life in your mind's eye any time you had to venture into a dark place. I also loved HBO's *Tales from the Crypt*, which often featured characters with poor moral compasses and what horrible ends said compasses led them to.

What is your favorite Halloween treat?

Food wise, things you can only get at Halloween. Count Chocula, Frankenberry, and Boo Berry come to mind. Pumpkin shaped cookies with the really sugary frosting. Yeah, you can get them all year long and they might look like flowers or Christmas trees or whatever, but I only want them when they look like pumpkins.

You are hosting the perfect Halloween movie marathon. What are the films you choose and why?

The perfect Halloween marathon for me would be based on films that have production designs and tone that invoke that Halloween feel. *Bram Stoker's Dracula* by Francis Ford Coppola comes to mind. I also would include *Monster Squad*. For a kid's movie, it didn't pull a lot of punches. It offers some of my favorite versions of the classic monsters and answers the age old question about whether or not Wolfman has nards. Other movies on my marathon: *Hocus Pocus, Halloween, Evil Dead, Evil Dead 2: Dead by Dawn, Army of Darkness, Cabin in the Woods, Sleepy Hollow, Trick R Treat, House 2: The Second Story, The Frighteners, Poltergeist* and *Nightmare Before Christmas*.

As a designer of horror theatre or experiences, explain your process.

The guests are a character. Plain and simple. That is why they come to haunts. It's not just to be scared. It's not just because they love horror… because some of them do not! They may have been dragged there by a loved one who does… no, I believe that the real reason people love haunts is to be the hero of their own perilous adventure. And my job is to create an excellent, terrifying adventure filled with the worst terrors and the most awful challenges. I am the villain and they are the hero of the story and when they leave that last room and hit the gift shop they should be panting, they should be exhausted and they should laughing. Not because it was funny, but because they are elated that they confronted fear and death and evil and came out unscathed.

Tell us about your contribution to our book. What was the inspiration?

When I was a kid, I took real delight in movies and comics. There were so many '*wow*' moments in the stories I loved. There was nothing like comparing notes with your friends after seeing something new at the drive-in. They would be equally traumatized and excited by the same stories. But kids today don't seem to have that excitement. Everything is old hat. They don't seem to care for the slow burning suspense of old fashioned horror. Something needs to happen right now and often, or it's boring. Yeah, they still get scared of the dark. Sure monsters still creep them out. It just doesn't seem to be fun for them anymore. They'd just rather the story get to the point so they can get back to their phones.

Describe the perfect Halloween.

Cool autumn air. Each tree crowned in an explosion of orange, yellow, and red leaves, some dotting the lawns and curbs of the neighborhood. Little monsters, superheroes, and strange characters running to and from doorways, candy in tow while parents give thankful waves. It's flickering glows from within jack-o-lanterns. It's finding that one house that gives out full size candy bars. It's taking all of this in from the porch while digesting a month's worth of visits to haunts and hayrides and pop up Halloween stores and the seasonal aisles department stores to buy even more crap for the yard you didn't need but really wanted. And maybe, without realizing it, we're doing what our ancestors did. Taking away the power of all things dark and scary by celebrating them instead of fearing them.

SCARE CRED: DAN CARRO

Dan Carro loves Halloween. His gateway into haunting was a scare actor position at Terror on Church Street over twenty-five years ago. Itching for more, he found himself at Skull Kingdom as part of the management team. Since then Dan's haunt habit has has spiraled out of control, careening him to creative projects for companies such as Distortions Unlimited, The Shallow Grave, A Petrified Forest, Spooky Empire, Dark Hour, Fear Asylum, and many more. Dan co-owned Legends' A Haunting at Old Town and is currently the creative director for Europa Park's Horror Nights: Traumatica event.

Zombie Activity Pages

BY DAVID COOK

He knows how to talk to the ladies

What a **MESS**! Help the zombie put himself back together. Make sure not to get any on you!

START

FINISH

A little girl zombie asks:
"Mama, do I have Daddy's **EYES?**"

And her mother replies:
"Yes, now **EAT THEM UP** before they get cold."

Here's a list of items that will surely come in handy.

Oh look, Bob has already found the first one!

```
C S E V F E O W N B P I
D R W A F V C Q U E D V
S U O I X A B B G T J O
W T N S M E R Z G E P L
J K E L S S W O H I G
B O R L F B A D H C S X
I N N L S S D S A T O
N X I Y N U M R M O A
C P A I K W B M V Q L O
S T A O Y W Z J H G J I
B H B T W U F M Q Y T H
C F G Q J X P O S O X E
```

☒ AXE
☐ BULLETS
☐ CHAINSAW
☐ CROSSBOW
☐ KNIFE
☐ MACHETE
☐ PISTOL
☐ SHOTGUN

a few words from

DAVE COOK

What do you love about the genre of horror?

I love the creativity. Horror is where the normal is turned upside down and anything is possible.

What is some of your favorite horror literature?

Comics like *Vault Of Horror, Tales From The Crypt, The Haunt Of Fear, Creepy,* and *Eerie.*

What are some of your influences?

Bernie Wrightson, Jack Davis, Rat Fink, and KISS.

What is your favorite Halloween treat?

Spiked apple cider with a side of fun-sized Baby Ruth bars.

You are hosting the perfect Halloween movie marathon. What are the films you choose and why?

The Monster (1925), *Abbott and Costello Meet Frankenstein* (1948), *Young Frankenstein* (1974), *An American Werewolf in London* (1981), and *Shaun of the Dead* (2004). I like my horror with a bit of humor.

If you could continue any horror story, what would it be?

Let The Right One In (2008). I would love to know what happened to Eli and Oskar.

As a designer of horror theatre or experiences, explain your process.

For zombies, a lot of the time it comes down to the eyes and the teeth. If you get those right – the rotting flesh and gore go pretty easily. The viewer needs to feel like - in that instant - they are not at the top of the food chain anymore.

When is the last time you were genuinely scared by something someone created?

I do a lot of work for a haunt here in Georgia – Netherworld Haunted House (http://Fearworld.com). They are a top-tier haunted attraction. This past year they moved to a new larger building, which gave them room to flex their scare a bit. I will admit to screaming like a little schoolgirl quite a few times. We went back repeatedly. They do such a great job and are really good people to work with.

Tell us about your contribution to our book. What was the inspiration?

As you can clearly see from my movie choices I like to have fun with my horror. I also like contradictions. So taking all the coloring book tropes with tongue in cheek dark humor – mixing that with zombies was a lot of fun to do for my contribution.

Describe the perfect Halloween.

At home with a nip in the air, not hot like it has been in Georgia these past few Halloweens. Decorations are up and spooky music on the turntable. It's a pretty "classic" nostalgic Halloween setting handing out candy.

SCARE CRED: DAVE COOK

Dave Cook draws monsters, beautiful girls, creatures, puppy dogs, and pretty much anything else you could think of. Flesh-eating-fun for the whole family! For nearly eight years he drew cute animals for Carter's/Osh Kosh baby clothes. As senior graphic illustrator at DS Cook Design, he now illustrates blood spewing zombies chasing half naked, axe wielding, pin-up girls. He has created artwork for *Stranger Things*, *The Walking Dead*, Jekyll Brewery, DragonCon among many more notable clients.

RETRIBUTION

BY RICK DANFORD

The large motorized raft lands suddenly on the white sandy beach. With the sun shining brightly through the trees, the passengers begin to exit the craft. The first three men are armed with 9mm's tucked in their waistbands and dark sunglasses. They lead the way for the final two passengers. Vince Colder, a 35 year old well built man steps out carrying a shiny metallic briefcase. His partner Jimmy who is a scrawny young man obviously nervous about their current situation follows him out of the craft.

All of the men are all dressed in dark suits, which in their current environment seemed incredibly out of place, but it was obvious this was a serious business trip. Across from them just outside the tree line sits a large wooden table. A large black man reclines in the only chair behind the table smiling widely at his new guests. Four large black men wearing dark sunglasses flank him to either side. They look pale and seem to be fidgeting ever so slightly as they stand focusing straight ahead. Their clothes are torn and dirty. Each dangles a machete at his side.

Vince makes eye contact with their host and is motioned to the table. The group slowly makes their way to the waiting party. The men open their jackets a little further to make sure the weapons are in plain view so as not to come across as hostile, only cautious.

"You must be Mr. Cloche," Vince says as he stands in front of the table across from the grinning man.

"And you must be Vince." Cloche says without losing his smile.

" My boss tells me we're to do some business today." Vince lays the briefcase on the table in front of Cloche and takes a step back.

Cloche sits up and pulls the case to him and opens it. He looks down into the opened case and smiles at the unseen contents.

"You understand the last time I attempted to do business with your boss it cost me five of my own men" Cloche says looking up at Vince.

"I know. It was unfortunate. He wanted me to express his sincere apologies about that and hopes this gesture will mend the relationship between you." Vince crosses his hands in front of him and waits for a response from Cloche.

Cloche sits back in his chair and looks up at him.

"With my belief's, the only way for he and I to continue our relationship would be for him to give me five lives in exchange for those that I lost."

With this Vince straightens up and his men look at one another not quite sure what they are hearing.

"This... gesture, as you put it, will help make the wrongs right and allow he and I to continue to do business."

Cloche sits back and raises his hands. With that motion, arms burst from the sand just below Vince's men and take hold of their legs. The men pull their guys out and try to free themselves from the death grips. Firing down into the sand as the corpses rise up and work their way closer to their meals. The men scream out as the bullets seem to have no effect.

Vince momentarily stunned by the attack turns to see one of Cloche's men raising his machete as he approaches him. Vince pulls out his gun and fires into the mans face. The force of the shot turns the mans head and causes his glasses to fly off but he does not fall. Instead he slowly turns back to Vince with half of his lower jaw torn away by the blast. Blood does not flow as it looks like dead flesh hanging from the mans face, but the worst part of all is the milky white eyes starring back at Vince. The eyes of a zombie.

Vince hears Jimmy scream out over his shoulder and he turns to see him being pulled down to the sand by two of cloche's men. The wounded zombie continues moving towards Vince and swings the machete at him just missing his head. Vince fires another shot into the chest of the creature with no effect. With his men and his partner screaming out in horror, Vince turns and runs for the tree line.

"Run Vince! Run!" Cloche calls out as he sits back enjoying the festivities.
Jimmy is pulled down struggling to the sand. He looks over at the other men as the reanimated corpses overtake them. The men are screaming as the zombies tear into their flesh and begin their feast. The screams begin to die down as the life is ripped from each man by the nightmare machines. The zombies hold Jimmy in place as Cloche walks over to him and looks down into his fear filled eyes.

"Rest easy my son. You will live again very soon. I promise you that."

Jimmy screams out as the zombies begin to tear his shirt off. They start clawing at his stomach ripping it open as his screams become high pitched wails. The creatures begin devouring him as he looks on, the life fading from his eyes. Vince is running through the trees as he notices zombies all around him in various stages of decomposition. They are all shambling towards him, all fixated on his every movement. He turns in every direction to see that everywhere he turns death approaches with dead hands and milky white eyes.

"They're coming for you Vince! The time for their debt to be paid is now!" Cloche calls out as he looks down into the briefcase, a smile creeps across his face as he looks at the stacks of newspaper cut to feel like the case was full of money. On top of the paper is a letter, 'Consider our debt paid in full.'

The End

RICK DANFORD

What do you love about the genre of horror?

I love the adrenaline, the edge of your seat suspense when you get anxious. There is truly something to be said about the emotions that fear and terror can create in you. As a filmmaker, it's that special feeling you get when you can make someone jump, shriek, or hide their eyes. Kind of like a badge of honor.

What is some of your favorite horror literature?

I was always a big Dean Koontz fan overall. But some of my favorite books are *They Thirst* from Robert R. McCammon, *Wolfen* by Whitley Strieber, and *The Stand* from Stephen King.

What are some of your influences?

I have a soft spot for 70's and 80's horror films. Some of my best movie viewing memories are from the drive-ins. Filmmaker-wise, my biggest influences are Tom Savini, James Wan, Matt Reeves, and George Romero.

What is your favorite Halloween treat?

My favorite Halloween treat is creating a cool haunted house to scare the kiddies. Yeah, that's me.

You are hosting the perfect Halloween movie marathon. What are the films you choose and why?

I would go old school because I'd like to have my friends experience where some of my roots took hold. I would play *The Car, Horror Express, The Tingler, Terror Train, It's Alive,* and *An American Werewolf in London.*

If you could continue any horror story, what would it be?

John Carpenter's *The Thing* remake. I know they came out with a prequel but I have a really cool story idea that picks up right where the Kurt Russell classic ended. Hopefully one day I'll get to make it.

As a designer of horror theatre or experiences, explain your process.

When designing something, I try to have a theme in mind and then try to imagine myself as a consumer and what I would want to see if I were them.

When is the last time you were genuinely scared by something someone created?

I truly can't remember. I know *Jaws* scared me out of the water. But even *The Exorcist* didn't bother me.

Tell us about your contribution to our book. What was the inspiration?

Retribution was a story I came up with when I was putting together my *Death Island* script. I also loved the idea of mashing genres what with horror and crime drama. This type of storytelling always intrigues me.

Describe the perfect Halloween.

The perfect Halloween starts and ends with a great Halloween party. A house full of your best friends, Halloween themed music playing, fog machine rolling, and horror movies on the television. I'm home!

SCARE CRED: RICK DANFORD

Born in New York and relocated to Florida at a young age, Rick has always dreamed of being in Hollywood. From filming his first film at the age of eight in his parents front yard with a Super-8 camera to working with the likes of Tom Savini, Ronnie Cox, Bruce Greenwood, and more. Rick is building a respectable resume in the indie film scene both in front of and behind the camera. He is an actor, writer, director and producer.

BENJAMIN

BY CHRIS DURMICK

"Please be brave, my little man," that's what my momma said.
She wasn't feeling very good, and early went to bed.

Morning came, and momma slept. She slept and slept all day.
And then men came, whispering, to take momma away.

In the dark I listened, 'til noises came no more.
They didn't know that I was there, behind the closet door.

When out I crept, the room was dark, and everything was still.
Tho' a candle was still flickering upon the windowsill.

In the light shined momma's hair lying near her bed.
It was soft and smelled like her; I put it on my head.

It hugs me tight like momma does when it starts to rain,
And I won't ever take it off, 'til momma's home again.

CHRIS DURMICK

What do you love about the genre of horror?

That it is primal. The triggers of fear exist within the most primitive part of the human brain, which is also closely related to the sexual/attractiveness drive. There is a reason horror movies make great date nights. Fear and horror are equal opportunists. They know no boundaries of wealth, class, race, or age. Religious folk have often ascribed the human reaction to fear as God's way of letting people communicate their terror without language. Horror is egalitarian and thus provides storytellers a perfect place to satisfy the human hunger for revenge and schadenfreude.

What is some of your favorite horror literature?

Anything by Edgar Allen Poe. This was a guy who was seriously fucked up and left his own issues right on the page. I would like nothing more than to resurrect Poe in today's world and see what nightmares he'd dream up.

What is your favorite Halloween treat?

My favorite conventional Halloween treat would likely be an Almond Joy, but the treat I enjoy the most are a bit more unconventional and come from scaring the bejesus out of the innocents who descend on my home for treats on Halloween night. So you think earning candy is that easy, do you? My home is always modestly decorated for the occasion, but that is only to create a McGuffin for me to hide in plain sight when the trick-or-treaters arrive. One year I buried myself waist deep as a mummy. Another, I lay in a coffin at an extreme rake to facilitate the jump-scare. This year, I built an oversized skeleton costume rig. I would stand stock still like a bad decoration and wait for the prey to slip past before lunging out. One has to be selective, of course so as not to traumatize anyone, and grown ups are always the more satisfying prey.

You are hosting the perfect Halloween movie marathon. What are the films you choose and why?

I'll limit this to ten, which is still quite a marathon. *Black Sabbath, The Haunting (1963), The Bride of Frankenstein, The Cabinet of Dr. Caligari, Alien, Eraserhead, The Nightmare Before Christmas,* John Carpenter's *The Thing, The Silence of the Lambs, An American Werewolf in London,* and *The Host.*

If you could continue any horror story, what would it be?

I have always wanted to make a sequel to *E.T. The Extraterrestrial.* Apologies to Mr. Spielberg, but if ET had been left behind, why wouldn't he try to pass himself off as friendly. My sequel starts with E.T.'s mother ship alighting in Elliot's backyard, with all the kids gathered around. E.T. steps out and his finger lights up as Elliot runs forward and then E.T. pushes his heart light right into Elliot's eye socket and flings his body aside. The rest is the *Mars Attacks* epic one would expect.

As a designer of horror theatre or experiences, explain your process.

I generally begin a project by first analyzing all of the objectives and characteristics of the thing. Among the first questions to ask (along with budget and total dwell time) are "what is this thing," and "who is it for." I then start with a complete and total brain dump, writing without any structure or form anything that comes to mind about the story we want to tell. Then I try to figure out the general story, the logline if you will, that defines the largest parts of the story like the basic plot and key characters.

I like to work with index cards as if I were writing a screenplay, and structure the event in much the same way, using three acts. From there it's a matter of figuring out the right beats, tempo, and physical scares or show action effects, and finally, writing the whole thing as a narrative that guests will never even know existed. I like to say that my main audience is the art director and design team, because they are the people who can benefit most from the details, but more than that, they can take a simple idea and modify it or improve it far beyond my capabilities.

Tell us about your contribution to our book. What was the inspiration?

My contribution was prompted by a simple concept; a friend of mine gathered thrift shop paintings and assigned them to different people to write a story to accompany the image. The results were staged like a gallery for a friendly get-together at his house. Although it's just a simple poem inspired by Poe, I find the result delightfully unsettling.

Describe the perfect Halloween.

My family and I have rented a cabin in a remote wood somewhere. We are hunkered down for a scary movie when the electricity goes out. The rest of the night is candles, ghost stories, and wind whistling through the loose windows.

SCARE CRED: CHRIS DURMICK

Chris is currently the Principal of Attractions and Museums at Thinkwell Group, where he has helped develop a myriad of attractions for clients including Warner Bros., Universal Studios, The Smithsonian Institute, The National Football League, and many others. Like so many other "carnies" in this industry, Chris' background has many twists and turns. A veteran of the "cardboard box in the garage" haunted attraction industry from his earliest days, his professional entree to themed entertainment was as a performer, wielding swords in Universal Studios Hollywood's *Adventures of Conan* show. He went on to develop and perform in *The Wild, Wild, Wild, West Stunt Show, The Flintstones Musical,* and *Totally Nickelodeon* before stepping into the full time role of Creative Director for Universal, developing the nascent Halloween Horror Nights mazes and attractions with partners like Rob Zombie, Clive Barker, Josh Whedon, Steven Somers, and many others.

A HANDY LOCATION

BY MICHAEL GAVIN

Nightclubs come and go all the time in downtown Orlando. Some say location is the key to success. Thus, one would think that a historic building just a few steps from the hustle and bustle Orange Avenue and at the back door to Church Street would ensure a lasting tenure. However, this two story structure at 17 W Pine Street in Orlando has endured many incarnations: the Blue Room, Deja Vu, Liquid Nightclub, Club Zen, Voyage, and Nightclub. What many may NOT know is that the location has a much darker, deadly, and twisted history. . .

Back in the late 1800s, a man named Elijah moved to Orlando. Being a skilled carpenter, he eventually set up shop in the very building that now still stands at 15-17 Pine Street in downtown Orlando. While his retail furniture business benefited homes across the community, Elijah had a far greater impact on Central Florida with his other, much more unconventional talent – he was an undertaker. Not just any ordinary undertaker – he was the first of his kind in town.

Prior to his arrival, family members who passed needed to be buried within a day or two of their death as there was no way to slow the process of decay. A new process of preservation called embalming allowed families to contact distant loved ones and delay burial for several days. This very skill was first brought to Orlando by the skilled undertaker. So it was, in 1905, on this spot on Pine Street that Elijah Hand set up his FUNERAL and FURNITURE business!

Elijah was eventually succeeded by his son, Carey in 1914. By 1920 a new funeral home was built across the street (in what is now the downtown campus for UCF) becoming the Carey Hand Funeral Home. It was the first in the region with a chapel, then a few years later adding the distinction of being the first with a crematorium. Prior to housing numerous bars, the cryptic venue served as a daycare, a school and a gateway for several phantoms and spirits.

Renovations in 1985 brought the property on Pine up to date with its current look and it would seem workers may have disturbed more than dust with their repairs. In addition to reports of hearing phantom footsteps emanating from the second floor, nightclub acts waiting in the upstairs green room complained of a heavy presence in the air. Some reported seeing ghosts of a woman or small children running about on that second floor. Internationally known psychic, Lynne Radar, did a segment of her cable TV show from the second floor of the former funeral parlor. Encountering several spirits during her walk through, she confirmed the name of one of the spirits as Robert.

As preparations began for the Orlando Hauntings Ghost Tours in October of 2000, employees of the Blue Room nightclub discussed firsthand accounts of cold spots and eerie activity. One employee befriended the young child of the club's owners (he would come running to eagerly greet her whenever she called his name). However, one day she called for the child and he did not respond. Alarmed, she called out for him several more times while searching the first floor. Up to the second floor she ran, concerned and calling the child's name again as she searched from office to office. She finally found the elusive child sitting cross-legged on the floor of one of the rooms and she was taken aback by the sinister grin on his face. She scolded him, demanding to know what he was up to. In a voice, clearly not that of a little boy, he reluctantly replied, "just playing . . ." After more intensive interrogation, the child admitted that he was entertaining an 'imaginary' friend by the name of Mr. Robert. The child was never allowed to play on the second floor again.

The building is once again active as the nightclub Ice Orlando, and the most popular "spirits" are those served to the patrons - perhaps a fitting final remedy to mask the cold spots that once haunted the Elijah Hand furniture store and funeral parlor? Will the new '"life" brought to 17 W Pine Street be enough to overcome its past, or will the building eventually succumb to its darker design and once again become deathly silent?

MY FIRST FRIGHT

BY MICHAEL GAVIN

For the longest time (even during research for the downtown ghost tours), I was a skeptic of most things that go bump in the night. I used to believe that, at least for most of the alleged hauntings I'd heard about, there was a logical explanation to what was transpiring. The following account relates how one incident changed my mind and opened my eyes to the possibility of things unseen or unexplained. I have changed the names of those involved, to protect their privacy. The Gaslight Apartments no longer exist; they have been renamed since this event took place. . .

I am not exactly sure when I met Lori; I think it was some time in 1996. Our first date took place one summertime Saturday afternoon and involved a casual lunch and light conversation. I was charmed with the opportunity to meet her then two-year-old daughter.

I seem to recall being intrigued yet skeptical when Lori first mentioned that the apartment she lived in was haunted. I was certain that there was a logical explanation for the apparent self-opening closet door in her daughter's room (perhaps the daughter opening the door in attempt to get attention?) Soon arrangements were made for me to be there for an evening to witness the events first hand (or, as I expected, gallantly dispel them). After dinner, the baby was put to bed and I made a point to inspect the suspect door to ensure it was secured and wouldn't budge unless the door handle was deliberately and completely turned. Lori arranged the covers over her daughter in such a manner that we would be able to tell if the child was the one getting out of bed and opening that closet door.

Anxiety and duty evoked the urge to check on the room about two hours later. To my shock and horror, the closet door directly in front of the bed was clearly and very much fully open! Lori had been with me the entire time and her daughter's bed sheets were completely undisturbed. Timidly we secured the suspect closet door again, and exited the room somewhat shaken and wondering if it would happen again.

We didn't have long to wonder - (note: this is about the time, in a movie, ominous music would begin to play). Later, upon revisiting the dark room, a sense of eerie déjà vu crept in as we were again greeted to a once secured closet door completely ajar and a peacefully sleeping little two-year-old girl, covers undisturbed. At this point Lori wanted to block the door, but caution prevailed (I didn't want anything to go flying into the child's bed). Instead, the baby was relocated to the couch and out of that room for the rest of the night. This game of opening and shutting the closet door continued throughout the evening, until we finally gave up around 2 a.m.

At one point, I recall noticing that a toy, which was resting against the far wall, had somehow made its way to the center of the room. All throughout the unnerving events, I recall experiencing a strong anxiety and kind of electricity in the air (a feeling I later came to know as the energy vibration associated with the presence of ghosts).

Finally, the sun began to break the night's darkness and it now felt "safe" to bravely venture into the small bedroom. What we discovered that morning astonished us beyond the previous evening's eerie activities. The closet with the mysteriously opening door had somehow shed all of its contents into a tangled heap on the closet floor. We found, on a nightstand next to the bed, a coloring book, conspicuously opened to page depicting a religious scene. It was the uncanny coincidence of the caption that caught our eye (and breath) "Jesus' friends were upset and suddenly he was there among them!" Was this a thinly veiled attempt at a message for the apartment's occupants? Even more bizarre was the earring that had managed to get stuck in the concrete ceiling as if it were a mere thumbtack upon a willing cork board.

Over time, the animated closet would prove to be the beginning of the challenge to my skepticism. Lori kept pictures of her daughter in ascending stages of maturity neatly lined on one of the apartment walls. Upon returning home from an afternoon outing, we were shocked to find that all of the framed photos had somehow become tilted at an odd angle.

However, the most mind numbing event came to my attention shortly after receiving a frantic call from Lori just as I was leaving work. She implored me to come over to the apartment immediately. When I arrived, I was stunned by what greeted me in her daughter's room.

In the center of the carpet was an upturned stool. Stacked very much like a house of cards was every toy the child owned, very delicately balanced. The toy sculpture reached beyond my ability to touch the top (and Lori is quite a bit shorter than me). This shook me to the very core and was the tipping point to a more open point of view towards the paranormal.

Shortly after that scare, we shared our other-worldly accounts with a local psychic. We soon learned that we were dealing with the spirit of a young girl, quite possibly hiding in the closet of that bedroom. What could have frightened this child so badly? Was she trying to tell us something? After discussing the events and information we had just learned, Lori revealed that there had been a fire some years ago that had damaged the apartment complex. Allegedly the fire started in the very same apartment she called home.

Lori and I drifted apart shortly after these events, though not for any reasons related to the insane and alarming activity in that apartment. In fact, I do not know if the events even still occur. I am, however, now a definite believer in the paranormal.

HILLTOP HAUNTS

BY MICHAEL GAVIN

Most people visiting Central Florida only think of theme parks and dinner shows, but the area has a rich and very interesting history. Part of that past hides a dark and disturbing secret.

Ocoee, located in Orange County Florida, just west of Orlando, has a population of roughly 36,000 residents. Many of those locals are probably unaware of the role the town played in 1920. Before this tragic tale can be told, it's important to know the key players:

July Perry – an African American labor leader. If workers were needed, July was the guy to go to;

Mose Norman – an African-American land owner/resident of Ocoee and prospective voter;

Col. Sam Salisbury – former chief of police in Orlando; and Judge John Cheney.

It was November 2nd and time to vote in the Warren G. Harding/James M. Cox Presidential election. African-American voters were being harassed and turned away from voting stations. Mose Norman initially refused to leave until he, and several others were forced away. Norman complained to Judge Cheney. The Judged asked Mose to obtain the names of those preventing him from voting. Instead Mose Norman returned with a shotgun. The weapon was wrested away from and turned against Norman, who fled the scene.

A white mob, led by Col. Salisbury, gathered to track Norman down. When they learned that Mose Norman sought refuge in the home of July Perry, 100 men descended on Perry's Ocoee home. In self-defense, Perry fired upon the attackers at the back door. Col. Salisbury was shot in the arm and two other men were killed.

Though he fled and tried to hide, Perry was apprehended, treated at the local hospital and then taken to the County Jail in downtown Orlando (now the location of Independent Bar) on the corner of Washington and Orange. However, he was pulled from his transport and lynched on the spot, his body left hanging from a nearby telephone pole. Mose Norman was never heard from again.

The incident incited riots with an army of white men surrounding, torching and setting fire to the African-American area of Ocoee. This intense injustice left the city absent of any black citizens for over sixty years!

Flash forward to "modern times." Greenwood Cemetery, the largest public cemetery of its kind in Florida, was purchased by Orlando in 1880. Within the gorgeous 26-acre park covered with towering, moss-covered oak trees are final resting places of many of Orlando's prominent historic figures. Among these are the grave sites of July Perry, Col. Sam Salisbury and Judge John Cheney. Cheney is buried atop the tallest hill in the park, near the Mott family mausoleum. Across the narrow, paved path rests Col. Salisbury. July Perry's gravesite sits at the bottom of the hill, near the sexton's office. All three within sight of each other . . . buried but, perhaps not at rest.

A Personal Perspective

I've had the privilege of enjoying Greenwood Cemetery's monthly moonlight historic walk on a few occasions. Other times, photography of the historic headstones and peaceful atmosphere produced scores of satisfying snapshots (some of which are currently used on the city's cemetery website).

I was always aware of the ghost stories surrounding Greenwood. Tales of phantom taps on the shoulder, disembodied voices and even an alleged sighting or two. With three dedicated children's burial areas and an unmarked burial area for former 'residents' of Orlando's Sunland Hospital (a now razed tuberculosis hospital turned into mental institution), these stories neither surprised or caused me much concern. However, around midnight, as one history walk was wrapping up, that would all change.

As I was chatting with one of the employees, he reminded me that it was close to "the hour." We both turned and walked up the cemetery's steep hill, towards the Wilmott mausoleum and Salisbury/Cheney gravesites. Though a typical warm, humid Florida evening, as we neared the top, we both were suddenly aware of a chill in the air. As the hilltop was reached, very tactile and significant waves of what can only be described as a light electric-like energy washed over us, seeming to bounce back and forth across the path. Was this the Colonel or the Judge (or both) or perhaps some other entity asking for attention? We never really found out, but then we also decided the short stroll should be quickly curtailed, agreeing that it would be best to leave these energies to themselves.

MICHAEL GAVIN

What do you love about the genre of horror?

Classic, gothic atmospheric and suspenseful stories. However, what I like best is that it usually shows that humans are the real monsters.

What is some of your favorite horror literature?

Authors Edgar Allen Poe and Owl Goingback. Ghost stories, haunted histories, and photo books such as Joshua Hoffine's *Horror Photography* and Misty Keasler's *Haunt*.

What are some of your influences?

Disney's *Haunted Mansion* and everything about it, Dick Smith, Tom Savini, Boris Karloff, Lon Chaney, and Lon Chaney Jr. I first discovered a love for horror at age nine when I found out that I could become the monster via a makeup book from the school book fair.

What is your favorite Halloween treat?

A fiendishly decorated sugar cookie is fun.

You are hosting the perfect Halloween movie marathon. What are the films you choose and why?

The Universal Studios classic monsters all the way. And maybe a few other classics like *Night of the Living Dead* and *House on Haunted Hill*. These "old" black and white films have a class about them that's missing with today's horror.

If you could continue any horror story, what would it be?

Its not really true horror, but I would love to see more from realm of *The Nightmare Before Christmas* more adventure was hinted at and the whimsical, haunting atmosphere is pure fun. Also the live-action *Addams Family* movies but only if done right.

As a designer of horror theatre or experiences, explain your process.

For ghost stories, local history research, cross referencing stories and as much as possible, first hand accounts. With the photography, am always looking for creepy cool, spooky locations (especially cemeteries) and events to shoot (or similar dark inspiration to create the environment). If shooting with a model, I like to work with the subject to involve them with story creation.

Tell us about your contribution to our book. What was the inspiration?

My love of horror, fueled by working with haunted houses and macabre make-up since the pre-teen days, guided me to find the best job ever - being a member of the "Eternal Dwellers Theater Company" - AKA Orlando's Terror on Church Street. The haunt was set up within a historic building that was once owned by Daniel Boone's grandson, which seemed to be haunted. After the attraction closed, I dove into local Orlando history and uncovered several other haunted locations. This led to, with the help of a few friends, the creation of Orlando's first ghost tour (most of the tales are from first-hand accounts after several interviews). Events and experiences since have yielded a few more stories like the ones shared. Imagined horror is fun and I love to create that environment with my photographs, but the true stories give the best chills.

Describe the perfect Halloween.

As a long-time resident of Florida - *no humidity* - and plenty changing leaves, cooler temperatures a decorated neighborhood, spooky music, treats and friends gathered around a bonfire (after trick-or-treating) while either swapping ghost stories or watching classic horror movies

SCARE CRED: MICHAEL GAVIN

As a fan of fear for over forty years, writing for an entertainment news site and fantasy/horror themed photography currently fuel Michael's passion for fright filled fiendish fun. With the help of a few fiends, he created and conducted Orlando's very first haunted history tour: Orlando Hauntings in 2000. A book detailing those spooky stories and first-hand experiences is in the works. Haunts and attractions like Terror on Church Street, Skull Kingdom, and Disney's Tower of Terror have all been Michael's "home" at one time or another. His photography and writings have appeared in *Playboy, Forbes, GHOST! Magazine, Orlando Weekly*, the *City of Orlando* website, *Gores Truly* and *Inside the Magic*. Michael's images have also been used to promote fan conventions, Pirates Dinner Adventure, and The Shallow Grave haunted attractions.

THE PUMPKIN TREE

BY KIM GROMOLL

KIM GROMOLL

What do you love about the genre of horror?

Nostalgia. It takes me back to Saturday afternoon matinee double features at Plains Movie Theater with my brother and cousins. It's that feeling of watching a monster movie like *Frankenstein, The Wolfman,* or *The Creature From the Black Lagoon* on a perfect fall night.

What is some of your favorite horror literature?

Stephen King, of course, but I also loved Edgar Allan Poe growing up.

What are some of your influences?

In my art, it's the early illustrators like NC Wyeth, JC Leyendecker, and Howard Pyle. In film, it's directors like Steven Spielberg, Ridley Scott, Guillermo del Torro, and Stanley Kubrick

What is your favorite Halloween treat?

Almond Joy.

You are hosting the perfect Halloween movie marathon. What are the films you choose and why?

For classic horror, I'd choose *Frankenstein*. For comic relief, I'd choose *Young Frankenstein*. For the scariest movie ever, I'd choose *Insidious*.

As a designer of horror theatre or experiences, explain your process.

I have been a designer of haunted houses for a theme park. I always liked to give guests a big entry statement. I like to immerse the guest in the experience. It helps to create that suspension of reality. Then I use misdirection throughout the maze to set up scares.

When is the last time you were genuinely scared by something someone created?

I had three or four jump startles in a haunt at Halloween Horror Nights in Universal Orlando this year. The house was the carnival house and it was by far the most beautiful and well thought out house I have experienced in years.

Tell us about your contribution to our book. What was the inspiration?

I worked with J. Michael Roddy on a scare zone in 2008. We wanted to create a traditional halloween from our childhoods. One aspect of the zone involved using over four-hundred jack-o-lanterns in a walkway. They flickered and blew out on cue and would then slowly come back to life. It is still one of the zones that i am most proud of and still is a fan favorite. I wanted to create that feeling in an illustration. Setting jack-o-lanterns in a dead fall tree at the beginning of a pathway leading into the woods.

Describe the perfect Halloween.

Crisp fall weather, autumn leaves, a bright full moon with wispy clouds, jack-o-lanterns in walkways, kids running from house to house in their costumes ringing doorbells and bubbling with excitement for the treats they get.

SCARE CRED: KIM GROMOLL

Kim Gromoll is a designer for all of the major theme parks. Over the past twenty years, he has designed hundreds of attractions, parade floats, shows, haunted houses and scare zones, props, sets, and just about anything associated with the theme park industry. Kim is also a fine artist. He paints limited edition prints for Lucasfilm and also sells original art in galleries. Kim lives in Orlando, Florida with his wife, Maryann, who is a college professor. He enjoys hanging out with his two adult kids, Nicki and Michael. Together, they like to go on adventures such as fossilizing in Wyoming, treasure hunting the Florida gold coast, visiting the 150th anniversary reenactment of Gettysburg, traveling to Ireland, and visiting Michael Skellig.

WHEN MONSTERS GET OLD
BY TIM HARKLEROAD

When monsters get old
they're not quite as scary,
and even sometimes
they're more fun.

They're too tired to chase you,
or jump and say "Boo",
and have trouble
trying to run.

Frankenstein's vision
is not very good
and he has to wear
glasses to see,

but he's still really cool
with those bolts through his neck
and those clamps on his
forehead are neat.

Dracula can't really
chew on your neck
cause his teeth might fall out
when he bites,

but he's still a great dresser
with that big awesome cape
as he flaps his way home
in the night.

The Wolfman, sadly, is
loosing his hair,
and what little he has
has turned gray,

but he still can do
that cool morphing thing,
and change back to an
old man by day.

Frankenstein's bride
is just like your Grandma
with her coupons and things
that she saves,

but she still has that
hair-do that goes on for miles
and lipstick that
goes on for days.

The old Lagoon Creature
has dried up a bit
and he has much
backache and pain

but he loves to go fishing
down in his lagoon
and he'll take you
if it doesn't rain.

The Mummy was old
to start with, you see,
but he's a lot
older today.

He wraps up in more bandages
or wears an old sweater
when the weather
is chilly and gray.

The Opera Phantom
might play you a tune
though it might be a
little too loud.

He has trouble hearing
without hearing aids,
but he's still a big
smash with the crowd.

The witch's old broom
like your grandmother's car
is slow and
noisy today.

but she'll take you neat places
like the mall or the park
while her signal light's
blinking away.

See? Monsters get older
like all people do
but older people
are cool.

They're always more patient
and do neat things for you
and teach things they
don't teach in school.

They take you fishing or shopping
or riding around,
or might read scary
stories to you.

So if you see an old monster,
just pretend to be one
and bow and say
"Howww doooo you doooo?"

TIM HARKLEROAD

What do you love about the genre of horror?

I'm reminded of my first encounter with *Famous Monsters of Filmland* magazine. My older cousin had an issue when we visited them in Maryland. It took me three days to work up the courage to read it. I was six-years-old at the time. Once I saw it, I was mesmerized and hooked on horror for life.

What is some of your favorite horror literature?

Anne Rice' *Vampire* series, some Peter Straub, a few Stephen King titles, Richard Matheson. To be honest, I preferred reading horror movie anthologies and classic movie scripts or transcriptions.

What are some of your influences?

Dick Smith, Boris Karloff, Christopher Lee, Tim Burton, Phil Morris, Harry Blackstone, and Jonathan Frid - all for different reasons. I realize none of these are writers per se, but also George Romero, Tobe Hooper, John Carpenter, Guillermo Del Toro, Quentin Tarantino, all the giants.

What is your favorite Halloween treat?

Candy corn and buttercream pumpkins.

You are hosting the perfect Halloween movie marathon. What are the films you choose and why?

The original *Halloween, The Legend of Hell House, The Nightmare Before Christmas,* The original *Woman in Black, Bram Stoker's Dracula, Bride of Frankenstein, The Ghost and Mr. Chicken,* and *The Howling*.

If you could continue any horror story, what would it be?

I would continue the original *Dark Shadows* television show, focusing on Barnabas Collins as he leaves his beloved Collinsport and travels back to Europe.

As a designer of horror theatre or experiences, explain your process.

I love startle scares, but I usually draw upon my own fears. Ghosts scare me. (I ghost hunt and I think we have one in our house) Giant creatures also scare me, just the thought of something so gigantic. That includes things like Godzilla, King Kong, the *Cloverfield* creature. Snakes also scare me. So when crafting a haunt I rely on creating an atmosphere conducive for the supernatural, in a rotted, decaying, formerly beautiful house. They I make them my customers scream like four-year-olds with good ol' startle scares.

When is the last time you were genuinely scared by something someone created?

Seeing Mrs. Drablow come over the end of the bed in *Woman in Black* turned my blood cold, but I gotta say the *The Blair Witch Project* also terrified me. Ed Sanchez is a genius. Wish I knew him. We chatted online a couple of times, but I would love to meet him and listen to him for a while. I talk too much but sometimes I remember to listen. I learn a lot from listening.

Describe the perfect Halloween.

Me in costume, I *always* dress up. Standing in the doorway, or backstage, of my haunted house, hearing the people scream, and me being the one responsible. I also like going somewhere with my wife, in costume, and then getting home in time to see *Halloween* for the millionth time, before Halloween cedes to November. Some of my best Halloween's were when I was a kid. I also enjoy teaching my children about the fun of it all. I want my kids to see in the holiday everything that I did. It's the one time of the year when I too am a child.

SCARE CRED: TIM HARKLEROAD

At the age of seven, after seeing magician Phil Morris perform, Tim Harkleroad decided he wanted to be a magician. He later toured with Phil performing throughout the south. At eleven, Tim received a cardboard skeleton, which he used to haunt his front yard the next Halloween. He later authored some of the most acclaimed "Haunted House How-To Books" in the industry including *The Complete Haunted House Book* and *Make Your House Everything You've Ever Haunted*. Tim has been a stand-up comic and ventriloquist, entertaining cruise ship audiences for twenty-seven years, owned and operated The Haunting of Krone House, and played banjo and uilleann pipes in Bluegrass and Irish bands respectively. Tim is currently the co-writer of and lead in the hugely successful *Hatfield and McCoy Dinner Feud*, where he also plays banjo. He lives with his wife Melanie in Seymour, Tennessee and is currently involved in writing new projects for Fee Hedrick Family Entertainment.

Brain Hurts

BY DAVID HUGHES

DAVID HUGHES

What do you love about the genre of horror?

It is no longer required that we, as a species, be hunter/gatherers to survive. As a result, we no longer have to go out into the wilds and brave the dangers within. We have evolved to the point that natural predators are no longer a threat to our daily existence, yet we have these deeply buried fight or flight survival instincts that are intrinsically woven into our DNA. Horror films tap into that instinct, and although we logically know that we are safe inside the theater, the best horror films are able to tap into that fight or flight impulse and keep us on the edge of our seat.

What is some of your favorite horror literature?

I have always loved the humanity of Stephen King's characters and the worlds he was able to build. Although they "dip" into the supernatural, most of King's stories deal with what's best and worst of humanity. I still haven't found that perfect "ghost story". The kind that just makes you afraid t walk in the woods at night

What are some of your influences?

I grew up a child of the 70's and 80's with a "healthy" dose of sci-fi and Saturday afternoon *Shock Theater* hosted by the amazing Dr. Creep. I always was enamored of the Universal Monster designs, but the make-up in *Planet of the Apes*, which was my obsession from age six to twelve, melted my little brain. I saw *The Poseidon Adventure* in 1972, which is when I realized that Roddy McDowall was the same actor that played Cornelius. I kept trying to see his face through the ape makeup and I just couldn't. He *was* Cornelius. It was amazing that the make-up could be so transformative. In 1977, *Star Wars* was released and like every other kid in the world it nearly became a religion. I was less drawn to the mythology and more intrigued with the '*How did they do that?*' question. I scoured every pulp magazine at the time to find behind-the-scene pictures of how they created this cinematic universe. I was so fascinated with every little detail that it subconsciously led me to pursue a career in set design.

The first true horror film I saw in the theater, at age fifteen, was *Friday the 13th*, and it was the gateway film to all the early 80's slasher films. I did not discover *Halloween* until several years later with the advent of home video and HBO. But I still hold John Carpenter's *The Thing* as the best of the modern horror era. A perfect setting, spot on casting & performances, and a creature that is arguably the best practical design ever to be put to film.

What is your favorite Halloween treat?

Reese's Peanut Butter Cup followed by a Butterfinger. Toasted pumpkin seeds are right up there too.

You are hosting the perfect Halloween movie marathon. What are the films you choose and why?

Bride of Frankenstein - great atmosphere, story, and fun. *The Thing* - same reasons. *Halloween* - great pacing, framing, music. *The Exorcist* - I love the audio design. *The Others* - one of my favorite "In an old house" ghost stories.

As a designer of horror theatre or experiences, explain your process.

As a designer of "haunted houses" I close my eyes and try visualize the setting, the character, and the action. I try to see all possibilities from different angles, and try to pinpoint what I believe to be the problem areas. If I can feel comfortable with what I see in my mind's eye, I move on to the next issue. If not, I keep hammering at it until the problem is solved, or until the realization that perhaps it is not going to work sinks in at which time I move forward with a new and different idea.

When is the last time you were genuinely scared by something someone created?

Scared? I don't "scare" easily. That being said, I will admit that *Hereditary* deeply affected me in the theater, and stayed with me much longer than any horror film in recent memory.

Tell us about your contribution to our book. What was the inspiration?

Have you ever felt completely defeated? That you have been utterly drained of all artistic thought, and that the imagination well has finally run dry? Well…..

Describe the perfect Halloween.

A cool fall night, with clouds skating across a full warm moon. Jack-o-lanterns flicker along a path as leaves crunch underfoot on our way to a campfire that glows in the middle of a forest clearing. The smell of wood smoke permeates my clothing, as I sit with a small group of close friends. We sit and stare into the flames sipping hot cider and apple jack, as we listen to classic radio ghost stories, and talk about Halloween memories.

SCARE CRED: DAVID HUGHES

David grew up in 70's Midwest Ohio, which meant nothing ever happened. Growing up before video games, cell phones, and the internet meant spending a lot of time outside and shuffling around in his dad's basement woodshop "crafting" things. Summer bicycle rides to Knollwood Pharmacy for candy, comics, and the perusal of *Famous Monsters of Filmland* and *MAD Magazine* led to a fascination with how fantasy worlds were created. In 1981, his older brother bought him the basic *Dungeons & Dragons* boxed game. This became an outlet to create worlds, weave stories, and inhabit them with a myriad of fascinating monsters. This love lead to a study of, and a career in, scenic set design. For the last twenty years he has worked for Universal Orlando in the Entertainment Art & Design Department as the manager of scenic design. In this role he oversees the design of Halloween Horror Nights, continuing his love of creating and exploring fantastical worlds.

Screwed

BY JAIME JESSUP

SCREEN: Screwed Act I

JAMES and DAVID, 30's, brothers, are placing items in a black
duffel bag. There is a chair nearby in the room.

> DAVID
> I'm just saying, I've never heard
> a story end well that begins
> with the phrase, "I was on OK Cupid."

> JAMES
> Well then how are you supposed to get
> girls online?

> DAVID
> You don't go online, retard - you
> suit up and look classy like me.

> JAMES
> Like you.

> DAVID
> Like me- you buy one of these stupid
> $40 ironic retro T-shirts from Urban
> Outfitters and they're all like,
> 'omigod, I love Zelda too!"

> JAMES
> Zelda?

> DAVID
> Or some faggy blazer with elbow pads.

James puts a roll of duct tape in the bag.

> JAMES
> Just to clarify, we're talking about getting GIRLS, right?

                    DAVID
          Shut up- you asked a question, I'm
          answering it. You go to a bar, pick
          your target, ignore her, you do NOT
          buy her a drink first thing, and then
          you separate her from her friends and
          make fun of her.

David loads some zip ties into the bag.

                    JAMES
          Seriously, this works for you?

                    DAVID
          Every girl's got flaws- just make your
          best guess and zero in on it. Is she a
          little fatter than her friends? She
          noticed it too, believe me. Find a subtle
          way to work that into the conversation,
          like a backhanded compliment.

David places a roll of black plastic trash bags into the bag.

                    JAMES
          And Mom wonders why we're single.

                    DAVID
          Bro- I swear to god- it works every time.
          Like, "Oh, I really admire your confidence,
          going out with all those model-types." You
          get her all insecure, she'll be dying for
          you to un-do the damage to her paper-thin
          self esteem by paying more attention to her.

                    JAMES
          Or, finally buying her a drink.

                    DAVID
          Exactly- always wine. And a NICE wine,
          too- because you're better than her and
          you're not interested in getting her wasted.

You don't care. You're the popular-
reference- shirt-wearing guy SHE needs
to impress.

David drops a ziplock baggie full of white powder into the
bag.

                    DAVID
          Then you drop in the molly and watch
          her pass out.

                    JAMES
          Meh. Maybe I should stay with e-harmony.

                    DAVID
          Internet's too easy to track, man. They're
          getting too smart about it.

                    JAMES
          Not the ones I've met. And they NEVER look
          like their photos. "More to love" my ass.

                    DAVID
          I'm serious James- we said we'd do it my
          way, and my way doesn't leave a paper
          trail. You wanna get caught?

                    JAMES
          Of course not.

                    DAVID
          Then go get a shirt from my closet, pack
          it up, and we'll find that same "more to
          love" girl who's "out celebrating being
          single and loving her life-"

                    JAMES

          Pfff!

> DAVID
> And stab the shit outta her.

James smiles and shyly adds a hunting knife to the growing collection inside the bag.

Lights Out

SCREEN: Screwed Act II

Lights up.

David and James walk back inside. David has the duffel bag. James is carrying a small box.

> DAVID
> You're an idiot. What are we going
> to do with a turtle?

James pulls a shell from the box and peers inside, trying to see the frightened animal.

> JAMES
> It's a tortoise- I dunno. Can we just keep it?

David puts the unzipped duffel bag on the table and starts unpacking. The items have been used- the trashbags are not neatly rolled, the zipties are in disarray.

> DAVID
> No we can't KEEP it. What are you gonna
> feed it? Do you even know what turtles EAT?

> JAMES
> Tortoises- and no. But I can look it up.

> DAVID
> You don't get souvenirs. We talked about
> that. That's the one rule- no panties,
> no hair, no jewelry. Why do you think we
> bury them in the first place?

                    JAMES
          (mumbles) It seemed like the right
          thing to do- and it's not a trophy
          David it's a turtle.

                    DAVID
          Wasn't it a tortoise 30 seconds ago?

James taps the shell.

                    JAMES
          Aww it's scared. If we'd just left
          it there in the road someone might've
          hit it.

                    DAVID
          We dumped that slut in the middle of
          NOWHERE, OK? NO ONE drives out there.
          Did you see a single pair of headlights
          while she was screaming?

                    JAMES
          No, but it was crawling in the road.

                    DAVID
          What, like her? "Oh, don't kill me,
          please, stop, I'll do anything!

                    JAMES
          (laughs, joins in)
          I don't want to die!

David suddenly pulls the bloody hunting knife from the duffel
bag and plunges it into the tortoise shell. James is horrified.

                    DAVID
          Take that you filthy whore!

                    JAMES

          Aw, you dick!

For a moment, David is lost in his fantasy- then he comes around and acknowledges his brother.

> DAVID
> No souvenirs. You brought something from there to here. That's a no-no. That will get us screwed.

James looks at the shell sadly.

> JAMES
> I only wanted to help.

> DAVID
> You wanna help next time? Call the crime hotline.

> JAMES
> What? Really?

> DAVID
> (joking)"Hello? My brother and I just violated a girl and she woke up halfway through and she keeps screaming while we're burying her- what should we do?"

> JAMES
> You're nuts dude.

> DAVID
> No, they want you to do it right. Why do you think the County puts all those "call before you dig" signs.

> JAMES
> (get the joke) Heh.

David wipes the knife on his jeans and starts playing with it.

> DAVID
> I hate it when they try and and tell you personal stuff.

JAMES

I couldn't even understand her. All that
crying with the tape in her mouth.

DAVID

Crying about how much she loves her sister.
It's Victim 101. They try and remind you
they're people too. Like I'm gonna change
my mind because you also have a first name?
Boo hoo. You still drank my wine, slut.

JAMES

Was that it? Bro I SAW her sister at the
bar. She was HOT, dude. Such a slut. She
wanted me so bad. (sulks)But we had to
pick the big one, I know.

DAVID

(dreamily) How amazing would it be to
have both- lay 'em out side by side in
the woods?

JAMES

What, do the hot one in the same hole as
the dead one?

DAVID

If by same hole you mean the pit we dumped
her in, yeah. That's the Maslow's Hierarchy.
That's the dream right there. Sisters in the
same grave, Jesus.

JAMES

I mean, we know what bar she goes to. I
wouldn't mind seeing her again.

DAVID

So we make the rounds every so often, and
she'll come out when she's done grieving.
Then, we have an easy way to rattle her.

                    JAMES
        "Oh, boo hoo, I'm a sad hot whore."

                    DAVID
        "Drink your cabernet you'll feel better."

                    JAMES
        Sisters. How awesome would it be?

                    DAVID
        Save it. We gotta get some sleep- we
        have church in the morning.

Lights Fade to Black.

SCREEN: Screwed Act III

Lights up.

David enters, looking pissed. He is followed by James, and
MICHELLE, 30's, who drunkenly hangs on him and stumbles a bit
in her heels.

JAMES
Hey, yeah, so have a seat, I'll get you something to drink.

Michelle sits, calling out to the brothers as they stand at
the counter.

                    MICHELLE
        It's like I just can't believe it's been
        a month since she's gone, right? Like,
        and you guys were there, you saw her that
        night, it's totally fate that I find you guys
        again. I just... she was so beautiful, you
        know? Seeing you again is like getting a
        little piece back...

David whispers angrily to James in the kitchen.

                    DAVID
What the hell are you doing?

                    JAMES
I never ask you for anything. We ALWAYS
do it your way- this girl WANTS me.

                    DAVID
You didn't even dose her and she's wasted.
She'd want anybody.

                    JAMES
You're jealous. You're jealous of me
because this time it's ME.

                    DAVID
OK, sure. Fine. She wants you- what are
you going to do with her?

                    JAMES
I dunno. Can we just keep her? Just for
a while?

                    DAVID
NO. You have your fun with her, we bring
her to the hole and then it's my turn.

                    JAMES
We always do it your way, in the dirt, in
the hole- you never let me decide anything.
You never let me have anything.

                    DAVID
Fine- you can have a nice pretty needle in
your arm when you fuck up and let her get
away. Is that what you want?

                    JAMES
...no.

                        DAVID
          You think that's what mom wants?
          Watching through a window while the
          State pumps her sons full of potassium
          chloride?

                        JAMES
          ...no.

                        DAVID
          What's that?

                        JAMES
          (shouts) I said no!

Michelle hollers. She's rooting around in her purse.

                        MICHELLE
          No means no! But I didn't say no so
          let's party!

James shoots a pleading look at David, who finally acquiesces.

                        DAVID
          You have 10 minutes. Molly. Go.

He hands his brother a bottle of wine and the ziplock bag full
of powder.

James approaches Michelle.

                        JAMES
          Here, Michelle, do you want some wine? It's a-

He hesitates, looking into the kitchen where a disgusted David
mouths out the pronunciation for him.

                        JAMES
          Caber-nay Soovig...

                    MICHELLE
        Sounds amazing- do you have a corkscrew?

David approaches and hands James a corkscrew with a brightly-
colored handle.

                    DAVID
            Right here.

He heads back into the kitchen area.

                    MICHELLE
            Perfect- lemme just pee first.

She exits, taking her purse.

                    DAVID
            I want my turn. This is SISTERS. Don't
            ruin tonight for us.

The lights suddenly go out- the stage is completely dark.

                    MICHELLE
            (laughing in the darkness)I hit the wrong
            switch. (giggles) Where are you?

                    JAMES
        Uh, I'll come over, hang on.

We hear him walking across stage when a ZOLT of flashing strobe
FX illuminates Michelle violently tasing him. He collapses.

                    DAVID
            What the- James!

In the flicker, we see David run towards his brother and
Michelle tases David. The lights strobe again with an electric
sizzle, showing Michelle using both hands to tase both
brothers simultaneously and all goes black again.

SCREEN: Screwed Epilogue

Lights up.

David lays on the floor, blindfolded, naked and spread- eagled in just white boxer shorts. The fly area of the boxers has a familiar brightly-colored object peeking out.

James is tied to a chair with his arms ziptied behind him. James has a wet green towel covering his head and face.

(*IMPORTANT: JAMES needs to have a breathing tube hidden beneath the towel- all the actor must do is pantomime the motions- his audio can be tracked in for his safety.)

Michelle saunters in, casually sipping wine from the now-open bottle. James starts to stir.

                    JAMES
          David? DAVID???

                    MICHELLE
          He's still out. Sorry.

                    JAMES
          Did you kill him?

                    MICHELLE
          Not yet. I'm not done with him.

                    JAMES
          Are you... done with me?

                    MICHELLE
          That depends. Are you sorry?

She approaches the seated man.

                    JAMES
          Sorry?

Michelle grabs him by the back of his towel, and his hair, jerking his head back and pouring wine into his mouth. She waterboards him for a second then lets him sputter for air.

                    MICHELLE
          Are you sorry for killing her?

                    JAMES
          Yes I'm sorry! I'm so sorry!

                    MICHELLE
          Why are you sorry?

She repeats the action, forcing more wine into his mouth before letting him have more air.

                    JAMES
          I just... wanted something to have.

Michelle drowns him a third time, and James gasps and chokes, screaming for help.

                    JAMES
          David! Mom! MOM!!! Stop it! MOMMM!!!

David starts to move and stir from his position on the counter.
                    DAVID
          (lifting blindfolded head) James- JAMES!
          Where are you? JAMES!!!

Michelle takes the hunting knife and plunges it into the top of James' toweled head. Crimson spills out from the wound, covering the winestained towel in a fresh vibrant red.

James, like the turtle, dies instantly, slumping forward. David is breathing hard- he knows he's next.

Michelle climbs nimbly, cat-like, onto the floor, positioning herself over David and removes his blindfold.

                    MICHELLE
          Peekaboo! I know you like the kinky
          stuff, so I tied you up.

                    DAVID
          You whore- you filthy c-

Michelle kisses him, shutting him up.

                    MICHELLE
          Shh. You kiss your mother with that mouth?
          I know what you did to my sister. And I
          know where you left her. In fact, I know
          pretty much everything about you by this point.

                    DAVID
          How did you???

                    MICHELLE
          You're SO much smarter than James- but
          unfortunately, you're both retards. I
          saw the two of you at the bar the night
          you took her. And I've been out every night
          since then, waiting to "run into you." And
          you're so predictable, with your patterns
          and your wine buying and your stupid
          T-shirts and your same dump site... Did you
          know James goes there much every day? Then
          drives straight here?

                    DAVID
          Oh my god.

Michelle shakes her head at him.

                    MICHELLE
          Mm-nnn. No God tonight. Not for you.

She rises, straddling above him like an avenging angel.

                    MICHELLE
          Just me. And your corkscrew.

                         DAVID
          My wha?

Michelle points down towards David's genital area, where,
hanging out of the end of what is obviously his covered-up
dick, is the brightly-colored corkscrew handle.

                         DAVID
          OH GOD OH GOD YOU BITCH- WHAT DID YOU DO?!?

                       MICHELLE
          Oh, David- looks like you got screwed this time.

He groans as she elegantly places a pointy high heel into his
stomach and bends over, takes the handle into her hand, and,
flashing him a smile, makes a sudden backwards RIPPING gesture
with her arm like she's starting a lawnmower. David HOWLS.

                       MICHELLE
          You think women are so stupid? Hunh?

She twists the corkscrew

                       MICHELLE
          This is for my sister. This is for the
          other girls in that hole in the woods.

David SCREAMS. She starts stabbing him in the chest with the
corkscrew.

                       MICHELLE
          Boo hoo! Have some wine.

David is in shock. Michelle grabs her purse. She exits.

                       MICHELLE
          You can bleed out- I'll come get you two
          and dump you later. I've got church in the morning.

The Lights fade.

GingerWolf

BY JAIME JESSUP

Since I knew I'd be leaving LA within a month, I wanted to use my night job as a "Scareactor" at Horror Nights as a dating experiment. I haven't been single since I was 16 years old, and if I was gonna crash and burn, I'd rather do it in LA and get it out of the way fast. However, like I said, I HAVEN'T BEEN SINGLE SINCE I WAS 16 YEARS OLD. I had no idea what I was doing, so I went balls-out and selected who I thought was the most attractive candidate: 6'4", broad-chested, broody, reddish hair and a werewolf. Operation: GingerWolf commenced.

I started by pointing him out to Elizabeth who said, "Oh, that's (**NAME REDACTED**.) I know him- he used to date one of my friends!" Elizabeth assured me that I had a good chance, as he dated mostly blondes. I was sold- I would practice on GingerWolf. Unfortunately, we were star crossed from the get-go. Elizabeth and GingerWolf were never there on the same night, so I never got my introduction. With the clock ticking down on the last week, I sucked it up and decided to introduce myself. KAMIKAZE!!!

Me: "Hey, I'm Jaime- I think we're both friends with Elizabeth?"
Him: "Uh... OK... yeah..."
Me: "She told me you might have a thing for blondes, so I thought I'd try my luck and see if you wanted to come to the diner tonight after work."
Him: "What? Really? Actually, I'm kinda digging brunettes these days..."
Me: "That's cool," I say. "Because I have a hat."
(I put my hat on at a jaunty angle, in demonstration.)
Me: "So should I save you a seat?"
(He pauses for a moment, realizes I'm joking, then laughs.)
Him: "Definitely."

His responses were somewhat slightly lackluster, but since I wasn't exactly looking at him for marriage material, I let it slide. I'd gotten a "yes," and I was mighty pleased with myself.

GingerWolf must've asked around to learn my last name, because later that night, I got a FaceBook message from him apologizing for not showing up - in his words, he was "surprised and turned on by my abrasive invitation." (Does he know what "abrasive" means? I was certainly agressive, but not abrasive. I let my grammar snob cool off and finished reading the message.) "But," (he continues) he has a girlfriend and their relationship is on the rocks- he wanted to let me know about his relationship and be up-front and honest. And he was sorry he didn't come to the diner, would I please text him that night and let him know I got the message. So I did- I texted him, thanking him for letting me know. I wished him the best of luck with his girlfriend and said something along the lines of "my loss- you're very pretty." (The text that launched 1,000 texts.)

A flurry of texts came that night from GingerWolf, well into 5:00 in the morning. He texted me his address asking me to come over and "just snuggle," he texted me all about how miserable he was in his "sexless" relationship, on and on and on. Highly amused, flattered and a little bewildered, I kept the conversation going from the comfort of my own bed- ALONE.

But the texts kept coming. And the phone calls. Apparently, I had grabbed a tiger by the tail. GingerWolf told me that he was "on a break" with his girlfriend, and really wanted to see me. He kept inviting me to come over at 3AM after I got off so we could talk and get high. He also wants me to send him naked photos of myself.

First of all, I don't get high. It's not my thing. Fine for those who do, but it's not my style. Also, I get drug-tested at a lot of my jobs, so I just can't. Second of all, naked photos? Really, GingerWolf? I don't have any naked photos. And if I did, I really wouldn't keep them on my phone. And if I did keep them on my phone, why would I send them to a near-stranger?

"Do u like anal sex?" he texts casually, at around 2AM. There's 2 things wrong with that text: One, NO. And Two, I can't stand it when people text "u." I'm a grammar snob with a tight butthole, what can I say...

I'd opened Pandora's Box instead of mine.

"Send me pics, pleeeez," whined a text.

He then sent me a photo of his wang. Taken from a southern vantage point, you could clearly see the entire GingerWang, as well as a daintily held limpwristed hand pulling a t-shirt up over pale ab muscles.

I'd suggested that GingerWang and I become FaceBook friends so I wouldn't just view him as a piece of meat, but he had yet to seal that deal, which made me wonder... Plus, Elizabeth warned me that he was a compulsive cheater, which was why it hadn't worked out with their mutual friend.

I teamed up with one of my housemates, who was pals with GingerWolf on FaceBook, and we selected the girl who posted the most items on his wall- a girl named Jamie (**NAME REDACTED**.) When we viewed her profile, it said she was "In a relationship with FUCKING GINGERWOLF!!!"

Oh! The ignominy! The shame! I'd been LIED to! Had I taken the GingerBait, I would've inadvertently become someone's Other Woman- not cool, GingerWolf! Not cool!

"So, who is Jamie (**NAME REDACTED**)?," I ask.

Loooong pause.

"Thats the ex," he replies.

"So it's OK if I FB mssg her and make sure it's cool if you and I go out for coffee?"

Immediate response: "NO PLEASE DONT DO THAT!!!"

I took the text photo of his penis as a gift from the Universe, and immediately became That Guy- the reason you DON'T send naked photos to people you don't know very well. Many a friend of mine got a GingerWang text on October 31st reading "Happy Halloweiner!!!"

A daintily held wrist became a popular handshake amongst my inner circle- everyone enjoyed a chuckle about GingerWang, and I washed my hands of it.

About 3 weeks later...

I get a text out of the blue from good 'ol GingerWang, saying how he's sad and he misses me. He asks me out for coffee, "nothing sexual," and just to talk.

I agree, knowing full well that this story would only get better if we met face to face.

A few hours later, he texts me asking to come over and cuddle.

"YOU HAVE A GIRLFRIEND," I respond.

He never asks me for coffee. However, on my way out of town, I stop at the diner to have brunch with some pals and apparently blazed right past GingerWang on my way out. Naturally, this prompts a text.

"I hate this rain... I'm sorry we never got each other," he says.

I say, "I suspect we value different things."

"Like what?"

"I like rain. And monogamy. Lil things like that. Happy Holidays, (NAME REDACTED)"

And I left it at that. I never got my sex tiger. But I never got an STD, either. Winner winner, chicken dinner.

EPILOGUE

A couple of weeks later, my good pal Chelsea and I got a little drunk. We'd been trying to figure out how to make an Ap out of the dick pic- something that would make it ejaculate confetti on someone's birthday, etc. Chelsea came upon the brilliant plan to text GingerWolf a douchey photo of HER ex, taken distastefully in front of a bathroom mirror in just his undies. We send it to GingerWang from HER phone (an unknown number to him) with the caption "5'11, 180lbs. Los Angeles area. Wanna meet up?"

We then distracted ourselves texting various pals to see if they had any good dick pics on their phones so we could flood GingerWang with texts of various images and invitations. My auto-correct made it sound like I was soliciting my guy friends for "Duck Pix?" Life got in the way, sadly, so we abandoned the pursuit and forgot about it until a few days later when GINGERWANG RESPONDED TO THE TEXT!

In his characteristic bad spelling, he asks (Chelsea) "What will u do?"

Chelsea responds: "Whatever you want."

A day later, GingerWang fires back. "bj."

WHAAAAAAATTTT!!!!

Upon receiving this news, I collapsed to the floor amidst a ton of latent pre-teen giggles. Chelsea then sent him the biggest, veiniest bastard our harvest had yielded, (a frightening specimen which dwarfed GingerWang's) telling me that she'd forwarded it along to GingerWang with the caption "You First."

And we never heard from him again. You learn something new every day, kids- but the moral of this tale is this: IF YOU SEND ME A PHOTO OF YOUR PENIS, I WILL MOST LIKELY BE IRRESPONSIBLE WITH IT.

Also, I DO NOT CARE FOR ANAL.

I think that about sums it up.

...Duck Pix?

JAIME JESSUP

What do you love about the genre of horror?

The first real film set I worked was a horror movie with Rick Danford and Tom Savini. Since I'd only just discovered the genre at the tender age of twenty-one, cutting my teeth with true masters left an indelible mark on my heart.

What are some of your influences?

I love torture porn and slashers, so Roth and Hooper, but the freneticism of Rob Zombie also appeals to me.

What is your favorite Halloween treat?

Marshmallow pumpkins. There's a bliss-point from the consistency and the taste that checks all my boxes.

You are hosting the perfect Halloween movie marathon. What are the films you choose and why?

The *Scream* trilogy as a warm up (to clarify the rules) then straight into *Halloween*. With the obvious exception of *Season of the Witch* because fuck *Season of the Witch*. I'd wind down with some good ol' fun ones like *House of 1,000 Corpses* and *Devil's Rejects*, then finish with *Last House on the Left, Eden Lake*, or *The Strangers*. The randomness of the cruelty always leaves a residual terror in my mouth. That's the way to wrap it up. You want people looking over their shoulder on the drive home.

As a designer of horror theatre or experiences, explain your process.

I'm a binge writer, so my process involves lots of background processing by enjoying and absorbing as many horror-based experiences as possible and soaking up all the fun. Then at some completely arbitrary point later in time I'll dream something or it'll pop into my head and I'll scramble to get it out on the keyboard before I forget. The feature-length script I'm working on now is the culmination of seventeen years of working haunt Events, and the relationships and real-life horror in between. It's going to be my opus and I'm deeply excited to finally have all of these memories coalesce into a story to share.

When is the last time you were genuinely scared by something someone created?

I'm incredibly critical, and usually I walk through an event or view a film with an appraiser's eye, like, '*Oh, hey, that's good quality,*' or, '*Meh, I've seen that scare done better.*' I'm also borderline emotionally crippled in that I'm so numb to the distraction/pop-out setup, it's extremely difficult to rattle me. I'll flinch if someone takes a cheap shot and shoves a prop in my face, but that's just them being lazy. I'll react, but I'm not startled. Most films and interactive haunts are fun for me, but they're not scary.

The things that get me, lately, are real life things. The first ten minutes of this season's *American Horror Story*, seeing Los Angeles destroyed by intercontinental ballistic missile's and the terror of people having minutes to live, everyone looting or calling their loved ones for the last time. That is an actual possibility, and seeing my worst fears on our flatscreen resonated with me. I've had nightmares about that before, and also our infamous California wildfires. I also legitimately think about the Golden State Killer and Richard Ramirez every night when I lock my deadbolt. These are the real-world monsters for which deadbolts were invented. But I wouldn't want to live anywhere else. This is literally (and geographically) life on the edge. The scary stuff is a small price to pay for a life with so much life in it.

Describe the perfect Halloween.

We don't really get to celebrate Halloween until it's over, because we're usually working. But when we do, we have a unique ceremony we like to perform. We call it "The Pumpkining." Each year after the final night of whatever haunt event everyone's working, all us night creatures take our jack-o-lanterns to work with us and at the end of our shifts, as the sun is rising, we pick a bridge and meet up. This is the end of the haunt season, and the full culmination of the Zodiac for the people who live for this time of year. We sit down in silence for a moment, and place our hands on the pumpkins to charge them with our gratitude and intentions for the next year.

At exactly sunrise, we line the pumpkins up on the river railing. Those orange bastards go sailing off the edge and down into the Los Angeles River. Usually there's not a lot of water flowing, so there's the deliciously moist SPLATTER and then all the ducks and egrets who sleep under the overpasses wake up and start calling out.

The sun's risen by this point and the bright birdsong echoes down the concrete riverbed throughout the entire city- these excited birds get pumpkin for breakfast! (I looked it up - it's safe.) The theory is, they'll eat these jack-o-lanterns, be filled with our thankfulness and good intentions, and go shit it out over Los Angeles. This is our way of spreading the love for what's next as we all transition back into day walkers. This has been our tradition for five years now, and it's the perfect finale for a perfect Halloween.

SCARE CRED: JAIME JESSUP

Jaime started scaring in 1999, so if she scared any pregnant women, their babies are now almost old enough to drink away the in-utero trauma. She's performed in mazes and on stilts for seventeen years at Universal Studios' Halloween Horror Nights (both Orlando and Hollywood) and also a few adorably un-scary years at SeaWorld Orlando's Spooktacular kid-friendly event, as well as a turn as a Not-So-Scary Storyteller at Lego Land, San Diego. Jaime has also had the honor of performing as a ScareActor at the last Halloween Party at the Playboy Mansion with Hugh Hefner. She's also acted or crewed on several horror films including *Zombies! Zombies! Zombies!* and *Never Sleep Again: The Elm Street Legacy*. She is currently a writer and performer in Los Angeles.

BELOW

BY RAY KEIM

Brant was surprised that Jake could open the gate so easily.

"I guess they never realized that iron locks wouldn't last an eternity," Jake said as they entered the gloomy, dark passage. A small shuffling of colorful wet leaves swirled into the portal with them, drawn in by a deep yawn from the depths.

"It's dank in here," said Jake.

"Dank? Thank's not even a word, stupid!"

"It is so! It means, um, smelly."

"Well, if it's dank in here it's because of you!" giggled Brant.

"Shut up and take this seriously!" hissed Jake. "And stop shooting your flashlight in my eyes!"

Brant's grin quickly dropped to reveal the anxiety he had been suppressing ever since they crawled through the chainlink fence.

The boys clumsily descended the gently curved stone stairway which was so narrow if forced them to descend in single file. The granite treads were barely wide enough for a footfall, and their height was nearly twice that of normal steps. Adding to the precarious design of the incline was a thin veil of viscous muck that draped everything. It teased their balance with every awkward step.

"Ugh! These walls are gross!", whispered Brant, as he brushed his hand along the irregular, slimy stonework for support.

At that moment his foot unexpectedly slid to the side a few inches and Brant nearly lost his balance. He was holding his flashlight in his left hand and carrying a small wooden box tucked under his left elbow. Jake deliberately ignored Brant's near disaster.

"It's probably not very far to the bottom. We should almost be there." said Jake, "I can hear the water."

"Water? You never mentioned water!"

Jake stopped dead in front of Brant, causing Brant to struggle for his balance again. Jake shot a fierce glare over his shoulder.

"It's raining, and we're underground in a two-hundred-year-old sewer! What do you expect?"

Brant shot back, "Stop pretending you know what we're doing! You don't even know if it's true! You don't even know if she's real!"

"She's real! You saw that sunken spot in the cemetery with your own eyes! Jake snapped.

"My dad told me that sometimes graves sink when the dirt settles! That's all it is!" Brant replied, in a condescending tone.

"Come on and don't drop the box!" Jake said as he turned and continued down the steps.

The pair reached the bottom of the winding stairwell. It was infinitely dark, but they could sense a large volume of atmosphere echoing with wetness. The cool, humid air was in motion around them, stirred by the circulation of a vascular network of ornately laid brick tunnels and ceramic ducts. Brant scanned the space with his flashlight revealing a narrow sampling of the chamber and casting frenzied shadows in the periphery of its beam. Jake removed his small backpack and revealed a small battery powered lantern. When the lamp flashed on, the boys felt a slight relief from the claustrophobic darkness, but it was replaced with an instinctual dread at the sight of the ancient brick walls of a vaulted sewer intersection. The circular room was about ten feet high and thirty feet across and pocked with several pipe outlets of various diameters, each releasing a small stream of foul dark tea. The chamber smelled of stagnant water and wet earth.

Directly in front of them was a dark, threatening maw of a large circular tunnel, tall enough to walk through, which lead into a horizontal abyss. To one side of the opening, there was an engraved number "17".

"There!" said Jake, with enthusiasm incongruent to the situation. "Tunnel seventeen!"

Brant pierced the tunnel's darkness with his flashlight and revealed a subterranean jungle of protruding gnarled roots and cracked warping brick masonry. Glistening tendrils of mold dripped from sinister, claw-like tangles. A small stream snaked into the menacing masonry monster.

"According to the map, tunnel seventeen goes north. We need to go in that direction. Then it shouldn't be very far." Jake said.

Brants only answer was a panicky, "You better come through with your end of the bargain, Jake, or I'll kick your butt when we get out of here!"

"Come on!" Jake barked.

Normally, Brant would have punched Jake on the arm for speaking to him that way, but they made a deal. The duo cautiously proceeded into the hollow, straddling their footsteps on the sides of the curved conduit, avoiding the thin, inky stream of water and ooze meandering through the gutter. The brick lining of the tunnel was becoming more irregular, slowly transforming into something that seemed less man-made and becoming more organic. Alive. Brant observed that within the velvet darkness of the tunnel ahead, glints of reflected light could be seen on the sweaty edges of the bricks and growth.

A moldy scent of sod was becoming more distinct.

Jake stopped abruptly and pointed ahead. "Look!"

Brant looked past Jake's shoulder and could see a distant amber glow through the bramble of roots and undulating brickwork, and he whispered, "I don't like this."

Jake resumed his trek toward the sickly light at a faster pace, leaving Brant paralyzed in a hesitant moment of regret. Brant watched as Jake's silhouette became illuminated in what appeared to be another large chamber. Jake stood facing the light on the left side of the room and calmly yelled, "You won't believe this."

Brant felt a combination of excitement and dread; the feeling you get at the top of the first drop of a roller coaster. He cautiously walked towards the light. As Brant approached, could see Jake's gaze alternate between looking at him, and looking at the source of the light. It was another open rotunda.

Upon entering the space, Brant was momentarily confused by the scene. Jake was facing a lit kerosene lantern on the floor, which was casting a dirty amber glow through its sooty glass globe.

Brant defensively crouched down and asked Jake, "Is someone else here? Who lit that?"

Jake was silent as the light flickered over his unbroken gaze. Brant followed Jake's stare. It was then that Brant noticed the pile of dirt and bricks next to the lantern. The left side of the vaulted room had collapsed at some point. A frozen avalanche of soil, roots, and stones were spilled into the chamber. Brant tried to make sense of the chaos he was seeing. After a moment of confusion, the full scope of the frightful scene in front of him came together. Jutting from the upper area of landslide wall were the ends of several boxes showing signs of metal hardware attachments. Jutting out of the top of the lower pile was a slightly reclined, half buried casket. Brant felt his stomach cramp at the sight. The top half of the split lid casket was open and partially torn from its hinges, revealing the desiccated corpse of a woman. Her arms were crossed over her chest, and she wore the clotted shreds of a once white chiffon dress. Her wispy gray hair was stirring slightly by the subterranean draft. The angle of the casket had caused her head to tilt slightly downward into an attitude of disdain toward the boys.
Jake and Brant stood for a moment in alarmed reverence.

Jake slowly approached the pile. "We're under the cemetery. That sunken grave we saw was hers."

Brant looked up into the small ravine created by the avalanche and could see a small blue-gray point of light shining through a very small opening in the dirt roof. A thin trickle of rainwater was spitting through. Jake tapped Brant's shoulder and pointed down to a headstone that had tumbled away from the mound. Brant walked over to it and flashed the beam of his light across the surface.

"Debbra Wagner 1849 - 1927".

Brant breathlessly whispered, "Oh my God. It's really the Wrentham Witch!"

"I told you so," said Jake.

Panic began to build in Brant's mind. This was too much to handle. He immediately wanted to be home with his dad watching TV.

Jake could see the uncharacteristic expression form on Brant's face, and he distracted Brant by smiling and loudly saying, "Give me the box!"

Brant's self-esteem regained control. He swallowed loudly; tasting the scent of mushrooms and pond water that filled his sinuses. He handed the box to Jake.

Jake approached the expelled casket. He climbed the small hillside and crouched next to the ghastly, mummified sentinel. Jake looked at the ghastly, gaunt face and said, "After this, we will be even, Brant. Are you ready?" Brant's eyes grew wide, and he nodded.

Jake opened the small oblong box, revealing a single red rose. He carefully removed the thorny flower from its coffin and placed it on the withered branches of the Wrentham Witch's crossed arms. For a few moments, the sounds of the echoed wetness became apparent again. Brant was mesmerized with terrified anticipation. At first, almost imperceptibly, the leathery skin of its sunken face began to twitch. Jake had a disturbing mad grin as he watched her sunken pruney eyeballs begin to inflate.

The lidless eyes were now bulging and glassy. They were a horrid brown with milky-blue irises. The rest of her face remained shriveled and fragile; a grisly, toothy skull covered in parchment-thin skin. Brant's legs gave out at this sight, and he fell to his knees, now paralyzed with fear. Tears began streaming down his cheeks, and he yelled, "Stop it, Jake! I changed my mind! Make her stop!".

Jake spoke in the deepest, most commanding voice he could muster, "Miss Wagner!"

Her eyes slowly rolled in the direction of Jake's voice, and her head lifted and turned with a long, nauseating creak.

"I brought Brant with me. He is over there", Jake calmly pointed. She slowly turned toward Brant who was still collapsed in the middle of the chamber. The witch grasped the rose in one hand and slowly raised the other arm from her chest, pointing at Brant. Her teeth parted, and she emitted a repulsive gurgling cry. Brant wanted to run but found himself unable to move.

Jake sat next to the corpse and regarded Brant smugly. "Did you really think I would let you use Miss Wagner's powers to help you?"

Brant was weeping and said, "I like you, Jake! I was just messing around and poking fun, that's all! I never hurt you or any of the other kids!"

It was true. Brant was a wise guy, but he wasn't disliked by anyone.

"Miss Wagner!"

The witch's head turned toward Jake with cat-like speed. Jake motioned to the pile of debris and said, "Brant was responsible for this. He was the cause of this indignation!"

The witch turned to face Brant again and let out a piercing cry of outrage. She then began to push herself up, out of the casket. Brant's paralyzed terror was beginning to make him feel lightheaded. He thought he might pass out. The witch clawed at the mud in from of the casket as she pulled her waist over the edge. Jake took on a furious, possessed expression, suddenly looking much older. No longer a boy!

The witch had just pulled one knee up on to the mound when a sloshing sound came from overhead. Suddenly a river of thick mud and sod began to surge through the torn opening behind the horrific scene unfolding. The small gray light from overhead suddenly expanded. Brant watched as a morbid landslide of mud, shattered caskets and corpses heaved over Jake and the witch. Within seconds the crypt's decayed atmosphere was replaced with the fresh scent of a sweet, damp autumn and the promise of daylight. Brant sat shivering at the base of the new terrible landslide, shocked that the threat ended so abruptly. He quickly regained his panicked energy and scramble over the reburied witch, and up the embankment to the surface.

It wasn't until he returned home that he noticed the rose, whose thorns had tangled on the sleeve of his muddy jacket. Brant never spoke of the incident to his father.

However, he did tell a skeptical Jake about it on the following Monday.

RAY KEIM

What do you love about the genre of horror?

Horror is primeval. It's in our DNA. The legends and cautionary tales which were told around campfires thousands of years ago are part of the human condition. We tell the same tales today with a few updated additions of what we fear now. They are survival lesson to be passed down.

What is some of your favorite horror literature?

Certainly the classics. *Frankenstein, Dracula,* and Poe. Stephen King has given me some amazing goosebumps too. While they may not be considered literature, I love reading "true" ghost story accounts. Books like *The Ghosts of Gettysburg* can give me the creeps, especially during an autumn visit.

What are some of your influences?

The movies of Doctor Shock, my Saturday afternoon horror host on Channel 17 in 1970's Philadelphia. Walt Disney and his *Haunted Mansion*s. *The Legend of Sleepy Hollow. A Christmas Carol. Scooby. The Great Pumpkin. Garfield's Halloween.* My friend's dad, Mr Jensen, who would rig up a glowing, blue, flying crank ghost that would float across his yard, while playing *Chilling, Thrilling Sounds of the Haunted House* on his stereo.

What is your favorite Halloween treat?

Sweetzel's Spiced Wafers, a Philly area treat. Hot apple cider with a pinch of cinnamon. Reese's, which are best at Halloween. Anything in those little orange and black treat bags.

You are hosting the perfect Halloween movie marathon. What are the films you choose and why?

So many possibilities depending on the audience. This list is the fun gathering with candles, donuts, red wine and pizza. *It's the Great Pumpkin, Charlie Brown.* Disney's *The Legend of Sleepy Hollow, Lonesome Ghosts, The Halloween Tree,* Corman's *Tales of Terror, and Carnival of Souls.*

As a designer of horror theatre or experiences, explain your process.

I like creating things that creep me out first. It always starts out with imagining myself in a situation and describing what I see and feel. Then I project it on characters and fine tune it to their personalities.

When is the last time you were genuinely scared by something someone created?

I'm not easily scared by things created for entertainment. The best I can do is get alarmed. For some reason, out of all of the many movies, events, and books I have partaken of, the scariest thing in recent memory is the female ghost from *The Grudge*! Freaks me the hell out! I get goosebumps up my back just thinking about it! I've lived in this house almost three years but wont dare poke my head up into the crawl space attic!

Tell us about your contribution to our book. What was the inspiration?

I grew up in a small iron/steel town in Pennsylvania. There were lots of natural and industrial places to explore. As kids we were always exploring train tunnels, pipes and culverts (never with flashlights). Usually it was on a dare to see who could go the farthest in. My story harkens back to the atmosphere, sights, smells and stupidity of being a kid who was lucky enough to not get killed. I just wanted to create a spooky scenario with a cool final scene that would make a great set design and special effects. Experiencing a cemetery avalanche!

Describe the perfect Halloween.

I had several years of perfect Halloweens when my two kids were elementary school aged. We would take them to my old neighborhoods in my home town. Running into old friends with their kids. Seeing older neighbors and showing them my kids. Hearing the echoes of chattering, laughing kids, running through crunchy leaves with their bags. Ah, the smell of the leaves and toasting jack o lantern lids! Then there were the three or four houses who owners loved Halloween as much as I, who would set up their own little front door haunted house experiences with spooky music, lights and home-grown performers. Then going home and greeting our own trick or treaters. Guessing their costumes and *never* giving them candy without a proper "TRICK OR TREAT"!

A perfect Halloween requires a full day of decorating and lighting the yard, setting up the music and fog machines, getting into a simple but creepy gentleman's costume, and standing in a menacing pose to great the kids. A glass of wine hiding behind the candy cauldron. And *never* giving candy without a proper "TRICK OR TREAT!"

SCARE CRED: RAY KEIM

Ray Keim is a seasoned entertainment designer who directs, conceives and produces digital illustrations, concept art, interactive game design, scenic design, props, and scale models for theme parks and attraction development. He is also experienced in film, television, live stage, and the web in addition to being a team leader, art manager, and design mentor. Online, Ray is known for his popular website, "Haunted Dimensions," which can be found at *HauntedDimensions.RayKeim.com*.

Ripon Lane

BY ADRIAN LEPELTIER

Calcutta, India around 1925. Ripon Lane was an established neighborhood of Colonial Calcutta. A large white two story house. On the second floor, a generous, wide balcony highlighted the house's appearance. It was here that my grandparents with their four children and my grandfather's mother lived. Great grandmother was very much the lady of the house and my grandmother was happy to allow her the position. Ruby and Norah, the daughters were sought after by the beaus in the area and their dance cards and social invites were profuse.

It was a late evening in August. The girls had gone to The Birkmyer Hostel dance. They had been escorted home by their dates of the evening. It was a warm, humid night. The girls asked their grandmother if they could sleep on the balcony, under mosquito nets on camp cots. Their grandmother assented and had the servants fix the camp beds. The girls undressed and climb into bed. Their grandmother decided to finish her last cigarette of the evening on the balcony. She enjoyed the warmth that helped take away the chill from her old bones. As she was finishing her cigarette, she felt the hair on her hands rise. She looked in the direction of the girls and saw a lady in white approaching the cots. "Who are you?" inquired the grandmother in an imperious tone. The lady moved close to Ruby's cot, peered in, then moved on to Norah's and peered in at her, completely ignoring the grandmother, who, again, demanded "Who are you? Why don't you speak?"

The next moment the person moved towards my grandfather's bedroom. Grandfather was awake and working on his accounting. He was the Collector of Customs for Calcutta. He felt the hair on his arms rise and he looked up to find a lady in white flowing dress looking at him. "Who are you? What do you want?" The lady looked at him and then moved towards the next room where his wife was asleep. My grandfather immediately jumped up from what he was doing and followed her into the room. As my grand father approached the figure in the room she vanished in front fo his eye.

Needless to say, enquiries were made about the apparition. They found out that the previous tenant of the house was a married lady called Jane Kerr. She had an unhappy marriage and committed suicide by drowning herself in the water tank on the roof of the home.

ADRIAN LEPELTIER

What do you love about the genre of horror?

Remember, I was born and raised in India till I was eighteen. Then I lived in London, England for seventeen years. I came to the USA from the late '50s to the early '60s for college. Halloween was not as popular then as it is today. Universal Studios was the first time I really became involved in Halloween. I am not a horror enthusiast. Universal required I be involved with the Halloween preparations.

What is some of your favorite horror literature?

Dracula - had to stop reading it at night and had to read it during the day it terrified. *The Amityville Horror* - anything with poltergeist seems so real and is so real. *The Monkey's Paw* - a wonderful one act play that I did in high school.

What are some of your influences?

Ghost stories told to me by my family as to their experiences and it sounded terrifying and so very real to me. *Dracula*. and *Amityville*. Then there was the time I went to sign a contract for Westcliffe on Sea. The producer was diagonally opposite me at one end of the room sitting at a desk. I was diagonally opposite him in a chair. I could see the door to the room out of the corner of my eye. He mentioned that the flat he was staying in, in Baker Street, London was once the flat of Alistair Crowley. Whilst telling me this I noticed what seems to be small lights appearing around the door frame. i mentioned this to him and he got up from the desk, asked me to follow him and started leading the way to the bedroom. I was following him down the corridor, down three steps. As I was descending the steps I felt a strong slap on the right side of my face. I stopped dead in my tracks and said, '*Peter! We are getting our of here! You are coming back with me!*' He refused and I headed with great alacrity to the from door and headed out of the flat!

What is your favorite Halloween treat?

Candy and chocolate.

You are hosting the perfect Halloween movie marathon. What are the films you choose and why?

Everything from the 30's and 40's. *Dracula, Frankenstein*, and *The Wolfman*. I remember as a teenager watching *Frankenstein* and jumping out of my seat in terror! *The Amityville Horror. The Haunting*. All Hammer horror films.

As a designer of horror theatre or experiences, explain your process.

I regret that most haunted houses have constant streams of people entering in groups. Therefore the shock has to come from surprise, which to me gets quite monotonous. If a haunt could be experienced individually, I feel like then the scare would be more palpable and far more powerful. When you look at horror movies, most of the fear and terror comes to the protagonist whilst they are alone and unaware of what is going to happen to them

When is the last time you were genuinely scared by something someone created?

It was the *Pitch Black* haunted house at Universal's Halloween Horror Nights XI. That was the most wonderful experience. Going through a completely dark environment and things happening to you out of the darkness. The darkness was so intense you were unaware of other around you.

Tell us about your contribution to our book. What was the inspiration?

J. Michael Roddy was my inspiration. I loved working with him and got caught up in his enjoyment of horror.

Describe the perfect Halloween.

Anything but brutality, gore, machines that go horribly wrong and injure people. Walking into the unknown with knowledge that all is not terribly right in the world you are about to enter, but curiosity insists that you enter this strange and intriguing domain.

SCARE CRED: ADRIAN LePELTIER

Adrian LePeltier began his entertainment career in London, England with live shows, modeling, television, and film. He studied drama at the world famous Pasadena Playhouse College of Theatre Arts. He first performed and later directed stage shows in both Las Vegas and Reno, Nevada. From 1992 to 2005, he was the director of entertainment for Universal Studios Florida where he and his team were instrumental in the success of the Halloween Horror Nights and Mardi Gras annual events. Adrian remains quite proud of his efforts cooking up memorable scares for Halloween Horror Nights over the years. He currently enjoys spending time at The Wizarding World of Harry Potter.

Pumpkin Pinup

BY JACOB MCALISTER

JACOB MCALISTER

What do you love about the genre of horror?

The fantasy aspect of it. Ghosts, creatures, and monsters drive a lot of my imagination and influence my art.

What is some of your favorite horror literature?

I lean towards comic books. There are so many great writers and illustrators showcased in that genre. Some of my favorite titles are *Locke & Key, Constantine, Hellboy, 30 Days of Night* and *The Chilling Adventures of Sabrina*.

What are some of your influences?

As an illustrator, some of my biggest influences come from comic art and illustrators. Mike Mignola, Stephanie Buscema, and Jeffery Allen Love, just to name a few.

What is your favorite Halloween treat?

It's the only time of year I eat candy and I eat *way* too much. I guess I'm making up for the rest of the year. I know it's usually a divisive candy but I look forward to candy corn all year long. We buy a bag at the beginning of the season and it's gone in a night.

You are hosting the perfect Halloween movie marathon. What are the films you choose and why?

The Shining - because it's my favorite. *An American Werewolf In London* - because it's my favorite. *The Thing* - because it's my favorite. *Cabin In The Woods* - because it's a brilliant and entertaining satire. *Child's Play* - because dolls are terrifying. *It* (2017) - because it's the best horror remake.

If you could continue any horror story, what would it be?

None. Sequels are never as good as the original.

As a designer of horror theatre or experiences, explain your process.

It's all about the research. I spend more time diving into the project and gathering influences than anything else. Execution is only a third of the overall process. The other two-thirds is the time poured into understanding my subject matter and finding out how I'm going to approach the project. Coming up with an educated, well thought out idea is key.

When is the last time you were genuinely scared by something someone created?

The last time I was genuinely scared by something would have to be a maze from Halloween Horror Nights 27 called Scarecrow: The Reaping.

Tell us about your contribution to our book. What was the inspiration?

I love vintage pin up artists like Gil Elvgren, and Duane Bryers. I equally love anything Halloween related and I'll jump at any chance to draw something inspired by it.

Describe the perfect Halloween.

Pizza with the kids and wife while we watch *Hocus Pocus* and get our costumes on. Trick or treating for hours in the cool crisp fall weather until my feet hurt.

SCARE CRED: JACOB McALISTER

Jacob McAlister has been working as a concept illustrator for Universal Creative for the past two years. Before that, he spent time in Universal's Art & Design Department contributing to Halloween Horror Nights as an illustrator for numerous houses and promotional pieces. Working sometime three to four jobs at a time, he taught for almost seven years at Full Sail University. You can still see him perform at Disney from time to time in Animal Kingdom's Finding Nemo: The Musical, which he has been a part of for almost ten years.

QUEEN MARY EXPERIENCE

BY SHANNON MCGREW

The Queen Mary is known for being one of the most haunted places in the world. For the past three years, I've been lucky enough to cover many events both on and off this famed ocean liner for my website, *Nightmarish Conjurings*. Up until recently, I never had any encounter of paranormal activity aboard the ship. The story I'm about to share is my account as it happened.

It was the evening of April 12, 2018, and I was running late for the Queen Mary's newest event, the unveiling of the notoriously haunted B340 Stateroom. Once I arrived and got situated, I breathed a sigh of relief and began to mingle with the other members of the press before our tour was to begin. Deciding it was probably best to use the facilities before embarking on a 3-hour event, I turned to my partner and excused myself with the promise that I would return quickly, and headed straight towards the restroom. Talking about bathroom activities is not something I normally enjoy doing, but in order for you to have a better understanding of what took place, I need to give you an idea of my surroundings.

I was located in a stall directly across from where the restroom door opened. As with most bathroom stalls, there are gaps on either side of the doors which allows guests to see out. I have no idea why this is, as it doesn't do much in terms of privacy, but alas, they are there. While I'm in the stall, I noticed someone walk into the restroom, turn on the faucet, wash their hands, and proceed to exit. Because of where I'm located, and the aforementioned gaps, I was able to see this person, who is of flesh and blood, come in and leave. With that person gone, I was the only one in the restroom; however, about thirty seconds after that, I watched as the restroom door slowly opened on its own free will and then close. I'm sure most of you reading this must think that there had to be something wrong with the door - it's an old ship, of course, so maybe there was a draft? Maybe it was a swinging door? I assure you, that door could only open if someone were to push against it using their weight. Definitely feeling somewhat spooked, I finished rather quickly, returned to where my contemporaries were and tried to forget what I had just encountered.

Like most people, I tried to start justifying what happened, if only to put myself at ease. Luckily, my attention was dragged away as it was time for my group to enter the infamous B340 Stateroom. There's been a lot of talk about this room - some believe it to be the most haunted area of the ship with some much paranormal activity happening there that the Queen Mary decided to close off the room from guests. Others claim that the tales of ghostly encounters were fabricated by the Queen Mary (and partly by Disney who used to own the ocean liner) to drum up business. Whatever the truth is, I do believe it falls somewhere in the middle, though from what I experienced I do think there is some validity to those who have experienced unexplainable encounters. My experience in this room differs greatly from the accounts of others. I didn't see a figure, the faucets didn't turn on by themselves, nor were the lights flickering. Instead, as soon as I entered this beautifully designed stateroom, I got hit with an intense wave of vertigo. I didn't want to cause a scene so I quickly made my way to the bed and sat down next to an Ouija board (because of course they would have an Ouija board). Deciding that I was NOT going to mess with that, I instead tried to focus on the design of the space. Throughout the room were written accounts of what guests and employees experienced in the stateroom and it's surrounding areas. In the bathroom, guests would find the famed urban legend of Bloody Mary on the wall adjacent to the sink, you know, just in case they felt brave enough to try to conjure up Mary for an evening of scares. I didn't end up wandering around much, mostly due to the feeling of vertigo, but also because I ended up getting an incredibly sharp pain on my left temple, which seemed to come out of nowhere. Luckily, our guide was rounding everyone up to leave, and to my complete surprise, I noticed that when I exited the room, the feeling of vertigo and pain immediately went away.

Our last event of the evening incorporated a paranormal investigation within the boiler room, located 40 feet below the water line. Having gone down there one other time, I wasn't overly thrilled with returning, mostly due to the fact that we were underwater and if anything were to happen… well, I think you know. We were brought to a small room located in the bowels of the ship where we were asked to sit around a table as the investigator discussed the different uses of his equipment and relayed stories of paranormal encounters that he and others had aboard the ship. I was sitting closest to the door and as I listened to him discuss his different techniques, I began to hear a noise coming from outside the room. To give you some perspective, there was no one else in the boiler room except for us and even if someone were to approach from outside, it would be easy to see/hear them. It was at this time that I heard a growling sound coming from outside the room, and I'll be honest, it sent a chill down my spine. Luckily, we were at the end of the presentation, and as the investigator was packing up, I approached him rather sheepishly and asked if he had ever heard a growling noise. He looked me square in the face, with no trace of humor, and said, "You've heard it, too?"

As the event came to a close, I found myself rushing to get off the ship. Having had three unexplainable encounters in such a short time there was nothing more that I wanted than to get off the ship. As soon as I got to my car and plugged my phone in, all the electronics stopped working. For the record, this is something that has never happened before or after this experience. It wasn't until I was about halfway home that the electronics (i.e. GPS, phone, music) started working again. As soon as arrived at my apartment, I went and saged myself, my partner, and the apartment, in hopes that whatever bad juju I experienced would not impact our lives at home. Unfortunately, I woke the next day feeling very sick, and a few days later I was hospitalized and diagnosed with double pneumonia and the flu. I'm not saying that whatever was on that ship got me sick, but the timing of everything, the experiences I went through, and the quickness in which the illness spread has always seemed questionable. It's been almost a year since everything occurred and I have since returned to the Queen Mary unscathed. I'm sure that my story could somehow be explained in a rational way to disprove what I went through, but I know what I felt. There are spirits aboard that ship, they wander those halls, and they reside in those rooms. One thing is for sure though, if I can help it, I'll never, ever, return to that boiling room as I truly believe there is something evil lurking there.

What do you love about the genre of horror?

I love that it is able to elicit emotions - whether that be terror, anxiety, laughter, sadness - it's all encompassing. Horror is more than just thrills and chills. It's a way to escape reality and, at times, it can even be a therapeutic tool.

What is some of your favorite horror literature?

Penpal by Dathan Auerbach is one of the most terrifying books I've ever read. *Summer of Night* by Dan Simmons is one of the best coming-of-age horror books I've ever read.

What are some of your influences?

When it comes to horror, H.P. Lovecraft is someone I admire for the way in which he crafts his stories. Where others create worlds, he creates universes which are inhabited by some of the most terrifying creatures imaginable.

What is your favorite Halloween treat?

Reese's Peanut Butter Cups, but I will also admit to having an affinity for candy corn.

You are hosting the perfect Halloween movie marathon. What are the films you choose and why?

Trick 'r Treat by director Michael Dougherty is a must. That is one of my all-time favorite films and one that I hold near and dear to me. However, if I really want to mess up my friends on the spookiest day of the year, I would sit them down for a triple feature of *Hereditary, Suspiria,* and *Overlord.*

If you could continue any horror story, what would it be?

Scott Smith's *The Ruins.* That book terrified me when I first read it and I think it would be fascinating to see that story expand. Just thinking about it makes me want to go and re-read it again.

As a designer of horror theatre or experiences, explain your process.

Though I don't design experiences, I do run a horror website and it's one of the most fulfilling areas of my life. I love that my site, *Nightmarish Conjurings*, showcases work from so many amazing creators whether it be indie or mainstream. My process is finding like-minded people who share that same level of passion that I have for the genre so that I can give them a platform to express their opinions and thoughts on a topics that are important to them.

When is the last time you were genuinely scared by something someone created?

Hereditary. Hands down. I watch *a lot* of movies and *Hereditary* destroyed me in the best way possible. I think about that movie at least once a day. You could say I'm a bit obsessed.

Tell us about your contribution to our book. What was the inspiration?

I've had some really crazy experiences with the paranormal in my life and it's something that I wish I talked about more. I'm fascinated by the idea of life after death and unexplainable encounters so it's something that I'm happy to be sharing with a much wider audience.

Describe the perfect Halloween.

A chill autumn evening spent exploring Salem, Massachusetts, going on a ghost tour, and staying in a haunted hotel with the one I love.

SCARE CRED: SHANNON MCGREW

Shannon is the owner and founder of the website *Nightmarish Conjurings* and has loved all thing horror since she was a kid. Growing up she was fan of *Goosebumps* books and movies/shows like *Killer Klowns from Outer Space*, *Poltergeist*, and *Are You Afraid of the Dark*. Shannon is an avid fan of horror attractions and has visited them throughout the country. She hopes to one day design such an attraction. Shannon is drawn to all sorts of horror sub-genres but her favorite movies include *The Exorcist*, *The Thing*, *Hereditary* and *Trick R' Treat*.

Visit Shannon at *NightmarishConjurings.com*

HALLOWEEN & WHY I LOVE IT

BY PAT MILICANO

Always loved Halloween, when one's imagination could run wild
The kind of thoughts usually suppressed by any normal child
When we feared the creature in the closet or under the bed
A beast or monster or unthinkable thing that'd leave us dead

But one day a year we could embrace those fears and face the dark
When together we'd find the courage to walk the creepy city park
Two Martians, a robot, and a pirate holding hands to face the worst
Eyes darting right and left and four hearts pounding ready to burst

The costumes made at home, by mom and dad or maybe a big brother
Underneath, wrapped up tight to beat the cold, surprised we didn't smother
The route was planned to include those that gave Snicker bars, full size!
And to carefully avoid the creepy house on Grant Street was always wise

We were certain the chances of surviving the night were incredibly few
But we went. We went into the dark finding a courage we never knew
Then like returning Vikings from a successful raid to steal and plunder
We'd gorge on candy, no monster got us, but the sugar near put us under.

I hope that the kids of today can fight off the commercialized version of this night
That they can have the simple pleasure of defeating fear in an internal fight
Because we learned we could be brave against the real fear that was unseen
I loved and learned a lot from my childhood clash with the night of Halloween

What do you love about the genre of horror?

It touches one of the few base emotions we humans all share. It also allows us to plan what we would do if confronted by a monster…. that's valuable!

What is some of your favorite horror literature?

Poe. Read him as a kid and couldn't get enough. *The Masque of the Red Death* messed with me for months.

What are some of your influences?

Believe it or not, *The Wizard of Oz* was a huge influence. While the horror aspect seems tame today, as a child it was frightening. But it also found ways to include comedy and it even wove a coming of age message into a story with witches and flying monkeys!

What is your favorite Halloween treat?

Candied Apples. These were a thing when I was a kid in Nebraska

You are hosting the perfect Halloween movie marathon. What are the films you choose and why?

Wow. Universal Classics and include *Idle Roomers* aka *The Three Stooges Meet The Wolfman*. I love a good comedy and horror mix.

If you could continue any horror story, what would it be?

An American Werewolf In London. I hated the ending. The curse should have continued.

As a designer of horror theatre or experiences, explain your process.

First I ask, who Is the audience? This informs every step of the process. If I'm working with a particular IP that obviously plays a major role. But in the end creating a show or an experience must be informed by the audience.

When is the last time you were genuinely scared by something someone created?

Honestly, it was *An Inconvenient Truth,* but I know that's not what you mean. I think that last time I felt fear was the original *Alien.*

Tell us about your contribution to our book. What was the inspiration?

I'm honored to be asked to contribute something to this effort. I'm contributing a poem because I like poems and I like Halloween. I was part of the team that brought Halloween back to Universal Studios Hollywood in the mid 90's. Possibly the hardest I've ever worked was on those first mazes and The *Bill and Ted* show. It is also probably the most fun I've had in this business. To complain about the commercialization of Halloween is wasted air. Halloween has always been somewhat commercialized, but I do often remember where my love for this crazy holiday began. I hope kids today catch the bug I caught that says once a year you can pretend to be anything and be either frightened and/or brave.

Describe the perfect Halloween.

My idea of a perfect Halloween has certainly changed over the years… but today it would involve experiencing a Halloween Horror Nights evening with my grandsons. To see it through their eyes would spark memories of my own childhood where my love for this genre was born.

SCARE CRED: PAT MILICANO

Pat has forty years of live show experience. He began his career in radio as an on-air personality, which led to several years as a professional stand-up comedian opening for major name acts. His interest in Hollywood let to becoming an actor and live stunt performer. Pat eventually moved into management where he was in charge of maintaining quality for all shows at Universal Studios Hollywood. While Pat has stunt credits in films like *The Usual Suspects* and shows like *CSI* and *9-1-1*, he has been more active with his acting over the last two decades. From recurring roles in *Married With Children* and *Who's The Boss?* to more recently *House MD*, Pat brings a credible acting presence to the process. Pat has produced and directed shows for Universal Studios Hollywood, Universal Studios Orlando, Islands of Adventure, Paramount Parks, as well as dozens of independent shows.

Hell's a Cabin

BY JOE MOE

"Get away from me!"

Cam swung the rickety door open, hard! The loose screen billowed, sifting dust, as he scrambled past, onto the porch. The door bounced shut with a clunk. Mia looked through the warped mesh of screen regarding Cam like a bloody dot on an egg yolk. Squinting, disgusted. "Cam, you're being so pussy-ish", Mia sighed. Have I ever done anything to make you afraid of me? No, I haven't. Irritable? Sure. Queasy? Maybe…"

But Cam was already down the steps, crunching gravel underfoot. His face yellowed by lamplight from inside the cabin. Bottomless worry lines lacing his forehead, messy silver hair reflecting flame, his back chilled by darkness. There were "yipping" noises somewhere in that darkness. Cam shuffled from side to side nervously, "The things you said, girl. They were more than words. They were like…ugly prayers."

Mia wrinkled her nose into a tiny red fist, "You're out of your mind (what's left of it)."

"Huh?"

"Forget it." Then Mia put on an ominous spook-show yodel, "Puh-lease come in from the co-o-o-o-ld"

Cam eyed the girl, maintaining a distance in case he had to run for it. Run? Standing there, his knees felt like the weakest chunks of his body. Held together more tentatively than that old screen door. He pointed a shaky finger at the girl, "Those things you said…"

A breeze blew the screen door open lazily. Its hinges shrieked like a distant squirrel fight. Mia stepped onto the porch and folded her arms, posing, "Look, I know I hurt your feelings…"

"Feelings?" Cam took a small step away, closer to darkness, "You said you were gonna kill me."

"C'mon, I said I'd "like" to kill you. There's a difference! Anyway, people say it all the time!" Mia blew wet air and sagged like a punctured wading pool.

Her wilting bolstered Cam a little. "Sure, people say they "wanna" kill you. But you said you were "gonna" kill me. I know you meant it. I know it!"

Mia bit her lower lip and turned away. Cam looked her over carefully. He leaned forward. "Are you… crying?"

"Huh? Oh, yeah. Sure. I feel so bad about upsetting you. I…" She lost it with an orchestral snort followed by honking laughter punctuated by another snort. Cam's eyes widened, sending his worry lines into the depths of oblivion.

"You're laughing at me!" Cam stomped his foot like a two-year-old in a mud puddle. He waited for the girl to think up an excuse for her outburst, but there was none coming. Just the continued shrill song a balloon makes when you milk air out of the pursing mouth of its stem. Mia doubled over, surrendering to fits. Now actually crying, but with laughter.

"Evil bitch!" Cam's curse conveyed a mist of spit into the air. A mosquito hummed through the dewy breath. Mia could think of nothing better to do but kneel down in mock contrition. Palms out. Emulating a religious figure in an old oil painting. "Sorry! Really! So sorry!" Still laughing, though.

Cam sputtered now, "I…I'm gonna go. I'm gonna leave here!"

Mia froze in mid-chortle. She perked up and shot Cam a look to shame winter in its deepest chill. The girl's storm cloud glare spun Cam's anger back toward fear. He stepped away again, completely into forest shadow. Yipping noises got louder. Closer. Cam recognized those sounds. A language? But he couldn't remember what it meant. He couldn't remember what the noisemakers were called, either. One more look at Mia's hovering menace and Cam leaked his own breathy whine. A desperate simmer that ripened into full-bodied siren as it went along, "Hnnghmee-ee-ee! The noise silenced the entire forest for a moment. The crickets were the first to resume conversation. Next, the…the…yippers? The whine and song filled Mia with a creeping shiver that culminated in glee. She smiled. "Yes. Go! Run quick, Cameron! Get away."

Before Cam could obey, and he fully intended to, the yipping grew still closer. Cam weeded his way through confusion and emerging panic. What was that damned sound? Why did it put his teeth on edge? Animals. Circling and…and plotting. Like the girl was plotting. To kill him! Coyotes! That's what they were! Coyotes that would eat him if he strayed into the dinner plate of night forest. Cam hustled back into the light. Mia was visibly disappointed, then livid. Cam ambled toward the cabin and grabbed a rake that was leaning against the porch banister. He skittered back in position to face the girl. "You want me to run out there with those…those…"

Mia rolled her eyes, "Coyotes?"

"Yeah! Coyotes!" Cam turned his back on Mia just long enough to swing the rake wildly in the darkness and holler, "Hi-eeyah! Fuck off, you…uh…uh…"

"Coyotes?" Mia offered, deadpan.

"Coyotes!" Cam stomped and rattled the musical tines of his rake until he was sure any living thing would have run off as far as four legs could take them. Cam impulsively threw the rake into the void of night, foolishly waiting to hear a cartoon yelp or squeal on impact. Empty-handed, he regretted it immediately. He turned back toward the porch, "What are you up to…girl?"

"Mia! Mee-yah, you moron!" She hadn't budged from kneeling in the doorway. But now she slumped off her haunches to stare intently at Cam. "Gristly ol' rabbit. Why didn't you just run for it, huh? You coulda' got away. Now you're stuck." Mia rose up again on her knees. Snarling half-heartedly before sagging back in resigned repose. "Aw, shit."

Cam straightened up with a jolt of a clue that had been missing until right then. "Are we "together"? I mean, in that way?"

Mia rolled her eyes wider, "As if I'd ever be with someone old enough to be my Grandpa."

Cam tiptoed to catch a glimpse of himself in a cabin window. Christ, he did look old! He sucked in air at the vision and put his hand to his mouth, changing the shape of his face. Realizing he had an upper denture, he plucked the false teeth out of his mouth to gawk at them in morbid fascination, like a big splinter you dig out of a toe. This was the better part of his grin? When was the last time these choppers saw sunlight? He couldn't remember the last time he smiled. Long time. He tried to put the plate back, but couldn't position it. The teeth swam around in his maw until they seated themselves. "Wh…Who am I?"

Mia considered. "A fireman. No, wait! Animal trainer. That's it. You are an animal trainer in a big zoo, no! Circus! Remember?" Mia nodded adamant confirmation.

Cam was so mixed up. "No, I can't remember." He shut his eyes and knocked on his forehead in frustration, dislodging his teeth again and having to make noisy mouth smacking to get them to settle back in. Dribble hung from the corners of his mouth and then floated away around his face. Glistening spider webs sailing on a gust of breeze.

"As a famous animal trainer I'd think you'd want to go out there into the woods and deal with those…"

"Coyotes?"

"That's right! Good, Cam. Deal with the coyotes." Mia nodded in the direction of the deep woods.

Cam looked over his shoulder considering it, but he didn't move. The two stood facing each other for a space unburdened by passing time. It went on and on. Inexplicably, Cam felt a spontaneous rush of sentimentality. He felt dampness in his eyes and a rise in his throat. In that thick moment, and for the first time this night, Cam felt a sweet reminder of some shadow of…love. Not love as a thing, per se. Rather, the foggy shape of a desire and ability to love. He relaxed and smiled at the girl. The girl stood up straight, seething. Balling her fists. Cam's false-tooth grin seemed to summon an actual demon. She flew down the steps landing eight paces from Cam. Her eyes fell upon a dirty pickaxe resting near a garden hose on a leaky spigot. Cam saw her eyes celebrate that pickaxe. He knew it was bad news. One side step and Mia was hovering over the ugly garden tool.

"Ooh, lookie?" Mia waved both hands over the handle of the pickaxe. "It's pointy, but not too sharp. It could really hurt somebody."

Cam was further terrified. "I don't like what you're implying, la…lady".

"Mia! You mindless asshole! "Mia" who is about to vent your empty head!"

Again, Mia gestured mysteriously over the tool. Cam turned to run, but stopped himself. Something "out there" scared him more than the threat of…uh…Mia's fury.

"Go! I'm gonna count to ten and give you a head start. If you're still standing here when I'm done counting, I'm gonna chop you. Oh, please, please, please just stand there. One…"

"I…I don't understand…"

"Two…"

"Miss…miss…"

"Mia! God-dammit! Three…"

"Listen…"

"Four…"

Something worse than bad knees and a pickaxe wouldn't let Cam make a run for it. The girl was inching her hands closer and closer to the handle.

"Fi- -six- -sev…"

Cam dropped to his knees (Ow!), "Please, sweetheart. I'll do anything…

"Sweetheart? Oh, you are really gonna get it. Eight…nine…"

Cam was sobbing now, "God, don't do this, Min…Min…."

"Mia! Mia! Mia! Get into that forest, animal trainer! Nine and a half…"

Cam prayed the shameless prayer of the doomed. Mia cringed hearing his intimate bargaining. As disconcerting as a burly man hollering, "Mommy!" during sex. But Cam didn't care who heard him, "Dear lord. Please forgive…who-whoever I am for any…whatchamacallits I may have committed in this life - sins! Yes, any sins."

"Ten!" Mia made a grab for the pickaxe. Cam couldn't budge. Even through his horror he lifted his head to see the girl grasp at the pick -- her hands…passed through…the wooden handle. Clean through! Like a bored neighbor's shadow walking through a vacation slide show.

Cam physically shook his head trying to vaporize the mirage. "You're not…solid!"

"If I was, I'd already have fertilized the forest with your brains." Mia huffed and stood up, making for the hanging lamp in the doorway, as if to bean Cam with it. Her hand passed through it, too. Cam still ducked. The world didn't even register displacement of air.

Mia stood above Cam now. Cam peeked through his guard to see the girl shaking with rage. Suddenly a rain of blows came. Mia flailed at Cam as if she had twelve automated arms with meat hammers at the end of each. Cam cowered. Covered up. That is until he realized that, like the pickaxe handle and lamp, Mia's fists passed through him like a mosquito through breath. Cam dared to look up at the girl's barrage as blows melted all about his head. He still cringed with every strike because they should have made contact. Knuckle to eye, then nothing. Mia stopped. Cam noticed she wasn't winded at all. He was sure she could have continued her windmill assault forever. But she stepped back and leered down at him." I…hate…you."

"I believe you." Cam unfurled and stood up on creaky legs, not much less afraid, "Are you a…a…"

Mia puffed a blast of air, "Tell you what, I'll answer your questions if you can say my name once. Just once!"

Cam struggled mightily, "M-m-m…"

"OK, I'll make it easy for you. Say your own name."

Cam couldn't. "Are you a ghost?"

"Oh, you wish." Mia paused, waiting for the next dumb question.

Cam held his head in his hands as if the girl's pummeling had gotten to him. "But you're not…solid."

Mia walked up the steps of the cabin and nodded at the flimsy door in wordless, impatient invitation. Cam followed tentatively, opened the door and without taking his eyes off the girl, entered. His anxiety gave way to disorientation. He now believed the girl couldn't hurt him physically. She wasn't flesh. She was liquid, but not wet.

Mia followed Cam inside. The old man walked straight through the front of the cabin toward the warm light of a fireplace and collapsed into a leather recliner as if he lived there. The seat felt so familiar. It swallowed him up in an overstuffed caress. He checked to see where the girl was before surrendering to the chair. He briefly closed his eyes. Very briefly. "So are you gonna tell me what's going…"

Mia shooshed him, finger to lips, as she stood against the frame of the glowing fireplace. She eyed the mantle, arching her eyebrows toward the contents, like a mom who can't help giving clues to her kid at an Easter egg hunt. Cam's eyes adjusted and he followed the girl's lead, regarding pictures and knick-knacks above the fireplace:

A photo of a happy couple near a beach. Was that the girl? Mena? A photo of the same couple near this very cabin. That's gotta be the girl. A large taxidermied salmon occupied a place of pride on the brickwork of the chimney. Pearly silver and blue in stark contrast to the red clay of brick. A photo of the now familiar couple by a river, holding up what must have been that trophy salmon when it was still a fish and not a trophy. A small wooden carving of a grizzly bear that Cam bought from a fake Indian named Rainbow Hawk in Manitoba – wait! Why did he remember that and little else?! A photo of Cam and Mia in a meadow, lavender petals dotting Mia's long hair which flowed over Cam's contented face as he piggybacked her through tall grass collecting foxtail burrs on his cuffs. God! The man in the photo was him. They were together! And in "that way", no less! "We were a couple!" Cam sputtered.

Mia made a lemon face, pulled herself together and melodramatically swatted at the photos on the mantle. As expected, her hand passed through them without consequence. "Crash! Tinkle! That's the sound of glass shattering on the ground." Mia remained unfriendly, but with less of the spite that had rivaled the blazing hearth a minute ago.

Cam rose up, or tried to. His old body, nested in a soufflé of chair, was stuck like a boot in deep mud. But he struggled and eventually made it to his feet. Cam walked toward the girl and reached for a photo. "What happened to us? We look so happy. And I was as young as you?"

Mia belched for effect, "They were taken nearly forty-five years ago, genius. You were thirty then." Mia slumped and pretended her tongue couldn't fit in her mouth and her eyes wouldn't focus. She blubbered in gibberish, "Bluh-buh-duh. Yoo-bah-do-bah-doo. Duh! Stupid!"

Cam was processing more and more, but not enough. And so slowly. He looked as far into the photo as his mind would reach. "You have to be a ghost. You're not flesh and bone and you haven't aged at all."

"Good try but wro-ong! I'm not a ghost." Mia performed a goofy, bouncy spazz, hopping up and down with her hands in the air.

"I have to know what's going on. Please?"

Mia stopped her interpretive dance, "I am not a fucking ghost, OK? Not a ghost. Next!"

Cam was near breaking, "I can't stand it anymore! I can't. Why are you torturing me?"

Mia flashed hot again. "Torturing you? Ha!" Mia lifted her blouse revealing a series of red welts up the length of her creamy white torso. "You got any of these to show for your torture?" Cam's eyes locked onto the brown mole beneath a perfect right breast. It was like a button that activated a flipbook of memories in him. Disjointed, but each one individually potent: the blond wisp of peach fuzz on the nape of her neck. The grimy chipped beef on burnt toast he pretended to love because it was all she could cook. How cool her palm felt against his warm chest. "Mia! Oh, Mia! I remember. I remember you. What happened to you?"

Mia smoldered, "You mean who made these?" She ran her hand up her side. One by one, each red welt opened up as her hand slid past it. The satin of her skin pouting with deep entry wounds. Her fingers obscenely penetrating some of the bigger stabs. A hundred yawning gashes like the gills of a trophy salmon. Rare, bloodless meat. The punctures made smacking sounds like Grandma tasting pudding as each blinked open then snapped shut. "Holy God!" Cam felt sick all over. "It's me, isn't it? I did that to you!" Without recalling the details, Cam was certain this was his handy work. The sight of the girl's wounds delivered such crushing remorse, he couldn't stand up anymore. He collapsed to his bad knees and immediately rolled onto his back in excruciating pain. The burning heartache reached past the electric, crushing agony in his legs. Both styles of hurt raged together in his core. Cam knew he deserved to suffer. He wept bitterly. "I can't remember. I know…I know I loved you. I just know it. How could I do that to you?" Cam tried to right himself, but only made it onto his side where he rested while his knees throbbed in itching pulses.

Mia knelt down in front of Cam. " Who knows why men do the stupid things they do? Who knows what makes their brains work – or, not work?" Mia shook her head sadly but without a drop of pity. "You were jealous. I dunno? Whatever got into you, got on to me. Ain't that always the way?"

"I'm sorry." Cam reached out for Mia. She backed away even though Cam's hand couldn't have touched her. "Not interested in your apology. Not interested in forgiving you. Nothing in it for me. Don't care about you."

Cam felt shock and despair, slipping in and out of comprehension. His emotions were constant and intense but his understanding of what was what, was intermittent. He chanted in his head, "My name is Cam. This girl was my love. I killed her. I feel it".

"Christ!" Mia yelled in Cam's face. "Do you know how many times we've had this little chat? Yes, you were definitely capable of stabbing me eighty-odd times with a steak knife. Yes, you suffered terribly from your guilt. Boo-hoo! Yes, you lied to my family and told them I'd abandoned you for a transient with drugs and promises of adventure. Yeah, you were remorseful. But you still fed me to the coyotes. They tore into me like a meat piñata. My bones are scattered all over this forest. A collarbone near the dried up well. A femur down by the edge of the wild berry brambles. The better half of my pelvis resting under the lilacs in that meadow we made love in. Is that ironic or morbid? Definitely weird, huh? So yes, you killed me, Cam."

Cam absorbed the story, incredulous. "Why…why should I believe you? You said you weren't a ghost and you obviously are."

"I'm not."

"You're dead!"

"Yeah, so?"

"So, if you're dead and still here to torment me, you're a ghost!"

"Nope."

"Then what? What?"

Mia stood over Cam and nodded toward the comfy chair, "You wanna know? Get up."

"I don't know if I can." Cam flopped around on the ground, finally struggling to kneel. He winced; sucking air through his teeth but quickly took some of the weight off his knees by throwing his upper body across the overstuffed chair. Groaning, he hauled the rest of himself up and flipped into the seat. He waded in upholstery as he shifted and settled, just as his dentures had puzzle-pieced in his mouth. Mia smiled at every bolt of pain that shot through the old man's body. But finally he found a semi-comfortable position and looked up miserably, "I've done what you told me to…so?" Mia stood in front of the fireplace. The heat radiated through her to warm Cam's face. "Story time, bastard."

Cam concentrated on Mia's lips. Waiting for her to speak. Mia took a breath, or pretended to. "Let's get the godammed killing out of the way, shall we?" Mia didn't wait for Cam to agree, "When we first got together, I had no idea you were so weak. In fact, only now do I realize the depth of it. Everyone has doubts, Cam. But you had convictions. You were dead sure that every man in the world had more money, charms and a bigger doo-dad. Well, weiners notwithstanding, I picked you, Cam. That insecurity of yours is why you moved us out here to no man's land.

"No, I wanted us to…"

"I wasn't really asking. Even out here in bumfuck, you found ways to imagine every man, woman or child was out to screw me. A dumb kid smoking reefer in the meadow. The bible salesman with the comical stutter. The farmer's teenage daughter who held my hand at a church bake sale. Even the septic tank service guy who smelled like his job. You never missed a chance to do your nut. Who knows what craziness finally drove you to it? I didn't get an engraved invitation. I was hanging wet laundry in the backyard when you decided to stick me. I dunno why? What I do know is that it hurt like hell until around stab thirty. That's thirty of eighty-three, bastard! My last sensation? Drifting on a dream. Last smell? Your sour beer-breath and my clean linens. Maybe blood? In the very end, I heard your breathing turn to whimpers. You musta' woke up from your idiot-trance right before stab number eighty-four, huh? That's the last time I saw your shitty face. And the last you saw mine, until a few years ago."

"I'm so sor…!"

"Oh, shut it! That's the vague and sordid tragedy of my death. Overkill, huh? Asshole!" Mia spat in Cam's face. As expected, no expectorate. Cam decided against pretending to wipe his cheek, paused out of a too late sense of respect, then asked, "So, what about the "not" a ghost part?"

"First, congratulations! You got away with murder. Clean and clear. Nobody came poking around. My relatives hated you from the get-go. Even more than they hated me. They never batted an eye at the news of me leaving you for a gypsy guitar player. Hell, they would've believed I left you for that stinky septic tank guy!"

"Ha! (Oh, shit)." Cam had laughed before he thought better of it. But Mia didn't seem to care at this point.

Mia shook her head knowingly, "Betcha' that's your last laugh of the night." Mia sat cross-legged practically inside the fireplace. The flames licked through her and continued on their way. "For years you went about your business putting me out of your mind. There was one time when you went out to those berry brambles and stumbled upon my toe bone. You tossed it so hard it hit the rainwater pond across the clearing and skipped four times on the surface before sinking. A salamander tried to swallow that toe, but it was too big. That bone is still there making moss. You went about your lonely life, occasionally going into town for provisions. Soaking up any sympathy you could from the townies that whispered behind your back, "There's that poor Cameron Fleming, all alone out there in the woods. Better let him be. He'll let us know if he has use for any of us.""

"And did I? I mean, have any use for anyone?" Cam asked earnestly. Mia didn't bother to hear him.

"About five years ago you woke up to the smell of smoke. You hustled to the kitchen to find black clouds billowing from the oven. I'd been dead for forty years but you still hollered my name like it must have been my fault. The minute you pulled that charcoal hunk that used to be a potpie out of that oven, you knew you'd nearly burned the cabin down yourself. You tried to put it out of your head, but it became harder as day by day these little gaps piled up. Kitchen door left open and raccoons ate a month's worth of food. Not once, but thee times! Lost your car keys for ten days. You got by pretending. Fooling yourself and the few townies you came across on rare trips to the store. This went on for three years until you got so bad, you'd sit at the fork in the road up there where Post Road meets Truman for an hour trying to figure which way to drive. And if you remembered, you'd usually forget how to shift into gear. You woulda' starved then, but for the grocer's son taking over the store and sending pitying deliveries. That's about the time you started hollering at me more regularly. You called, I showed up. From then on, I've been with you. Waiting to see you die. Trying to help you along."

"For chrissakes! Are you trying to tell me that you're in my head?" Cam already knew the answer. He was shaking.

"Yep. Not a ghost." Mia stretched further back into the mouth of the fireplace.

Cam thought, "If you're my hallucination, then I can think you away! I can stop you from haunting me."

"You try every time. Going on six months now. Jeez. If I were alive, I would be so fuckin' tired of going over this pathetic story, day after day. I think I'd kill myself. You don't know how many times we've been through it. Your conscience tolerates it. Craves it. No other person, living or dead could."

"Go away now!" Cam concentrated on the girl being gone. "Gone!" Mia did flicker intermittently along with the bed of flames she was sitting in. But she didn't disappear. Cam was weak from trying. "Why?"

"Don't worry, shit head. You'll succeed soon. Try again…"

Cam did try. The veins in his neck strained to the surface and oily perspiration beaded on his face. A blood vessel burst behind his eye. It was electric, sharp and painful and sent white stars into the corners of his vision. Cam slumped back into his chair, sputtering.

Mia stood up from the fireplace and approached the exhausted man. "Here's how it will go. You're old and tired to begin with. Now you're completely spent trying to wish me away. Soon you'll fall asleep. You can't help it. So old and tired. Tomorrow you'll wake up, a blank slate, and we'll start all over again from scratch. At first you won't remember that I can't hurt you and I'll try my damndest to talk you into the forest. By the way, you feeding me to those coyotes gave em' a taste for people-meat that'll be the end of you yet."

Cam could barely muster the energy to speak, "No…"

"Yep. Your mind is already wandering away. Scattering like my bones. All of your memories are leeching out. Soon you'll be empty. Ooh, I can feel myself going as we speak." And Mia was indeed fading.

"Ghost."

Mia's transparent image knelt close to Cam, "Your guilt is what summons me. And in the image you think you deserve. Angry, vengeful and righteous, as I would have every right to be." Then Mia leaned in close. So close that the shell of Cam's ear penetrated her melting lips. "But if I were the actual ghost of Mia, despite what you did to me, I would forgive you and see you home peacefully, honey. Because I always loved you, Cam. Always. Even in your dimming mind you know it…the girl always loved you…" Despite his delirium, Cam knew the truth of those words. He knew that the Mia he'd known and loved could never commit cruelty toward him or anyone. The Mia he had fed to those…those…she never could hold a grudge or hurt a fly. She had loved him completely. Cam reached out as far as he could. Through the fading aura.

"Stay…please…"

But she was gone and Cam was going fast. He wept violently then. As if all the answers he had been grasping for were restored. In that moment, Cam took a sobbing breath that seemed to draw in every memory that had been hovering out of reach for so long. He cried and cried…and then stopped abruptly as he forgot why he was crying. He tried to hold on to any grain of information he'd been given. So very much to remember. The girl. His… potpie? Those…things outside. Outside? Would he really have nothing left when he woke up tomorrow? What's happening tomorrow? Salamander. Beer. A girl. Toe bone. So tired…potpie…

JOE MOE

What do you love about the genre of horror?

It's intellectually, emotionally, and viscerally stirring. It inspires the broadest flights of fearful fancy and requires a willful suspension of disbelief that keeps us plastic and young in our imaginations. It invests us in the relationship to creator, monster, and victim, unlike any other genre can.

What is some of your favorite horror literature?

Mary Shelly's poetic and harrowing *Frankenstein*. Emily Brontë's gothic and atmospheric *Wuthering Heights*. The dense dread of Poe or H.P. Lovecraft. Oscar Wilde's sophisticated *The Picture of Dorian Gray*. Thomas Tryon's sadistic *The Other*. Anything from pop-horror phenomenon Stephen King. Poppy Z. Brite's sultry torture in *Exquisite Corpse*.

What are some of your influences?

Heroes I never met: Lon Chaney, Stanley Kubrick, Marcel Duchamp, Oscar Wilde, Andy Warhol, Federico Fellini, and David Lynch. Heroes I've met: Ray Bradbury, Van Dyke Parks, Mel Blanc, Kenneth Anger, Dick Smith, Jean Noguchi, Kermit Love, and my best pal and mentor (who influenced many of my influencers) Forrest J Ackerman.

What is your favorite Halloween treat?

A perfectly fresh Milky Way bar, for deliciousness – or a razor blade apple, for the story.

You are hosting the perfect Halloween movie marathon. What are the films you choose and why?

The Legend of Hell House, The Exorcist, and a *Dark Shadows* marathon!

If you could continue any horror story, what would it be?

Burnt Offerings! Who wouldn't want to put the new occupants of a haunted house in the malevolent path of a freshly dead (and pissed off) ghostly Oliver Reed, Karen Black and Bette Davis? Deluxe!

As a designer of horror theatre or experiences, explain your process.

1) Make something I've always wanted to see. 2) Make something without stuff I never want to see again. I always think of the audience as kids demanding magic. I try to take their expectations and exceed them by innovating scares they already love OR defy them by taking unexpected detours to unique terrors. I respect their intelligence while pushing the emotional scare-buttons we all share. You've gotta love your "victims" to truly get under their skin.

When is the last time you were genuinely scared by something someone created?

I love to be scared. I am the first one through any haunted house. Recently, my Mad Monster convention partner Eben McGarr created a Kane Hodder "Sack Head Jason" photo-op. It was like a time machine back to the set of the movie. You walked into the cabin and Kane approached fast - with a pickaxe! Before you could get your bearings, the amazing Dee Wallace popped out of nowhere dressed as "Mrs. Voorhees"! It was disorienting and frightening before settling into delightful.

Tell us about your contribution to our book. What was the inspiration?

I hope my story portrays the best and the worst that passion inspires and proves that regret can be a ghost of it's own making. It's about how love might be the last vestige of our humanity even as we fade away. Our past relationship to love can determine whether it is a spectre to embrace…or to hide from.

Describe the perfect Halloween.

Each Halloween, I grab my kit and create a spontaneous greasepaint makeup. Sometimes an abstract ghoul, sometimes a likeness of Lon Chaney, Jr., sometimes I just spirit gum trash to my face. I watch kids hooting and hoarding candy and recall the sense of wonder we all possessed in our youth. I wish more of us fought to preserve it. I thank my lucky scars for the fulfillment the genre has brought me.

SCARE CRED: JOE MOE

Born and raised in Hawaii, Joe Moe is a third generation Polynesian entertainer, studio vocalist, screenwriter, FX artist, designer of dark-rides for international theme parks, and co-promoter/host of *Mad Monster Party* horror conventions countrywide. Joe's a regular contributor to the granddaddy of all monster mags, *Famous Monsters of Filmland*. For years Joe lived in "Horrorwood, Karloffornia" with the late genre legend Forrest J Ackerman, in his "Ackermansion of Sci-Fi, Fantasy & Horror." Through "Uncle Forry" Joe is privileged to have met many classic horror heroes including Christopher Lee, Vincent Price, Roddy McDowall, Ingrid Pitt, Ray Bradbury, Gloria Stewart, Robert Bloch, Ray Harryhausen, Fay Wray, and others. He is proud to be a three-time Rondo Award recipient including "Monster Kid of the Year" (2008). Joe is senior editor of the catalogs for Profiles in History, the world's leading auction house of Hollywood memorabilia.

THE BLOOMINGDALES

BY BERNIE NOGA

INTERIOR DAY. A large Department Store on a busy shopping day. Set in the 1950's. A tall man JAMES, his wife MARY, and their little girl SUSAN stand next to each other wide-eyed at the shopping that awaits them.

> JAMES
>
> Mary... Susan... It's getting late. Suddenly the store will be closing soon.

> SUSAN
>
> There are so many things here Daddy I wish we could stay forever.

James and Mary LAUGH as Susan picks up a DOLL.

Suddenly the light goes off.

> JAMES
> (Quietly)
>
> Damn.

> SUSAN
>
> Daddy, I'm scared!

> MARY
>
> Don't worry Baby. Daddy's here.

> JAMES
>
> Hello... Hello...

                              MARY
                           (Quietly)
           James, I'm a little worried...

                              JAMES
           Well, the doors are locked, no one will be
           here till morning. I guess you got your
           wish. You have the whole store to yourselves.

Mary and Susan look at each other and smile. Both scurry off
happily in slightly different directions. Susan plays on a
mountain of toys. Mary tries on dress after dress. James sits
in an overstuffed recliner, smoking a pipe reading a paper.

A STRANGE NOISE is heard.

They all stop with what they're doing and rush together.

                              JAMES
           Hello. Hello? Can you hear me?

There is no answer.

There is a struggle between James and an unseen MAN. He grabs
James by the neck and starts to twist. Mary SCREAMS, Susan
starts to cry.

                              JAMES
              Stop!

James' face goes pale, and his head rolls across the floor.

Susan drops her doll.

They stand motionless as the Man picks up James' head... Revealing
James Mary, and Susan are a family of Mannequins.

                              MAN
                           (V.O.)
              Bloomingdales!

What do you love about the genre of horror?

Horror takes us on an emotional rollercoaster. It takes our insecurities and fears and manifests them for us to see and experience, most times in iconic characters. Freddy Krueger, Jason Voorhees, Michael Myers. Hell, sometimes even as a shark!

What is some of your favorite horror literature?

I've read Stephen King, but I tend to gravitate more to the works of Rod Sterling, and Anne Rice.

What are some of your influences?

Alfred Hitchcock, Rod Serling, John Carpenter, Roger Corman, Wes Craven, and Vincent Price.

What is your favorite Halloween treat?

Blackened candy apples.

You are hosting the perfect Halloween movie marathon. What are the films you choose and why?

Dementia 13 (1963) Directed by Francis Ford Coppola. A little slow by today's pacing, but a nice little start. *The Abominable Dr. Phibes* (1971) Fun, quirky, and Vincent Price. *Phantasm* (1979) Bizarre at times, but fun to watch. *Poltergeist* (1982) Stephen Spielberg, creates terror in the suburbs. *The Exorcist* (1973) Classic favorite. *Thirteen Ghosts* (2001) Update of old Castle film. *The Thing* (1982) John Carpenter directs this remake of film. Nice performance by Kurt Russell. *Night of the Living Dead* (1968) Romero directs film showcased in Museum of Modern Art. *The Fly* (1986) Jeff Goldblum and Geena Davis in remake of classic film. *Cabin in the Woods* (2011) Awesome fun film. *The Blair Witch Project* (1999) Breakout film for some former students of mine.

If you could continue any horror story, what would it be?

Phantasm.

As a designer of horror theatre or experiences, explain your process.

Usually I can come up with a random idea that I write down. I look at my location, think of the characters in that world, and I let the thoughts flow like blood. I like to think of the stories behind the demons, who they are and what made them.

When is the last time you were genuinely scared by something someone created?

I had just gotten off work and was headed over to my second job, a scenic shop called Cinnabar, when I walked up the ramp and saw a body laying on a gurney. Water was coming out of it. Looked just like my friend Paul Pollette. My heart starts beating fast and there's a lump in my throat. It looks like he drowned. I come to find out its a body for the first Halloween Horror Nights. Scared shitless.

Tell us about your contribution to our book. What was the inspiration?

Coffee inspired story. Insomnia while driving through a closed shopping mall. Had to pull over as characters were slowly taking shape in my mind's eye.

SCARE CRED: BERNIE NOGA

FilmGuru (film goo-roo) Noun. A Frizzy Blond Haired Filmmaker who creates Stories through multimedia art, animation, photo, and video imagery. A personal spiritual teacher, adviser and mentor to those pursuing the art of indie filmmaking.

ROACH

BY ALAN OSTRANDER

"Roach" was a rather disgusting little old monk that was one of the 'ickiest' of the "Eternal Dwellers." Rumor has it that he was found onsite when Terror on Church Street was first created and was so endearing that they just had to put him to work!

a few words from
ALAN OSTRANDER

What do you love about the genre of horror?

I enjoy the roller coaster of emotions that horror evokes from people. It is always interesting to see what is frightening to each individual person as everyone has different fears. What is horrific to one person inspires laughter in another.

What is some of your favorite horror literature?

My favorites are the 'old classics' that I grew up with like Edgar Allen Poe, things that really get into the reader's psyche and mess with their head! Sometimes, the reader's own imagination can bring forth more frightening images than if the writer went into extreme, explicit detail. I've always been a fan of Stephen King's work for this reason. He leaves enough blanks for the reader to fill in with their own experiences, thoughts, etc.

What are some of your influences?

I have influences from all areas of the genre. Directing/design: David Clevinger from the original Terror on Church Street attraction. Makeup/FX: Dick Smith, Rick Baker, Stan Winston. Performer: Vincent Price

What is your favorite Halloween treat?

Reese's Peanut Butter cups!

You are hosting the perfect Halloween movie marathon. What are the films you choose and why?

I would provide a mix from the old psychological classics like *House of Wax* to more gore-centric 80's slashers as well as Asian/Japanese horror that tends to focus more on spirits and ghosts. That way there is something for everyone!

If you could continue any horror story, what would it be?

Hitchcock's *The Birds*! I always loved the movie, but felt it never really had an ending.

As a designer of horror theatre or experiences, explain your process.

The biggest key I have found in making haunted attractions/shows is to make everything relatable to the audience. Using iconic figures and known stories provide the most impact – tapping into persons' pre-conceived ideas and thoughts. I always try to define my audience as much as possible and learn everything I can about that demographic-culture/age/etc. so that I can play to those fears. I have given several lectures to attraction producers of why "Chainsaws & Killer Clowns aren't scary in China." The best horror must relate to and resonate with the audience.

When is the last time you were genuinely scared by something someone created?

Not so much something someone created, but more by actions. A good, unexpected "startle scare" or sudden impact in a well-designed haunt always gets me.

Tell us about your contribution to our book. What was the inspiration?

Roach was a very fun character I created back at Terror on Church Street. He was originally supposed to work in the gift shop, but later became one of the crazy icons of the attraction entertaining the queue line with a mix of comedy and the macabre. Roach has since been spotted at various haunted attractions around the world, as well as appearing on the "Great Wall" of China, and lurking around Argentina.

Describe the perfect Halloween.

For me, the perfect Halloween would be where everyone just has FUN! Without any negativity, name-calling, protesting, etc. by those that do not share our love and enthusiasm for the Holiday.

SCARE CRED: ALAN OSTRANDER

Alan Ostrander has been a professional theatrical artist since 1984, specializing in all aspects of Special FX Makeup for live productions and film/television. Throughout the US, Thailand, Japan, Hong Kong, Argentina and more, he has worked as an actor, set designer, stage manager, prop master, artistic/talent director, and many other positions in the entertainment production industry. He is the founder/creative director of AEO Studios, a one-stop theatrical shop, and is known as Hong Kong's "Father of Halloween" for his thirteen years introducing/cultivating this western holiday in East Asia.

UNUSUAL SUBJECTS

BY DARREN PERKS

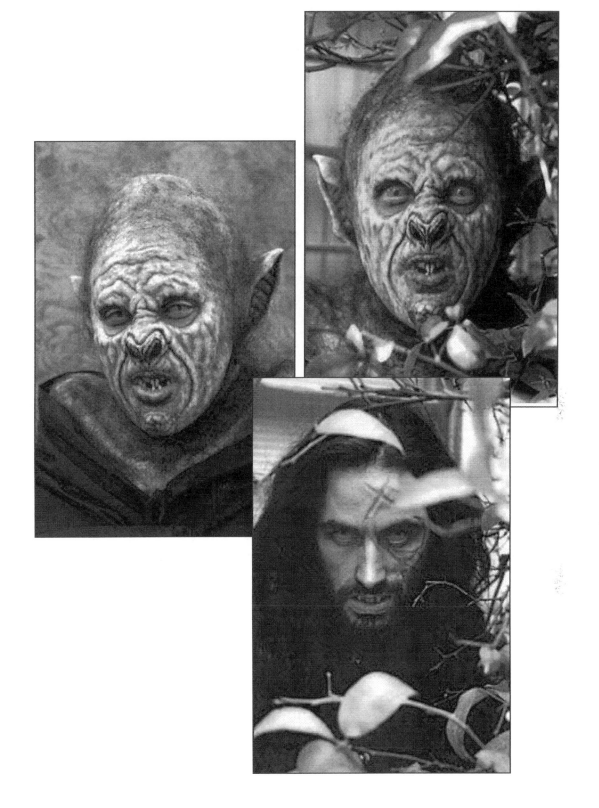

DARREN PERKS

What do you love about the genre of horror?

Everything below my answer nails it and the fact that, artistically, it's endless. Your imagination is limitless and horror adds the element of uncertainty and fear that is always present (in the background of everyday life) that is ignored until it's forced to be dealt with. There is nothing more unknown than death or situations completely foreign to an individual. If it can't be seen or rationalized, your forced to come up with your own rational explanation or beliefs for protection (imagination kicks in).

It's intellectually, emotionally, and viscerally stirring. It inspires the broadest flights of fearful fancy and requires a willful suspension of disbelief that keeps us plastic and young in our imaginations. It invests us in the relationship to creator, monster, and victim, unlike any other genre can.

What is some of your favorite horror literature?

Anything that is vague in detail, but sets the characters, mood and situations deep enough so you feel immersed. Let's you fill in most of the blanks with your own imagination/experiences.

What is your favorite Halloween treat?

The treat of the entire event and fabricating my costume when I was a kid. Seeing cool stuff pop up in the stores.

You are hosting the perfect Halloween movie marathon. What are the films you choose and why?
The Exorcist, Something In The Woodwork (*Night Gallery*), *There Aren't Any More MacBane's* (*Night Gallery*), *The Thing* (Carpenter), *The Fog* (Carpenter), *Halloween 1* and *3* (Carpenter/Wallace), 1979 *Dracula, Jaws*.

As a designer of horror theatre or experiences, explain your process.

Think of the atmosphere, surroundings and overall feel of the particular place where the story/scene exists. Imagine being there and visualize what type of character/creature, etc. would most likely inhabit it. Open spaces where you feel out in the middle of nowhere, but there are areas of cover in the far distance that can be seen (trees/tall grass/decrepit buildings-walls, etc.) where things can be hiding and watching you. Character driven designs that would exist as they actually would. Long matted hair, dirty and unkempt, something wrong with them in appearance that is not symmetrical in design. Nothing organic is truly symmetrical, something has to be off (at least slightly) to help further push it into reality. If a mistake occurs while designing/sculpting/fabricating and it lends itself to the overall appearance, or helps push the piece closer to reality or uniqueness - leave it alone and don't feel a need to copy it on the mirrored-side. Nothing is perfect, or symmetrical - if a push to "perfect" is the goal, it tends to look more like it was made specifically (such as a toy or other perfectly balanced design). Symmetry and hard lines work well in architectural and machined style design. I think the two design styles can be merged as well for a semi-realistic look - which helps push the uniqueness of the character.

When is the last time you were genuinely scared by something someone created?

The Exorcist is the only movie that remained disturbing to me into my early/mid twenties. The last time I remember being extremely scared by another artists creation was this make-up and film and it was back in the early nineties. Watching it in bed, late at night in complete darkness. Not a problem until I fell asleep and awoke (I thought) with Regan standing right next to me with her face beside my pillow. I was obviously dreaming, but awoke in a dream within a dream (*American Werewolf* scenario). I overwhelmingly thought that I woke-up and she was standing over me with a blank expressionless stare - just a few feet from my face. I leaped out of bed and jumped to my feet (as I actually woke up) and it took quite some time to get back to sleep.

Tell us about your contribution to our book. What was the inspiration?

It's a fun subject that I enjoy and has influenced me and my career goals. I'm honored to take part and share with so many other contributors that share the same passion.

Describe the perfect Halloween.

Having time to build a cool costume for my wife and I - and hosting/or going to a highly decorated/detailed party. Watching horror movies the week or weeks leading up to Halloween night.

SCARE CRED: DARREN PERKS

Darren has worked extensively for thirty-five years as a key special effects make-up artist in the motion picture, television, commercial, theatre, print and marketing industries. Darren also designs and fabricates custom scenic displays and effects (through Dynamic Design International) for the leading theme park and haunted attraction clients including Disney, Universal Studios, and Busch Gardens. A key position as a lead designer and sculptor at Don Post Studios further inspired Darren to begin the Dynamic Design International Halloween manufacturing portion of the company. Customers included Spencer Gifts, 7-11, Kroger, and Halloween Adventure Stores. Don Post Studios was one of the first and most widely known Halloween design and manufacturing facilities established in the US. Some of the projects headed by Darren during his four years at Post included the Universal Monsters' "Calendar Mask" licensed re-issues, *Star Wars Episode 1: The Phantom Menace* licensed series, a re-design on the officially licensed Michael Myers *Halloween* movie mask, plus numerous Halloween mask, prop, costume and décor designs.

THE LEGEND OF FEAR FARM

BY LEONARD PICKEL

The Legend of Fear Farm
By Ben S. Kared Clayton Town Historian

Daddy of 13, Forest Phear was a farmer, and a fine-un too, till the bottom dropped out of the stock market in '87 and made millionaires homeless overnight. Many good people even killed they'self, rather'n face the hardships ahead-um. But people still needed to eat, and the government needed to feed-um, so farmin' subsidies was increased and many a once proud man went on the "government dole." With so many mouths to feed Forest took the government's handout. He had to. But when he did, something inside him died.

There are many ways to kill yourself. You can use a gun or a rope, or you can climb into a Jack Daniels bottle and never come out. Forest just seemed to stop livin'. It was a slow cruel death - just waistin' away day after day, witnessed first-hand by his kids. The oldest Phear boy, by 6 years, was Seymour Phear. Named after his mama's daddy, Seymour had dreams of becoming a doctor, but those hopes was dashed when he was forced to take over the family farm at the ripe old age of 15. Forest was buried in'92, but Seymour told people "He was good as dead long before that." The death certificate said that Forest died ah old age, but what killed him was a broken heart.

Try as he did, framin' did not seem to work for Seymour. Tobacco, wheat, corn, even hay seemed to refuse to grow on the Phear Farm. Either Seymour did not have the green thumb that his daddy did, or maybe the dirt missed old Forest just as much as the rest of the family did. Either way, there were hungry youngin's in the Phear home, and no one else to feed-em but Seymour. One thang you could say about Seymour was he left no stone unturned when figerin' out how to make a dollar. Unable to grow much worth sellin' the Phear roadside produce market went through a variety of restarts, worked by the Phear children. Lemonade Stand, Ice Cream Parlor, Gift Store, Plant/Flower Store and Tourist Trap were the most successful incarnations, and Seymour was always looking for the next get rich quick scheme to save the farm that had been in the Phear Family for over 100 years. None of these schemes ever worked, but that did not stop Seymour from trying something new. By 2002, what had been a thriving 50-acre farm had been sold down piece by piece as money was needed. All that is left is at is left was the dirt the Phear Farm House sat on, a large cemetery with 100 years of dead Phears, a shallow lake and some dense forest.

The one single thing that Seymour was good at was huntin'. He just loved to hunt stuff, and to make ends meet he and the other Phear boys would stay out in the woods for days at a time, shootin' and skinnin' anything that moved, from squirrels and rabbits, to deer and even a wild pig or two. Seymour would field dress the meat and sell it to the other farmers in the area. Finally, this seemed to catch hold and make some money for the family, but it was not long before the wild game on the Phear property just ran out. The Phears had even fished dry the lake on the property and was havin' to go further and further out to find somethin' to shoot. Committed to his position as head of the household, even when Seymore had nothing to sell to others, he made sure that the Phear clan had enough to eat. Even in the leanest of times, the Phear children seemed quite portly.

Seymour was the oldest child with 4 brothers and 8 sisters. You could spot a Phear kid from a block away. They all had skin so pale that it looked white against their jet-black hair. If you got closer up, you would also notice their sunken eyes and prominent almost canine lookin' teeth. Rumor was that all Seymour could feed'um was stuff that he killed, and a diet of mostly meat turned the kids into animals themselves.

Growin' up, Seymour was never a bad kid. No more than the usual runs in with the law that happens in a small community with littler' nothing to do, and plenty of moonshiners willing to sell White Lightin' to anyone with change in their pocket. Resentful for havin' to drop out of school to run the family farm, Seymour Phear hated his life and most of all, hated that farm. It was not long before he started actin' up. Fights was the largest category on the Seymour Phear's rap sheet, with strangers mostly. Seems Seymour also hated people that he did not know, and at the slightest provocation would fly into a murderous rage and have to be pulled off to keep from killin' the poor guy that crossed him.

For a while, you could find Seymour in the city lock-up purty much every Sunday mornin'. The local Sheriff, Alan Quilyah, had been lifelong friends with Seymour's paw and took pity on the boy forced to be a man. Al would be sure to sober Seymour up and let him out in time for Church.

There was some suspicion of an armed robbery or two that Seymour was most likely to have been involved with, but the most serious thing Seymore was accused of was murder, in the disappearance of Tain T. Rite. Tain and Seymore was both courtin' Sally S. Cream at the time and most people swear that Seymour just "cut out" the competition. No body was ever found though, and with no more than hearsay, Seymour was never charged with nothin'. But the town folk knew, and so did Sally who would not have nothin' to do with Seymour afterin' that.

It was about that time that, Sheriff Quilyah started seein' an increase in people showin' up missing after traveling through the area. Bein' so close to Raleigh-Durham, they had always had more-in their share of runaways and out of towners passin' though, many of who found the end of Seymore's fist, but reports of people not showin' up at their final destination seemed to swell up about the time that things got toughest for the Phear family. It seemed an odd coincidence at the time, but it made the hairs on Sheriff Al's neck stand up. From years of police and detective work, Al knew that this was a sure sign that he was on'ta somethin'.

After askin' around, Al came realized no one had seen hide nor hair of Seymour or any of the Phear clan for that matter since a week Tuesdee at the hardware store. Fall was settin' in but some of the thangs Seymore was a buyin' didn't make no sense this time a year. It didn't hurt nun that Al was up for re-election and the town folk had been demanding he do something about Seymore for a while. So, the Sheriff decides to visit the Phear Farm and see if'in there was anythang a goin' on up there.

Arriving at the farm Al was surprised to find the roadside store locked up and none of the Phears in sight. Pokin' around a little deeper, Al finds all of the barns locked tight as well. Just then the Sheriff heard the unmistakable sound of a distant chainsaw, coming from a clump of trees near the Phear farmhouse. A freshly graded dirt road disappearin' in'ta the tree line was too muddy for the squad car, so Al hoofed it out to investigate on foot.

Now a chainsaw is a very common farm tool and hearing one work out on a farm is not unusual, even in the fall of 2003, and Al was not more interested in talking to whoever was using the thing than he was afraid of what the saw was being used for. But when he got into the woods, Al suddenly drew his gun at the horrible sight he seen. It was an archway over the path made entirely of bones… human bones; the meat scrapped off'um cleaner than a butcher could do it. Al's first thought was that he wished he had brought the squad car to call for back up, but other then his worthless Deputy there was no one worth callin' anyway. And it was just Seymore Phear. Maybe he's gone a little nuts, but he could handle him as AL had done on many a Saturday night after beatin' somebody near death.

Pushin' further into the woods, Al passed crime scene after crime scene. The killin's looked fresh, but there was no need to check for a pulse on these poor victims. In some cases, there was so little of the pour dismembered soul left; a pulse would be impossible. A cold shiver ran down the spine of Sheriff Quilyah remeberin' the wild stories that Seymour had came up with to keep from getting' arrested for those robberies. Some of them were whoppers, and Al wondered what excuse Seymour would come up with this time. Aliens he thought to himself! It would have to be that aliens from outer space had done all this and Seymour just happened to be chasin' them off with a chainsaw right before in Al got there.

The sounds of the chainsaws got louder and louder as Al passed scene after scene of mutilation, so many corpses that he gave up countin' at 24. Or was it 25, too many body parts for that pile to be just one person. Either way, this makes Seymour a bigger serial killer than John Wayne Gacy, and as Al moved along the path, he could not help but think that there was a book or even a made for TV movie in all this. He would have to remember to take lots'a notes and photos.

Al could see movement through the trees in the direction of the whirrin' chainsaw. He decides to get off the path and cut though brush to reconnoiter the best way to get the drop on Seymour. At the edge of a clearin' Al hears the voices of Seymour and a few others he couldn't make out. From behind a tree he stops to take a read of the situation. There on the fresh cut trail was a wagon, hitched to an old farm tractor. A group of Kids was sitting on a hay wagon.

As the Sheriff reached a clearing he recognized the ones on the tractor to be the Seymour's hefty siblings. With his revolver still in hand he scanned the area for Seymour. Suddenly the doors of an old house burst open and the sound of a revin' gas powered engine was heard. From out of the door rushes a maniac in a blood-stained apron wheedlin' the longest bladed chainsaw Al had ever seen. Wearin' what looked like a Leather Face mask from Texas Chainsaw Massacre, this guy was charging the wagon full of now screaming kids. Al stepped into the clearing leveled his gun and hollered "Freeze!" The kids on the wagon turned lily-white faces toward Al, as he screamed "Freeze!" at the still advancing lunatic. A single shot rang though the woods. The sound of the saw was silenced, but the screams from the wagon full of dark haired Phear children continued!

The next day, radio stations started airing ads for a brand-new Halloween event called the Farmer Phear's Horror Hayride. They buried Seymour in September, as reservations started piling up for what the commercials called the most realistic murder scenes of any hayride in North Carolina." The newspapers said it was an honest mistake. Al did it buy the book, and Seymour could not hear the Sheriff over the sound of the chainless saw.

Seymour was gone, but there were still 12 mouths to feed on the Phear Farm. So, the event will go on as planned. Take a tour…If you dare!

Ben S. Kared, Clayton Town Historian

LEONARD PICKEL

What do you love about the genre of horror?

What I love about the genre of horror is that it allows people to safely experience a life or death situation, without the risk of actual harm. Fear is an emotion and like any emotion it needs to be experienced, experimented on if you will, so a person knows how they will react when they are confronted with a fight or flight.

What are some of your influences?

Stephen King has been the biggest influence on my style of attraction, but I am also influenced by Alfred Hitchcock. I would not be where I am today without architect Walter Netsch. In college I studied his field theory, which was the inspiration for triangular grid system that I am know for throughout the haunted house industry. I also attend as many as two-hundred haunted house events in a season. I am inspired by many of them, but a few stand out. Ed Terebus of Erebus Haunted House comes up with the best scares of anyone I have meet, Dwayne Sandburg of Thirteenth Gate has done some incredible out of the box concepts and Jim Warfield of Raven's Grin Inn taught me not to take myself so seriously. As fright attraction designers, we are not trying the mess people up for life. The goal is to entertain people, tell them a story of survival and raise their endorphin levels to a maximum, but let them survive unscathed.

What is your favorite Halloween treat?

My favorite treat is pumpkin pie with whipped cream on it, but I hate pie crust, so I just eat the filling. Is that weird? I used to love banana taffy as a kid. Hated the orange and black paper twisted candy. Mom stole those anyway.

You are hosting the perfect Halloween movie marathon. What are the films you choose and why?

It would have to include the original *Changeling* with George C Scott. Very creepy move. I'm pretty hard to startle and the conquering got me three times, so I would add that. And one of the early zombie films, can recall which one, they all run together, but the kid was trying to get out of the crypt by standing on the coffin and fell through it and the corpse, yuck. And the movie about the girl that get cursed by the old lady for dies and ends up in the grave with her… creeps me out talking about it.

As a designer of horror theatre or experiences, explain your process.

A themed attraction is a movie (or play) that you walk (or ride) from scene to scene. I do a great deal of brainstorming with the client to get their likes and dislikes about frightful experiences and develop a backstory that describes what evil lurks in the structure. What effects does it have on the location, as well as the inhabitants? What minions are created by the evil to do its bidding? The backstory outlines the who, what, when, and where for the storyline. The storyline drives the action in the attraction and blueprints the them of each space. Then I design from each room from the inside out. I develop what the scare, the action, will be in the room, then I plot a pathway past the scare that best facilitates the scare, then I place furniture and props to force the patrons past the scare at the best angle. Then and only then do I draw the walls around the room.

I have a list of three hundred scares that I have either used or thought of over my forty-plus years scaring people for a living, and I run through those to see what might fit as is, or what can I twist, using the theme or the story, to create something new. I love to combine two old concepts to create something new.

Tell us about your contribution to our book. What was the inspiration?
The story I submitted was for a 2003 attraction called Clayton Fear Farm in Clayton, North Carolina, which I provided consulting and design services to. The event included a hayride, haunted house, spinning tunnel, and haunted green house. The client insisted on the event being called Fear Farm, but there were several other attractions using the name in other states. When I write backstories, I enjoy coming up with hidden meanings in the character names. I proposed a family name of Phear with Seymore Phear as the protagonist. This gave the client a dot com address that was available to purchase. The funny thing was that the client remarked for years on the number of people who believed that the story was real, even with the tongue in cheek names in the "history" of the event.

Describe the perfect Halloween.
The perfect Halloween would be one that I am neither exhausted from twenty-four-hour work days leading up to client openings or traveling the country looking for new ideas for future scare concepts, which runs into November now. I have never put so much as a tombstone in my yard for Halloween. It would be fun to decorate the house and scare the neighborhood kiddies, but then again, it would be hard for me not to go overboard, which would defeat the purpose. I did hand out candy at a friend of mine's house once and had a blast. Maybe the simple things are the best.

SCARE CRED: LEONARD PICKEL

Leonard Pickel has amassed a lifetime of Haunted Attraction Design and operational experience, with October seasonal events to year round haunted attractions, museums and dark rides. He has designed over one-hundred successfully creative events since his first attraction in 1976 and has provided consultation for hundreds more. Always an innovator, Leonard is constantly experimenting with new technologies, and searching for fresh new approaches to making money in the business of haunting.

A TALE OF TWO HAUNTS

BY JEFF PRESTON

In 1973 the Jaycee's haunted house opened their first haunted house in my hometown of Gallatin Tennessee, it was somewhat of a nationwide trend at the time. I was 14 and jumped at the chance to work in the haunted house. For a monster kid this was a dream come true. I was placed in a coffin beside another coffin with a mannequin...mainly because nobody else would get in the coffin. One night a lady with her son came in and leaned over the ropes saying, "I swear this one looks real" I then reached up out of the coffin she hit the wall behind her and fainted dead away... I was instantly hooked on the art of the scare!

A couple more years followed working with the Jaycees who gradually utilized more of my creative input. From a kid in a coffin to designing rooms and the scares that went with them, I literally was like a kid in the candy store. Of course then came high school, adulthood and like most things of youth just kind of faded away.

In 1994 I attended the nations foremost model kit show "Wonderfest" in Louisville Kentucky. That year as it was every year Bob Burns was the number one honored guest. The banquet proved to be a milestone for me Bob treated us to footage of his legendary Halloween shows in Burbank California. Everything magical about Halloween was captured in that footage. The style and craftsmanship that when into the shows was remarkable. The sets costuming and makeup were of Hollywood quality, which they should have been. Most of Bob's friends who helped out were working special effects professional in Hollywood including a young future multiple Oscar winner for make-up Rick Baker. The one thing stood out was the fact that everyone involved was having a blast, especially Bob. The seed was planted I want away from Louisville with one goal in mind to create the Halloween magic I remember as a youth.

That fall I started by carving a few pumpkins (the Pumpkin Masters carving tools we're still relatively new to the market), decorated my front hallway and dressed up as a welcoming ghoulish host. I had the time of my life and thrilled the dozen or so tick or treaters that graced my door. How could anybody to be excited over twelve visitors? The fact of the matter is I lived on the dark dead end street and had never had any trick-or-treaters before so for me this was a significant victory.

The following year enlisted the help of six friends. We blocked off most of the walkway leading to my front door. We had a fog machine, Black lights and strobes, custom fangs and a hidden microphone that altered my voice to a chilling demonic echo. We had over a hundred visitors, word was starting to spread.

1996 was a pivotal year. Monsterscene, a magazine I did illustrations for released a Bob Burns special at the end of the previous year. I illustrated the cover enabling me to become involved with Bob on a one-to-one basis. It was a dream assignment, and the cover turned out to be my most significant work to date, not to mention my first monster magazine cover! More than anything it opened a dialogue between Bob and myself by this time my skill as a pumpkin artist had grown. I was asked to do a demonstration on Nashville based noon talk show. I showed how to carve a Bob Burns face on the pumpkin and talked about my Halloween shows at the house. Attendance that year grew to over 300 we were now firmly entrenched as a Halloween tradition.

In 1997 we expanded our production to the backyard this allowed me to use the new deck I had built that spring. We wove our way in and out under the floor and blocked off the entire back of my house, creating a terrifying journey of mazed horror! Our production value significantly increased. Again, I gave the pumpkin carving demonstration on television plugging the show in the process. Attendance exploded! We ran 700 screaming terrified visitors through in two and a half hours, another hundred were turned away after we shut down for the evening I was starting to get the feeling I just might be onto something here I kept the same blueprint in 1998.

The same route was taken by visitors, but we redesigned our scenes and polished the show two an even higher level. I had a new friend that came on board that worked heavily in theatrical set design and lighting. His expertise, not to mention his lighting equipment, brought us to where I would've stacked the show against any local commercial attraction. Our exit polling confirmed this. The comment most commonly heard was "I went to all the haunted houses in Nashville, but this was the best! You guys scared the crap out of me to me!" That was a standing ovation. Our numbers declined that year, but the quality of visitors made up for the drop in attendance. From opening to closing, all we heard was constant screaming.

In 1999 I was indecisive. Having spent a great deal of money and sweat equity landscaping my home I did not want to disturb my efforts, The passion just wasn't there. I had run out of ideas, and my desire to start production was entirely absent. Then I ordered the video series "Hauntworld: The Movie" a series spotlighting the various haunted attractions across the country, and the bug bit! Suddenly new ideas start popping up, and my creative juices overflowed. My crew, now 35 Haunters, came back for more. I had been consulting with Bob Burns every season always asking, how do you do this or that, he was always gracious sharing his knowledge and expertise. We expanded the show around the house and reversed the route our exit the previous year became the entrance and vice versa. We started production earlier reducing my Halloween season anxiety I knew inside I taken the show as far as I could at the house so this was the final year of the "House on Haunted Hill." We fine-tuned, polished the show and when about to present a Halloween night deserving of Bob's Seal of approval. The attendance that final year was off the charts. Emergency management directed traffic in front of my house and at the end of my street where cars were lined up for almost half of a mile. Close to a thousand people in a little under 3 hours, for a road that never had a trick or treater this was amazing. Since that final year, there hasn't been another as a matter of fact.

Let's venture back to the HOUSE . . .

Entrance to the
House on Haunted Hill

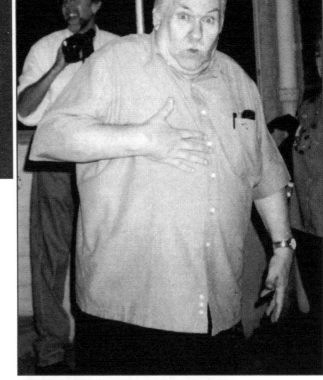

Horror historian
Bob Burns at the Exit.

The line to get in.

The haunted maze.

Jeff catches a nap.

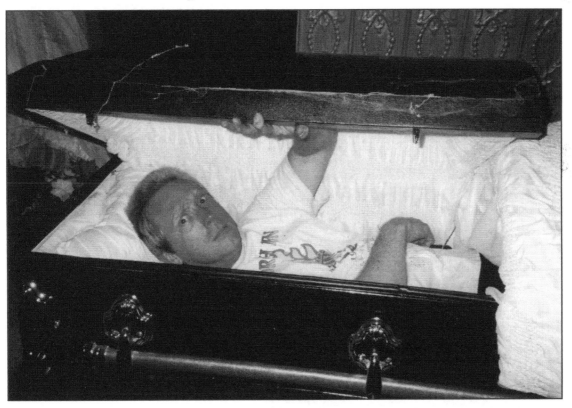

THE BARTENDER

The bartender… the last location on 2nd Ave Nashville had a built-in bar, couldn't move it so we had to utilize it. I had the bartender on an animatronic arm that shot up and over the bar…sounded good in theory. It was just too slow to be effective, looked good though.

THE SHIP'S CAPTAIN

The ship's captain was the way I started the attraction going along with the VERY short storyline that final year. Utilizing the old mirror illusion, it did look like just a torso remained on the ships wheel.

In the fall of 1923 along the Nashville Riverfront a barge was found in the mist. Run aground, it's lifeless crew lay strewn about from bow to stern with throats torn out, the ship's captain bound to the wheel with his own entrails, his face frozen in horror at the bloodbath that took place before him. Locals spoke in hushed whispers of these hellish deeds and feared that their city would soon be overtaken by the hell spawn that was responsible for this massacre. Through the years that followed this was but a tale to be told to keep children in their beds at night. The ancient doors of evil have opened.

THE HANGING BRIDE

THE WEREWOLF SCENE

The under the deck werewolf scene also worked really well. The werewolf was built on a PVC pipe armature and would move in a twist motion when activated by a hidden string, A happy accident, the movement was VERY realistic and effective. With the lighting most thought it was a real person…the real one though was on them as they turned the corner with attention still on the scene.

While posting my promotional flyers on the town square, I kept noticing the availability of building space. The little voice in my head spoke- this is where I need to move the show! A building on the square that was actually haunted was secured, and plans began for 2000 and "Terror On the Square." Now was the building that "Terror on the Square" located *actually* haunted?

The storylines that were written to design the attraction around were interwoven with actual local history. The "Lackey Cave" was real although probably not as widespread as legend made it out to be, running underneath the entire town. Of course, I didn't care one way or the other I just embellished the tale tenfold. That somehow got the attention of area ghost hunters. One day I got a call from a lady wanting to investigate. She told me she was a psychic. I explained that the story "The Mortuary of Madness" was totally fictional but she still wanted to come and

take a look. The day arrived, and there was a knock on the door. Just my luck she reminded you of "Tangina," the older psychic lady from "Poltergeist." She did bring a friend with her and immediately told her when she stepped inside the building, "Oh it's upstairs."

Now let's backtrack a few weeks. One Friday night I was doing a radio interview during halftime at the local football game broadcast. My right-hand man, Mark King, was busy working on the steps to the fake elevator we had built a few days before. I left him there to work while I slipped out to do the interview. When I came back in an hour or so he was gone. I immediately called and said, "Where are you, get back up here we've got to finish this tonight!" He said dead seriously, "Look I heard you on the radio, all the doors were locked, and I knew I was the only one here, but I heard someone walking directly above me, and I got the hell out!"

I laughed, called him a wuss and to get back up there. He did, we continued to work without incident, but I could tell he was legitimately spooked.

Now back to the "Run to the light" lady. When we got upstairs, she walked a few steps in and grabbed the side of the left side of her head saying "I have a pain here" and then proceeded to say the same thing about her right arm. I thought to myself "Oh brother what a load of cra......." Then it dawned on me she was standing directly over where Mark had been working on the elevator steps and heard the footsteps. The hair immediately went up on the back of my neck.

Still skeptical I took her along the rest of the square and when we hit the upstairs entrance to a corner bank she immediately grabbed her throat and said she couldn't breathe. What she couldn't have known this was where a bank president had hung himself years earlier, it wasn't publicized, and very few knew about it. She could be the real deal after all.

The next year, I continued the storyline incorporating the Civil War and Union General Eleazer A. Paine who held my hometown under a siege that reminded me of Vlad the Impaler! Ah Ha…Civil War vampires, I had my theme! In my research, I found something interesting. After the war there was a caretaker, a Confederate veteran of the war, that took care of the downtown buildings. He had lost his right arm and suffered a wound on the left side of his head during battle.

That year as the one before Mark wasn't the only one who heard someone walking upstairs, seemed everyone did but me. However, I was upstairs when the phone rang on a postseason evening, one of my workers went to answer it then realized the phone wasn't even plugged in! We called it a night.

Let's revisit the SQUARE. . .

MAUSOLEUM ENTRANCE

This is where the lead vampire actress would appear at stage right and walk along the elevated platform speaking Italian Setting the mood!

THE DOLL WALL

The dolls wall started at the home haunt and carried through every year at TOTS.... Too creepy not to use it! Dolls were painted in fluorescent paint to glow under black light then hung on a black was that was hunted so when the wall was released at the top, the dolls swung forward towards the patrons and loss of bladder control usually followed! The last two sound effects were added of screaming echoing babies and the effect was even more effective.

PUMPKINHEAD

Pumpkinhead was also carried over for the home haunt. It was basically a giant puppet that was operated from behind. The torso was built via tips from Bob Burns form his day of working with Paul Blaisdell. Cut foam, contact cement, and heavy tissue paper and you cam make anything….best made outside where air is plentiful!

THE SKULL WALL

The skull wall was built to great visitors when they stepped off the fake elevator to make them feel like they walked in "Lacky Cave" the cave system that ran beneath the town and in this case the city cemetery! Built with plywood, skulls, ribcages and spray foam. Three 4 X 8 panels attached then blended together with wire and drywall joint compound created a long seamless... VERY creepy scene. In fact, I vividly remember the night we put them up and chills ran up and down my spine.

THE SPIDER

First a hanging Skelton behind bars, inspired by the "Forgotten Prisoner of Castlemare" Aurora Model kit of the 60's. No scare involved just a mood setter. The spider Victim, the animated giant spider would spring to life directly overhead when the motion detector was set off by patrons.

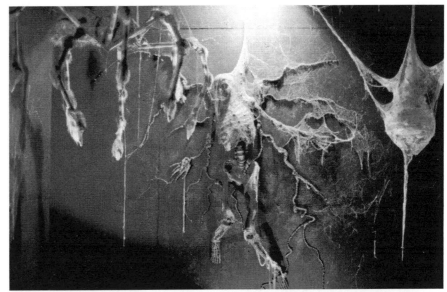

THE FORGOTTEN PRISONER

THE RAT VICTIM

The rat victim…. What you can't really see is the 50 or so rats attached to the walls are scurrying towards the victim. The dark hall wall also was cover with the fake rats so if a patrons touched the wall they would be touching a rat. An out of site haunted would hit the ankles of the patrons with a rubber rats tail (since I couldn't afford the Epcot Center "Honey I Shrunk the Audience" air power rat tail slapping the legs) add the sound effects and patrons who hated rats hated me even more after going through this scene!

JEFF PRESTON

What do you love about the genre of horror?

How do you go about describing the love for something that you've had since early childhood? I can vividly recall at age five going back home while my parents played cards next door to watch *Shock Theater* hosted by the eye patched clad Dr. Lucifer in Nashville. Upon his command of "turn off your lights" I dutifully ran though the house doing just that until I planted myself in front of the television awaiting all the glorious back and white Universal films.

What is some of your favorite horror literature?

If it counts, the Warren Magazines, *Eerie* and *Creepy* were my sources of horror literature and still hold that special place in my heart and creative mind. Stephen King, of course, as I got older but honestly I'm not that much of a reader, I'm more visual.

What are some of your influences?

Frank Frazetta, Basil Gogos in the horror art realm. With haunting, Bob Burns!

What is your favorite Halloween treat?

Fun-sized Baby Ruth's. Although trick or treating at Johnny Cash's house as a kid and getting a full size Black Cow holds a special memory, I kept the wrapper for years.

You are hosting the perfect Halloween movie marathon. What are the films you choose and why?

Frankenstein vs the Wolfman - the opening scene in the cemetery holds a vivid memory. It would set the tone for a creepy night ahead. *Dracula has Risen from the Grave* - classic Hammer, great visuals that even today rank high on the shudder scale. Dracula pulling the stake out, the priest dumping the female corpse out of the new dug up coffin… still sends shudders up and down my spine! 1979's *Dracula* with Frank Langella makes the cut for one scene alone - Mina in the mines… for me the creepiest scene of all time! *The Exorcist* - reasons not needed, the uneasy horror of this film stays with you YEARS after seeing it for the first time. I'm still apprehensive about watching it, but I'm hosting the marathon and I'm out to scare my guests! *The Omen* - classic horror that cannot be excluded. Then *Trick R Treat* - this film to Halloween is what *A Christmas Story* is to Christmas. It *has* to be included. Finally, *Halloween*. After remakes and countless sequels, going back we can really appreciate the genius of John Carpenter in making this film. It fires on all cylinders and is a perfect final for the marathon.

If you could continue any horror story, what would it be?

The really good ones need no continuance as they stand alone. That's why sequels rarely work or rise to the level of the original. The only exception would be *The Bride of Frankenstein*. My answer would be 2011's *Don't Be Afraid of the Dark*. I would like to see this continued because the teeth coveting Homunculi are such cool little creatures

As a designer of horror theatre or experiences, explain your process.

Home haunting, the goal was to set a mood and just scare people with various scenes. As a professional, I tried to design he attraction around a storyline. That made for a flow and purpose to the haunt. How many took the time to actual read the story I haven't a clue but from a creative standpoint it gave structure to the attraction

When is the last time you were genuinely scared by something someone created?

Never, I'm a haunter's worst audience for a scare. I'm more taken by the creation I'm seeing, the scene - the detail, the costuming, the makeup - to even be remotely startled.

Tell us about your contribution to our book. What was the inspiration?

The concept of gathering stories from haunters, who are the most creative group of people I know, is a noble effort that I'm honored to contribute to. Haunting is a true art form and shinning the spotlight on its creators will hopefully bring a whole new appreciation of the creativity and ingenuity that goes into it.

Describe the perfect Halloween.

Going back to the roots of home haunting is a dream I have. An elaborate yet simple yard haunt that trick or treaters have to navigate to get their candy. It creates golden memories that are never forgotten.

SCARE CRED: JEFF PRESTON

Born in Ohio in 1958 and raised in Tennessee Jeff Preston has had a lifetime fascination with monsters and all things 'spooky". He has been a professional illustrator for over thirty-three years. Inducted into the prestigious New York Society of Illustrators in 2006, he also serves on the membership committee. Having enjoyed a prolific career in publishing and advertising his monster art is what he is best known and awarded for. His art has appeared on the covers of *Famous Monsters of Filmland, Little Shoppe of Horrors, Monsterscene* and *Monsterpalooza*. From home haunt to the professional attraction "Terror on the Square" in Gallatin then Nashville Tennessee (2000-2002), his approach was the same as in art. Highly Detailed, dramatic lighting and atmosphere, all trademarks of his creative endeavors. His home studio is based just outside of Nashville and he is always open for work.

THE LAST TIME WE SAW HIM

BY J. MICHAEL RODDY

The magnificent creature was falling. He tried to spread his mammoth, black wings, but the weight of the attacking beast prevented that. Anger, mixed with searing pain as the violent foe continued to dig razor-sharp claws into his body. The mix of the sensation of falling and the great, searing pain was at once exhilarating and tormenting. Falling. How many times had he easily sailed on the night wind, but that was without the extra weight of this beast. He turned to try and throw his attacker off but felt the snap of his left arm. Pain shot through him. The turbulent ocean of darkness was below, and any second, the two great beasts would be smashed upon the hidden rocks and waves. He had faced greater foes, some more powerful, that had tried to take his life, but this one was fueled by something none of the others had… his opponent didn't want to win, he wanted to die.

Another slash of claws dug into his back, and for the first time, he let the attacker know he was in pain. He screamed in defiance. Had he finally been bested? No. He would not let this be his last battle. No. He would not allow the legacy of his rule to end this way, not here, not tonight. He forced his wing to move and felt the pain of the shattered bone, turning and baring his glistening fangs. He bit deep into the fur of the attacker, causing it to release its grip. A second was all he needed. He pushed with his mighty strength and the beast cascaded against the wall of the castle. There was a sickening sound of a meaty thud that was quickly swallowed by the sound of the surf. He knew the creature didn't die. He could sense it. But, he also knew he only had a few seconds before he would break against the rocks below.

The pain was filling his brain. He had to recover and quickly. His left wing was now useless, but if he could right himself, he could use his right to possibly save his life… Yes. HE would not die tonight. He turned, and with his massive wing, he pushed outward against the rushing wind. He felt himself lift missed the jagged rocks within mere inches. The wing gave him enough thrust to move farther away and crash into the sand. He felt bones break as the wet, cold sand swallowed him. Lying there, a wounded, black mass, he looked up at the moon. It was full and bright. It was always beautiful. How many moons had he seen, nights like these where he was the predator, not the prey. He would be again. Twisting in the sand, he righted himself and slowly let the cold take over. His body ached. He stretched and felt the torn muscle and bones start the healing process.

He stood and listened. He heard the movement of at least a dozen creatures nearby, but no sound of his main predator. He would face him again, another night. But now, he needed to feed and to find his sanctuary. It would be dawn soon. Dawn. For a hesitant second, he thought of letting the sun rise and feeling the warmth overtake him. But, that would indeed be the end. No, he would live for another night. He was the King of his kind.

POP

BY J. MICHAEL RODDY

Parker Hamilton was melting. His skin, his internal organs, his brain all felt like a warm puddle of wax. He shifted in his shoes as he stumbled along the back alleyway. With each step, he felt a sloshing internal shift. His vision was getting blurry. Must keep going. Get back to the 24-hour clinic. They could help him… but, how?

The process had started to accelerate. Skin felt like it had been disconnected to the muscle underneath. Loose. Everywhere felt loose. He felt like he was dripping. His fingers drooped off his hands. His ability to grab and control was gone. He couldn't drive. Only choice was to give up or keep walking, slopping forward. He forced himself forward.

Had it really only been two days since he felt the small sting? It was early that morning, the room was dark, and he was running late. He had pulled a shirt from the dark and then felt it. Something moving across his abdomen, almost ticklish. Then, a slight pain. Annoying pain. Something had bitten him. It was a small black bug, which he instantly crushed between two fingers. There was an immediate gratification to feeling the small life pop between his forefinger and thumb. Hey, it had attacked him first. He never even really regarded what type of insect it was. It was small, and had caused him discomfort and he was late. The problem was solved and then wiped away in a Kleenex and tossed away unceremoniously.

He tripped under his weight and the inability to support it anymore. Somewhere in his shoe, he felt a warm and wet sensation. He imagined his feet like jello and his size 11 oxfords a costly mold that contained them. He steadied himself against a garbage dumpster.

He slid down the side of the dumpster and sat. The dim streetlight cast shadows down the alley, and he could see that his hands were now loose and spindly. His insides ached. There, protruding from his belly was a mass. It hurt. The pressure was becoming unbearable. It was like every muscle, and organ was liquifying and slowly pushing towards that mass. He couldn't take it anymore. He ripped open his shirt and saw the mass. It was coming to a whitish head. He reached to touch it, and it seemed to tremble, but the pain was excruciating. He cried out. The agony gurgled in his throat.

It was late. His cry was met with only the distant sound of a car. He had gone to the doctor and was given a topical cream. "It would be fine in a day or two," the doctor at the 24-hour clinic said. If only he knew what type of insect had bitten him, maybe he could…

He wiped his mouth and felt his lips move. Something clattered to the street. Teeth. His eyes were starting to iris into the dark, and he would be blind soon.

The pressure building up under the mass was unbearable. It was trembling, needing to be released like a pressure valve. He couldn't use his fingers, they were useless and would not be able to do the job. He thought to himself how good it would feel. He thought of the doctor on television that specialized in filming "popping" pimples and cysts. She would have a field day with him. No, he had to do it. It was driving him mad.

He shifted against the wet dumpster and prepared himself. A small pool of light allowed the faintest glimpse of his torso. There it was. Begging. Please release me. With all of his strength, he put his elbows on each side and at the base of the mass. The pressure was tremendous. There was a rush of pain and relief. Then he slowly felt the entire contents of his abdomen rush out. He saw his entrails; his guts rush out and spray across the street. The smell of sour rot filled him and he gagged. It kept oozing out. He was dying. And then, in his last moments, he saw the most horrific sight…

Free. That was all it could think. Free. It scurried up the wall and looked back for a second. Its eight eyes focused on what was below. What a perfect host. Warm and delicious. It scurried over the wall and searched. Tonight. It was time. The invasion had begun.

HAUNTED PHOTOGRAPHY

BY J. MICHAEL RODDY

"Lonely Ghost"

"Visitor
Parking"

"Locked
Graveyard"

"Little Girl Lost"

"Trick or Treat"

Dead Wrong

BY J. MICHAEL RODDY

INT. MASTER BATHROOM - NIGHT

A pair of hands. Washing with soap.

CLOSE ON DRAIN

Water mixed with soap.

UP AT FACE

We see a MAN. 30s. Handsome. Dark intense eyes. He is dressed in green hospital scrubs. He is slightly manic as he washes his hands.

> MAN
> I have to get going soon. I am due
> at the Hospital tonight.

He looks back over his shoulder.

CLOSE ON FEET

Two bare foot stick out, lying on a rumpled bed.

BACK TO DRAIN.

We see water, now mixed with blood.

CLOSE ON HANDS - FINGERNAILS

The fingernails are dirty with fleshy material. The man continues to scrub.

BACK TO BARE FEET

We slowly move around and see the Woman's legs. As we move around we can see the spattering of blood covering her thighs.

CLOSE ON BLADE

The blade of an exacto knife. A small hunk of fleshy material is seen on the tip. The Man places the tip under the running water and the flesh is washed away.

BACK TO BARE FEET

We move around completely and find a sheet covering the rest of the motionless body.

The Man turns off the sink and smiles.

                    MAN (CONT'D)
          Gotta get a move on. Gotta be at
          the hospital in a few hours. Time
          to take a trip miss...?

He picks up a discarded purse and opens the wallet. We see a Driver's License.

CLOSE ON PICTURE

A smiling, attractive Woman, 30's.

                    MAN (CONT'D)
          Miss Cooper.

CLOSE ON MAN He smiles.

CLOSE ON PICTURE

Two beautiful children.

CLOSE ON MAN

For a moment we see sadness in his eyes. Remorse. The moment quickly subsides as the darkness takes over.

>   MAN (CONT'D)
>   Keep on Trucking.

EXT. DRIVEWAY - NIGHT

>   CUT TO:

The man places the sheet covered body in the trunk of his car.

INT. CAR - NIGHT

He gets in the car and starts it. The radio is loud. For a moment we hear an announcer.

>   RADIO ANNOUNCER
>   The national health advisory has
>   not made a comment yet, but reports
>   are coming in more frequently.

He is not listening. He slides in a CD.

EXT. - HIGHWAY - NIGHT

>   CUT TO:

Lights play across his face as he drives. On the seat next to him is a newspaper.

CLOSE ON NEWSPAPER

We can see an article that reads - "4th Local Woman Missing" He continues to drive.

CUT TO:

EXT. DARK OPEN FIELD - NIGHT

The car pulls into an open field. He gets out holding a flash-light.

A flash of lightning illuminates the area. Behind him is a dark open field.

He opens the trunk and removes the body. He dumps it down and gets a shovel.

LONG SHOT ON MAN DIGGING

He digs as another flash of lightning lights up the sky.

MEDIUM ON MAN

Behind him we see three forms standing in the distance. The Lightning flashes again and the three forms are closer.

CLOSE ON MAN

He is oblivious as he digs.

The three forms grab at him. He spins around and screams.

CLOSE ON WOMAN

Her face a twisted mask of snarling hunger. She grabs at him. He falls onto the body. He looks up at the three bloody and decomposing women. The bag rips open and Mrs. Cooper grabs him. He screams. She snarls and then takes a bite out of his throat.

We pull back and up into the night. A full moon hangs sentinel as the man's screams become muffled.

FADE TO BLACK.

J. MICHAEL RODDY

What do you love about the genre of horror?

I have been a horror fan since my earliest memories of discovering stories. The anticipation and excitement, the rush of adrenaline all led me to darker stories and films. I love that the genre is cathartic. You make it through a great book, film or piece of theatre and you feel you have survived. Maybe this helps us in some way face our fears and be prepared for them. When a good story has you, and you are there with the characters, you feel the threat and danger. You allow yourself to immerse yourself and suspend disbelief… but at the end the lights come on and you are safe.

What is some of your favorite horror literature?

Ray Bradbury's *The Halloween Tree*, Stephen King's *Pet Semetary*, Robert McCammon's *Mystery Walk* and Clive Barker's *Coldheart Canyon: A Hollywood Ghost Story*. Lovecraft is also such a powerful author. His descriptive passages of slimy, black organisms in many cases make no sense in the conformity of the mind and allow you to try and visualize which then creates terror.

What are some of your influences?

Steven Spielberg - *Jaws* continues to be an example of perfect visual storytelling and how effective your imagination can be. Think about those yellow barrels and that theme. They complete the shark's image. John Carpenter – The best horror director. His films are textbooks in how to generate tension and fear. I love them all. And, his music is always playing when I write. Stephen King – one of the best at creating horror with words. Tom Savini – The modern-day showman. He is everything I want to be. Magician, make-up artist, actor, director. *Abbott & Costello Meet Frankenstein* – Proving along with *Ghostbusters* and *Evil Dead II* that horror can also be funny.

What is your favorite Halloween treat?

I love Almond Joy and Hershey Chocolate bars.

You are hosting the perfect Halloween movie marathon. What are the films you choose and why?

It's The Great Pumpkin Charlie Brown – perfect way to start the evening. *Dracula* – the film actually creaks. Such a magnificent example of gothic horror. John Carpenter's *Halloween* – this film is at the top of the list. Carpenter created a masterpiece that seems to capture the essence of the holiday. Frankenstein – the original and best creature feature. *Trick 'R Treat* – when Michael Dougherty created the Sam character with "Season's Greetings" he gave us the perfect image and character for a night of ghouls and goblins. *Abbott & Costello Meet Frankenstein* – it has all of the favorite tropes of the Universal classic monster films with the delightful humor of Bud Abbott and Lou Costello. The best thing is that the monsters are never made fun of. They are scary and threatening.

As a designer of horror theatre or experiences, explain your process.

I always look for ways to connect to the guest/reader by using my own unique experiences. I love being an audience and put myself through all of it before I start to commit it to design. First, I look for the theme, the essence of the idea. Next, I figure out the location and the history. Where do I want to venture… a graveyard, a carnival, a funeral parlor? What happened? Then, I plunk the audience in the middle of that moment and let the ghosts have at them.

Tell us about your contribution to our book. What was the inspiration?

The Last Time We Saw Him - I love *Abbott & Costello Meet Frankenstein*. The one thing that I always imagined was the fact that plunging into the ocean would not destroy either Dracula or the Wolfman. So this is my tribute to that fight between two titans of terror. *Pop* – One of my scariest fears is sickness. I survived cancer at an early age and this stems form that and my fear of spiders. It is terrifying when your body becomes sick and it almost seems to be alien. You lose control of it. *Dead Wrong* – A short film I wrote and set in a computer folder. What would happen if a terrible crime had been committed during the beginning of a zombie apocalypse. I still want to produce it someday. *Haunted Photography* – I have always loved the art of telling a story with a single photo or frame of art. Here are a few that I have attempted and feel are worthwhile to generate effective creepiness.

Describe the perfect Halloween.

I live in Florida and Halloween is rarely what I would consider my perfect setting. I want the coolness in the air, the orange dusk and the deep blue midnight. The crackling of the fire and the hint of supernatural in the air. Then, there's a crunch of fallen leaves somewhere in the distance. Was that a cackle overhead?

SCARE CRED: J. MICHAEL RODDY

J. Michael Roddy began his entertainment career as an actor. His encyclopedic knowledge of pop culture brought him opportunities to write and direct. He has been a prevalent member of the design team for Halloween Horror Nights at Universal Studios. There he created and implemented over one-hundred haunted attractions and scarezones. He has also created successful shows and attractions for Walt Disney Creative Entertainment involving *Star Wars*, *Frozen*, Pixar, Marvel, and Disney Cruise Line. He was also a producer on 2011's award-winning documentary *The Shark is Still Working: The Impact & Legacy of Jaws* and 2017's award-winning *MonsterKids*. In 2018, he won a Rondo Hattan Award for Best Documentary. He recently formed Roddy Creative LLC where he provides creative writing and directing for live shows, attractions, exhibits and marquee events. He is also the creator of MonsterKids - a podcast that delves into the positive influence of horror genre on culture. He lives in Central Florida with his wife, two kids, three dogs, and two cats.

FIVE ARTWORKS

BY CHAD SAVAGE

"31"

"HALLOWEEN EAGLE"

"HALLOWEEN SPIRITS"

"ANN MARIE & FRIENDS"

"DOOMSPIDER"

CHAD SAVAGE

What do you love about the genre of horror?

I was always drawn towards a darker aesthetic (even at an early age, I loved Halloween more than Christmas), so to an extent I don't have a simple answer. It's just in my blood. Having said that, one of the many things I love about horror is its adaptability - you can tell *any* kind of story you want within a horror framework, mix in other genres, use familiar tropes or take those tropes and use them against your audience's expectations... the possibilities are only as limited as the storyteller's imagination.

What is some of your favorite horror literature?

Some of my favorite authors are Clive Barker, Stephen King, Neil Gaiman, Brian Keene, Tim Lebbon, Ray Bradbury, Poppy Z. Brite and John Everson, just to name a few.

What are some of your influences?

Clive Barker, H. R. Giger, Gerald Brom, Chet Zar, Edward Gorey, Tim Burton, Alan M. Clark, Joseph Larkin, Marshall Arisman, Francis Bacon, Michael Parkes, Chris Mars... this list could go on for days.

What is your favorite Halloween treat?

A good scare!

You are hosting the perfect Halloween movie marathon. What are the films you choose and why?

Michael Dougherty's *Trick 'r Treat* because it captures the spirit of Halloween better than any other movie I've seen. *Hocus Pocus* because it's just not Halloween with the Sanderson Sisters. *Something Wicked This Way Comes* because nobody does Halloween like Bradbury. *The Lady in White* because it hits all the right nostalgic notes. *The Haunting* (original) because it's one of the greatest haunted house movies ever made.

If you could continue any horror story, what would it be?

In the movie adaptation of Stephen King's *The Mist*, there's a woman that leaves the grocery store in the first act to get to her children - you see her (and her children) on the bus in the final reel of the film. I always thought her story, from the grocery store to the bus, could've made for a great sequel.

As a designer of horror theatre or experiences, explain your process.

That's an awfully broad question, so the awfully broad answer is: I try to balance (a) what my client wants to see with (b) what I know pushes people's buttons and (c) without falling into cliches or over-used tropes.

When is the last time you were genuinely scared by something someone created?

That doesn't really happen anymore - between real-life scares and the fact that I work behind the scenes on this stuff on the daily, fictional frights don't really get to me (as long as it's entertaining, I'm good). That said, though, I was thoroughly unsettled by the film Hereditary.

Tell us about your contribution to our book. What was the inspiration?

In Autumn 2017 I was invited to participate in a group dark art show themed around phobias; *DOOMSPIDER* is a combination of common phobias (spiders, death, clowns) in one unsettling image.

Describe the perfect Halloween.

Temperature in the mid-60's, a bright moon with scudding clouds and breezy enough to kick up some leaves. Trick or treaters aplenty, and AFTER dark. Hot cider, caramel apples and the scent of singed pumpkin meat in the air. Glowing jack o' lantern faces and illuminated decorations everywhere you look. A creepy sound effects record playing somewhere in the distance - just far enough away that you can only sort of hear it, so it actually becomes spooky. Ghost stories and scary movies. And, if you're me, acting at a haunted attraction and giving people at least one good scare!

SCARE CRED: CHAD SAVAGE

Chad Savage is an award-winning dark artist and visual designer who has been in the service of all things sinister and spooky since his first Halloween. His illustrations have appeared in/on numerous books and magazines, his custom-made horror fonts are ubiquitous and if you've been to a haunted attraction recently, there's a very real chance that he designed their marketing materials and website. Find out more at SinisterVisions.com

203

A GOOD CAST IS WORTH REPEATING

BY SCOTT SIMMONS

The names of our characters are
often hilariously on the nose.
Hence "Dave the Clown."
(actor: Dave Archer)

ScareHouse Bunny

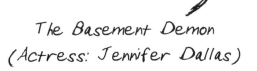

The Basement Demon
(Actress: Jennifer Dallas)

a few words from
SCOTT SIMMONS

What do you love about the genre of horror?

It's often so playfully subversive. The so-called great works of literature and drama are often preening and self-important, the stuff of pristine editions and oscar ceremonies. Horror is the wild ride on the rickety roller coaster, the stuff of hot wings and rock n roll. Horror is rarely the cool kids or the trendy celebs, and it's definitely not the authority figure. If pop culture was a college campus, horror would be the Delta Tau Chi House with John Belushi smashing guitars. It's not the most prestigious or the wealthiest, but it's definitely the wildest and messiest party in town. That's not to say that all horror needs to be explosive and wild - but something that all horror shares, from the graceful whispered poetry of Shirley Jackson's prose to the throaty gargling snarls of Leatherface's chainsaw, is the willingness to undermine expectations and accepted behaviors. It's not the fart in church. It's the clown in the sewer.

What are some of your influences?

As an adolescent I was raised on films by George Romero and John Carpenter and writings from Stephen King and Alan Moore, and I realized recently that all of those guys love to blur the territory lines between genres and frequently mashed-up disparate elements from wildly different sources. (Quoting the character of Chinese sorcerer Egg Shen: "We take what we want and leave the rest. Just like your salad bar")

What is your favorite Halloween treat?

When temperatures are low and my stress is high, I will devour an entire pumpkin pie in one sitting. I regret nothing.

You are hosting the perfect Halloween movie marathon. What are the films you choose and why?

Something Wicked The Way Comes, Salem's Lot, Pumpkinhead, The Fog, 13 Ghosts, and *The Legend of Hell House.*

As a designer of horror theatre or experiences, explain your process.

For me it often starts with either an image or conceptual contrast. Some of the most potent ideas at ScareHouse started with just a single, seemingly random image popping into my head -- often it's very clean. Clown on swing. Possessed woman crawling up from basement. Easter Bunny with axe. There is a thin line between humor and horror, and I think both operate from a place of surprise and contrast. A joke is essentially a short story with a twist ending. A scare is something that breaks our expectation. A bunny is cute and passive. He's the bottom of the food chain. A bunny with an axe is no one's meal. My favorite ScareHouse characters and moments evoke nervous laughter and/or screams - sometimes simultaneously.

When directing actors I'll often push them to go past the expectation or cliche and find the contrast. If you're a demonic-looking girl with burning eyes and rotting teeth the first instinct might be to go all creepy and weird ... but what happens when you giggle? When you seem happy to be there? When you flirt?

208

One of our current haunted attractions is filled with demonic children and creatures, and we rarely allow them to act menacing or traditionally "scary" -- they're more often giggling, playing, and having fun. If you were a demon released from hell you wouldn't really be worried about being all menacing and terrifying, I figure you'd be like a dog who finally broke free out of the yard running amok through the neighborhood ... it's the best day ever!

So my process usually starts with gathering images and ideas or character beats that seem fun to explore, that the actual attractions and stories that contain those experiences and interactions are constructed in some way that will connect everyone and everything together.

When is the last time you were genuinely scared by something someone created?

My brain is a jerk. It frequently uploads horrifying images into my brain without warning, usually when I'm just about to sleep. One night, several years ago, I had a sudden and very vivid image of creepy man standing in the doorway of my bedroom...not moving ... just grinning ....eye twinkling ... and watching me. Last summer I saw "Hereditary" in theaters and there was a shot in that film that quite literally brought that nightmarish image to life and I damn near died. I'm a 47 year-old, grown-ass man and I barely slept the night after seeing the movie.

Tell us about your contribution to our book. What was the inspiration?

I hope that I can inspire and encourage others to mash-up, montage, and meld inspirations together. Don't repeat and remake what you or others might have done, but take all those elements and inspirations and attitudes from others and make something that is new and exciting -- yet still very much your own.

Describe the perfect Halloween.

I live in western Pennsylvania which means I grew up surrounded by that classic autumn atmosphere that's really only available on the east coast. Changing leaves, cool and crisp air, the wind in the trees. The perfect Halloween? Lets warm up this apple cider with a little whiskey, enjoy a spooky hayride with a bunch of college kids in rubber masks jumping out to scare us, then fall asleep listening to *Sounds to Make You Shiver* on vinyl.

SCARE CRED: SCOTT SIMMONS

Scott is creative/marketing director and co-owner of ScareHouse in Pittsburgh, PA, which was named one of the best haunted houses in America by Travel Channel, Buzzfeed, and ABC news and regularly praised by horror icons such as Guillermo del Toro, Michael Dougherty, and Elijah Wood. Located in a century-old Elks Lodge building in suburban Pittsburgh, ScareHouse comprises three walk-through experiences plus a separately ticketed attraction known as "The Basement," an ultra-intense and immersive experience that is not for the weak of heart. "Pittsburgh's Ultimate Haunted House" is open select dates from mid-September through early November. Tickets and info at ScareHouse.com.

ROADSIDE

BY JEFF STANDARD

Creepy. But if it gets me off the road for a while, maybe I will survive the drive. Blinking red lights distort through the rain streaked windshield. There are three or four other cars in the dark parking lot. So at least I won't be alone, if this place is being run by a murderous cannibal family. The sign over the ticket window reads 'A Happy Place'. A second sign had been awkwardly nailed onto the end adding 'To Die'. The building is either genuinely falling apart or has had one hell of a good scenic paint job. Faintly discernible figures line either side of the door. Their phantom appearance lending themselves to being lost souls or the risen dead.

Getting out of the car into the steady rain, an older woman in the nearest car rolls down her window halfway and waves me over. She smiles sadly as I approach. She holds a ticket out the window.

"Please take it. My husband wanted me to go in with him, but I decided I didn't want to leave the car."

I reached out. "If you're sure," I said "I can buy it from you if they-"

"No." She pushes the ticket into my hand "Good Luck"

"Thank you," I reply as she rolls the window up and her face seems to fade behind the streaks of rain on the glass. I jog over to the porch and while stepping up a pain shoots through my knee, a pressure like it's about to dislocate and then it eases a bit as I limp over to the window. The opening is shaped like broken glass and I carefully place the ticket through the center. At first there is no movement. Quickly a bony hand grasps the ticket and part of my hand. Startled I jump and then laugh nervously at the first scare of the night. The front door slowly creaks open. Crossing the threshold I think maybe I should have just slept off my tiredness in the car.

Slivers of light cut into the large room from holes in the roof, or so it seems. Water drips, from the ceiling, into the musty room. Faded cartoon characters emerge sporadically from the molding walls. A sudden crashing sound occurs to my right and I am blinded by light as a wall set drops beside me revealing the front of a truck. A blood covered figure halfway out of the shattered windshield is sprawled onto the crumpled hood. On the other side of the light several small dark forms stand...were they mannequins or people? All at once young voices speak in unison,

"Stay with us forever."

My neck hairs stood on end and I stumbled, out of the light, beside the truck. A bloody hand grabs my arm and gargled voice spews the words "Get out." I see my arm is now covered in fake blood as I pull away his nails scratch my arm.

"This is a little much, don't you think?" I try to wipe off some of the blood, but he collapses back on the hood. The headlights slowly dim leaving an eerie darkness. Turning to my left another door creaks open and I fall toward it. Stepping just inside the door. The floor has fallen away in many places throughout the room. Small furniture and toys collapsing in with it.

"How is this safe?" I call out to no response.

I just want to go back, but the door has now locked behind me. There is just enough light again to make out the floor that is left and faint blinking red lights coming up from beneath the floor.

"This is more extreme than I thought, could you please just let me out!" I call out.

Slowly I test the floor and plot my way forward to avoid falling in. The floor groans under my weight. Softly the sound of static filled radio stations start to rise from beneath the floor. Different eras of songs and different qualities of sound all start to blend together. I pause and the first hand shoots up from the darkness.

"Oh come on," I shout. If I were not alone this might be scary fun, but I am alone. Where the hell are the others from the cars. Another hand pops out of a hole, followed by moans blending with the jumble of radio sounds. My knee begins to hurt worse and I am finding it hard to maneuver between the holes and multiple hands reaching out for me. My pant leg is grabbed, causing me to tumble forward to the ground, with a yelp. I begin to forget this is not real as I hover face first, over a hole, staring into a horrible decaying face. I flail and scramble to get back up, half dragging myself to the next door, which swings immediately open against my weight. I am sent sprawling, this time to the rain soaked ground outside. The shoulder of my already bloody arm smashing into the ground first and exploding with pain.

"What's wrong with you people?" I screamed out, half believing I will look up and see that family of murderous cannibals surrounding me, but there was only the sound of the rain. No one emerges to help. The back of the building is fenced in with chainlink, overgrown with vegetation. Dilapidated playground equipment juts out from the dead vines covering them. Is this still part of it. From the shadows I sees one of the small dark figures from the first room, then another and another, their arms and necks at impossible angles.

Trying to get to my feet becomes impossible because of the pain from my knee and shoulder. The only exit from the yard is a hole in the fence I spotted, but it is at the back of the yard near the woods and away from my car.

"This has gone too far.....I need help!" The figures only come closer and I can not tell what is real anymore. Dragging myself through the fence, there is a light but it is distant. Fear makes me keep pushing forward until I roll and look back to see that the entities do not cross the fence. I do not know why I am so weak. What if I pass out here in the mud.

Boots squish into the mud near my feet.

"Thank God someone found me. The mud and rain half blur my vision as I strain to look up at the dark figure above me.

"I have to save my wife..." a scratchy old voice pleads "she's still in the car"

He drops to his knees and collapses next to me, his empty eyes and face decomposed beyond recognition. A sudden rush of adrenaline kicks in and I fight my way through the briars that are tearing and ripping at my clothes and skin. I soon crash out of the underbrush into a yard, still moving toward the light, feeling the blackness closing in at the corners of my sight. I feel boards beneath my fingers...they will find me....then a voice.... "You gonna die here on my porch"...and everything fades.

"Hey..you still alive" A large gray bearded man shakes the bloody mud soaked figure on his porch. A woman joins him in a house dress.

"I told you I heard a crash" she scolds "You should have gone to see" "Woman, It's raining!" he snaps.

She bends to take a closer look "He's a mess...must have gone through hell to get here. That place is cursed...all those poor kids".

"That curve's been taking out folks for decades" he scowled "who was dumb enough to build a child-care in such a horrible place. What did they think would happen? Let me get my raincoat and I'll bring the truck around. I think I should just drop him at the funeral home, the hospital seems like a waste of time."

"You'll do no such thing" The woman swats him on the shoulder. "Obviously he wants to live if he made it all this way.

"Yeah..." the man concedes "the way he looks, I don't think he could have crawled ten feet without a wild bear scaring him....or something else" He looks out and scans the darkness of the woods before heading back in the house to get his jacket.

a few words from

JEFF STANDARD

What do you love about the genre of horror?

True horror can come from within or it can come at you from without.

What is some of your favorite horror literature?

I grew up reading Stephen King, Clive Barker, and Anne Rice.

What are some of your influences?

The original *Twilight Zone* series is, without a doubt, the greatest influence on any writing I have ever done.

What is your favorite Halloween treat?

Reese's Cups!

You are hosting the perfect Halloween movie marathon.

I would pick *Abbott and Costello Meet Frankenstein, Halloween, The Howling, Pumpkinhead,* and *Hocus Pocus.*

If you could continue any horror story, what would it be?

I think I would be interested in continuing the idea of the first *The Howling*. The idea of colonies of werewolves living among us blending in a horrifying concept.

As a designer of horror theatre or experiences, explain your process.

With any story process, I just need to hear the parameters of what is needed and my mind starts filling in the blanks.

Tell us about your contribution to our book. What was the inspiration?

I wanted to combine the haunt experience with real horror.

Describe the perfect Halloween.

Passing out candy and then watching *Hocus Pocus.*

SCARE CRED: JEFF STANDARD

Jeff Standard is a member of the Universal Orlando Design Department. He worked with the Prosthetics Dept. for fifteen years and has spent the last nine years as a creative fabrication artist. Jeff has also been integral in the production of twenty Halloween Horror Nights events.

Who do you

It is loaded

compassion

How are so

Edgar Alla

What is

As a kid

memorie

You migh

Something

the smart

crafted po

because

me very

For a

Each pr

speaking

large eno

out of sig

emotiona

to room u

character

scenic, lig

rooms wi

the exper

WE HOPE YOU ARE ENJOYING THE BOOK SO FAR... DID YOU REMEMBER TO LOOK UNDER THE BED?

BEAST WITCHES

J. Michael Roddy

I AM WAITING

BY SCOTT SWENSON

Tied to a wooden chair

Darkness pulls the ropes tighter around my chest, I can almost hear them creak as they stretch

I never saw my captor, but I know I am the captive

Alone

I wait

I am waiting

Anticipation starts as a dull rapid pounding in the back of my head

It grows and the heavy silence reaches in as the pounding pushes out

The pain of these opposing forces is building behind my eyes but I can neither run nor cry

So

I wait

I am waiting

After an eternity the pain subsides. Perhaps I am just too tired to feel it anymore

The dank cold emptiness now fills the room, my head, and my heart

Blackness is my world, I can even taste it

And

I wait

I am waiting

A sliver of light cuts through the pitch overhead creating a sheer veil through the air

Suddenly, a heavy metal door creaks and slams fully open sending a pelting barrage of light down on top of me

I am paralyzed by the sudden opposition

Screaming

I wait

I am waiting

Slowly I am able to open one eye then the other to see the damp dark concrete floor and the large metal drain near my feet

A white ember seems to glow from the edge of the illuminated island surrounding my chair

With effort it comes into focus, it is a single human tooth

Silently

I wait

I am waiting

Something shoots out of the darkness behind me as my head is covered with the stench of sweat and musty burlap

This sack has been used many times before, it is wet and adheres to my face

Breathing becomes difficult, this bag is tight around my neck

Gasping

I wait

I am waiting

There is a sharp pain in my right wrist which is tied to the back leg of the chair. I feel a warm liquid begin to puddle into my fingers and slip to the floor

Another stab in the left wrist, more wet warmth, more puddling

I am bleeding

Panicked

I wait

I am waiting

As I struggle, I hear someone else in the room breathing. The short rasps and chuffs are filled with anticipation

I am the focus of an enthusiastic spectator

I fight against my ropes like a trapped animal but I am held fast

Exhausted

I wait

I am waiting

The ringing in my ears approaches like a distant train as I feel my strength flow towards the floor

My thoughts are now jumbled but I am able to whisper, "What are you doing?"

The breathing stops, and just as I drift away, I hear

Quietly

"I wait"

"I am waiting"

a few words from

SCOTT SWENSON

What do you love about the genre of horror?

It is loaded with passion and emotion. In order for us to explore fear, we must understand love, lust, anger and compassion (or the lack there of). Horror seems to be where all emotional states come crashing together.

What are some of your influences?

Edgar Allan Poe, Dr. Seuss, and my own nightmares

What is your favorite Halloween treat?

As a kid I would always dig through the trick or treat stash to find the Butterfingers and Reeses. I also have fond memories of making popcorn balls in the fall.

You are hosting the perfect Halloween movie marathon. What are the films you choose and why?

Something Wicked This Way Comes - a nice way to ease into the night. *Let the Right One In* (the original) - one of the smartest and most compassionate horror films I have ever seen, plus wonderful visuals. *Poltergeist* - perfectly crafted pop horror. John Carpenter's *The Thing* - fantasy/sci-fi gore at its best. *An American Werewolf in London* - just because I love this movie! *Freaks* - because it's an awkwardly quirky classic. *The Exorcist* - this film has always made me very uncomfortable. *Halloween* - end the night or early morning with Jamie Lee.

As a designer of horror theatre or experiences, explain your process.

Each project has its own idiosyncrasies and needs, so each project requires a slightly different approach. Generally speaking, I try to imagine a world and then plan the guests' journey through it. I want to make sure that the world is large enough so that the actual experience won't show everything…just like the real world. I like having things "just out of sight" so that the guests can use their own imaginations to fill in the wretched details. I then try to create an emotional map. I ask "What should people be feeling now?" I try to make the emotional content build from room to room until there is a climax. I then try to create a transition back into the real world. Usually I am very actor and character driven, so I try to create a "performance playground" in each room, with several ways to connect with the scenic, lighting, atmospheric, etc. I also think very cinematically and I am always trying to find new ways to reveal rooms with transitions that only really exist in film. Overall, I try to make the guest feel as though they are part of the experience, that they live in this newly created world.

When is the last time you were genuinely scared by something someone created?

Although it isn't exactly a haunted attraction, the final scene in **Sleep No More** by Punchdrunk is still very unnerving to me. It is partially because I became totally immersed in the experience and partially because I wonder how they can pull this effect off safely night after night. (Yes, I am intentionally being vague so as not to spoil the experience for those who haven't seen it yet.)

Tell us about your contribution to our book. What was the inspiration?

This was originally written to be read out loud…slowly. Since I wrote it in first person, I think it plays on all the things that freak me out. I hate having my face covered. The removal of teeth is an unpleasant concept. I am totally grossed out by the feeling of my own warm blood in my hand.

Describe the perfect Halloween.

1974, wearing a cape and a sweaty latex vampire mask, my friends and I take to the streets of a Chicago suburb to fill our pillowcases with free candy and push the boundaries of how far our parents told us we could roam after dark.

SCARE CRED: SCOTT SWENSON

For over thirty years, Scott has been bringing stories to life as a writer, director, producer and performer. After twenty-one years with SeaWorld, he formed Scott Swenson Creative Development LLC. Since then, he has been writing live shows, creating and implementing themed festivals, and developing communication-based training classes. Much of Scott's work has focussed on haunted attractions. He was part of the original development team and creative leader for the first fifteen years of Howl-O-Scream at Busch Gardens Tampa. From 2014 to 2017, he was the writer and creative director for the historically based atmospheric theatre piece - *The Vault of Souls*. Scott has also written and consulted for haunted attractions at at Valleyfair Theme Park, SeaWorld Texas, and ZooTampa. His most recent projects include DARK at Fort Edmonton Park and "UNDead in the Water" at The American Victory Ship in Tampa. He is a regular contributor to *Seasonal Entertainment Source* magazine and his podcast, *A Scott in the Dark*, continues to grow in popularity. Scott has self-published three books of dark poetry and prose. In 2017, he was presented a Special Recognition Award from The Haunted Attraction Association. He is a sought after panelist and presenter for entertainment trade shows, especially those focused on haunted attractions and atmospheric theatre.

PATIENT 666

BY MELISSA & TRACEY TANNER

Sister Mary Margaret was born to an Irish Catholic family in Chicago, IL. She decided to join the convent at the age of twenty-two after graduating from Loyola with a Psychology degree. For the next six years she taught psychology at St. Thomas Aquinas in Chicago, IL. She was then sent to Ocoee, FL to run the Asylum.

After years of running the facility, a young girl, Stephanie, was brought in by her family because of acting erratic, falling into a coma like state, throwing objects, and foaming at the mouth. Family pets had become afraid of her. The family had taken her to several doctors for examinations but no one could come up with an answer. They took Stephanie to their local priest and he suspected she was possessed by a demon. The priest, Father Joel, immediately had the family take Stephanie to the Asylum and Sister Mary Margaret.

Over the next few months, Father Joel, the Asylum's doctor, and Sister Mary Margaret attempted an exorcism to save Stephanie from the torment of the demon. Unfortunately, they were not successful, and Stephanie lost her fight with the demon. At that time Sister Mary Margaret lost her faith, her mind, and eventually her soul.

Within a few days the other staff members at the Asylum noticed significant changes in Sister Mary Margaret's behavior. It was becoming very clear that the demon decided to take over the sister's body, mind, and soul. The demon in kind drove her mad and then decided to move onto the next victim. This left the sister a shell of her former self.

The Asylum Haunted Hospital:

The Asylum Haunted Hospital used to be run by Sister Mary Dementia but after a horrible incident with a patient she lost her faith, her mind, and eventually her soul. She now wanders the halls and grounds of the Asylum looking for some peace from her madness. Sister Mary Dementia is just one of many poor souls that have lost their mind at the Asylum. We invite you to come out and meet her and our patients. This haunted hospital is unique as it is in 100% darkness and all you have is a small flashlight to light your way through the halls of the Asylum. Are you brave enough to try it? To learn more, visit Facebook.com/AsylumOLC

CASE NUMBER: 666

PATIENT NAME:
SISTER MARY DEMENTIA
(AKA SISTER MARY MARGARET)

CURRENT DATE:
OCTOBER 25, 2018

GENDER:
FEMALE

BORN:
JULY 12, 1970

MELISSA & TRACEY TANNER

What do you love about the genre of horror?

Both: Halloween is our favorite holiday and our entire family is into it. We watch horror films the entire month. Our yard is decorated and conducted as a scare zone and we love to see it when people stop by to look at our creation(s). We discuss the characters we will be on Halloween night and design the costumes, makeup, props, etc. Now we are running The Asylum Haunted Hospital. We love creating scary characters and to use them to scare others.

What is some of your favorite horror literature?

Tracey: Anything by Stephen King

Melissa: The classics like Mary Shelley's *Frankenstein* and Bram Stoker's *Dracula*.

What is your favorite Halloween treat?

Tracey: Caramel apples; peanut butter/chocolate

Melissa: Candy

You are hosting the perfect Halloween movie marathon. What are the films you choose and why?

Tracey: *Halloween*, movies based on Stephen King's novels, M. Night Shyamalan, *Insidious*, *The Conjuring I & II*, Rob Zombie films, *Beetlejuice, Ghostbusters, Hocus Pocus, The Shining*, any true (murder) crime docu/movie

Melissa: *Halloween I* and *II* and *Prince of Darkness* by John Carpenter, any film based on a Stephen King novel, films based on Anne Rice novels, several of the M. Night Shyamalan movies, and *Underworld*.

If you could continue any horror story, what would it be?

Melissa: John Carpenter's *Prince of Darkness*. I would describe what happens in the future. How the *Prince of Darkness* returns in the form of the girl and how he works to take over the earth and leads the world to its doom.

As a designer of horror theatre or experiences, explain your process.

Tracey: I enjoy making the characters come to life and definitely love working with makeup. I know what scares me and I hear what truly scares other people, so I do my best to re-create those scares. Flow is important to me when placing characters within a haunt. I'll start with a layout of the house and then place the characters accordingly. Spacing out the scarier characters can result in a more even scare experience. I also listen to feedback from my actors. I really encourage them to get into character and tap into their creative side for in doing so.

Melissa: I am more on the prop side with Tracey being more on the character side. I think about the concept we're projecting and how can we do it. From there I research to find examples and/or samples that can inspire me to build the house and props required. I will then draw it out and work on dimensions. Once the concept is storyboarded, I would then determine the materials I would need and start to build it. For instance, with The Asylum I wanted a nurse's station. So, I started collecting medicine bottles and making case files for the patients (characters). I then assembled it all together and installed shelves for behind a desk that was the nurse's station.

Another idea that came up was to install a "padded wall" to simulate the padded rooms that a patient might be placed in for their safety. We did a lot of research and the built the wall panels using foam bed toppers, buttons, wire, and paint.

Tell us about your contribution to our book. What was the inspiration?

Tracey: I LOVE Halloween and horror. I look forward to seeing props, different makeup, different kinds of scares, the sets (if it's a Haunt), etc. Every year we design the yard/scare zone for Halloween (complete with a real coffin) and the inside of our home is also decorated. We religiously visit Universals Halloween Horror Nights every year since living in Florida. At Christmas we have a black wreath and a black Christmas tree with some Halloween ornaments. I enjoy being around others who adore Halloween as much as I do.

When is the last time you were genuinely scared by something someone created?

Tracey: I think Valak, the demon in the Conjuring 2 movie, got to me a bit. Like I said before, we have a paranormal team and I have been more shaken by real events that have happened to me than a movie created by someone.

Melissa: It's hard for me to be genuinely scared by a film or book. I am more affected by Suspense/Thriller films. For instance, the movie Frailty really shook me to my core. The concept that Demon Hunters could be walking among us and killing demons disguised as humans. These demons are committing crimes of a horrible nature. It truly messes with your mind. Another film that affected me was The Mothman Prophecies. The thought that some supernatural creature knows that bad events are coming and goes to the area to warn those that will be affected.

Tell us about your contribution to our book. What was the inspiration?

Melissa: We are submitting a bio and pictures of one of our main characters of the Asylum Haunted Hospital, Sister Mary Dementia. For me it's my love of Halloween and the horror genre. I love to see props, costumes, makeup, etc. For years I have been a fan of haunted houses and the characters presented such as Halloween Horror Nights (Orlando), Statesville Haunted Prison (Crest Hill, IL), and Basement of the Dead (Aurora, IL). I have also decorated our yard, as a haunt for decades now and we run it as a "scare zone" on Halloween Night. Last year we decided to get involved with a local haunt and this year we ran the entire operation.

Describe the perfect Halloween.

Tracey: Perfect scares whether at our own scare zone or the Haunt we run, great company, cool weather, lots of candy for those brave enough to come close, unique decorations, and us enjoying the holiday as a family.

Melissa: Warm weather, good friends, good food, awesome decorations, and scaring those that come to our house.

SCARE CRED: MELISSA TANNER

Melissa has held an interest in Halloween and horror/suspense since she was a teenager. As she moved into adulthood, she began to research how to make her own props to decorate the inside of her home for Halloween. Then that interest grew into building props for the outside of the home and the yard. Melissa really enjoys making the props vs buying them at a store or online. Her first big prop was an old west style coffin that featured lights, skeleton, and a removable coffin lid. She would eventually add tombstones, zombie containment areas, directional signs, and pumpkin patches.

Over the last two decades the decorations and props have grown and her and her family started dressing up on Halloween night and offering a free scare zone in their front yard. These scare zones became very popular, so additional actors were added. In 2017 Melissa and her family had an opportunity to work as scare actors at the Asylum Haunted House run by the Ocoee Lions Club. Then in 2018 Melissa and her wife Tracey, co-managed the Asylum Haunted House; with Tracey doing the design, makeup, and costume work and Melissa building and setting up props.

SCARE CRED: TRACEY TANNER

Tracey has held an interest in Halloween and the horror/suspense genre since she was a young girl. She absolutely loves the special effects creations that are in film, haunted houses, etc. Besides enjoying watching horror films, she loves to read and collect books by Stephen King; of which she has read anything and everything he has created. Over the last few years, her and her family started dressing up on Halloween night and offering a free scare zone in their front yard. These scare zones became very popular, so additional actors were added. In 2017 Tracey and her family had an opportunity to work as scare actors at the Asylum Haunted House run by the Ocoee Lions Club. Then in 2018 Tracey and her wife Melissa, co-managed the Asylum Haunted House; with Tracey doing the design, makeup, and costume work and Melissa building and setting up props.

EDGE OF DESPAIR

BY JOHN TARPLEY

Outside I stood, I had heard stories of the family farmstead yet never been, it seemed perhaps it was part of my imagination, the kind of scary places kids make up in their heads. This was no make-believe though. In front of me stood the most ominous house, one of unnatural beauty and clearly a labor of love yet taken back by Mother Nature through years of disrepair and vacancy.

Pushing the iron gate open as I walked into the front garden it appeared as if it hadn't seen human existence in over a hundred years. The smell I could make out to be mold hanging in the air as the ivy had strangled any other competing life from the woodwork around me. What was once a beautiful fountain, now sat as a vast stone monument overgrown with dead twigs littering the basin. I could sense no other life form in there with me, yet I remained uneasy as if something was indeed in there watching and waiting; for what I didn't know.

Finally making my way into the house, I realized it was dark (not the kind of dark from no electric lights but the nature of unnatural eerie darkness as though no light permeated the area for what must have been an eternity). I explored the old house as best I could, stumbling in a few places, and going down what seemed like endless hallways only to be created by doors locked by time itself. It wasn't long before I stumbled upon the old metal box in the attic. It seemed as though it hadn't been moved in the last century. After feeling around for a moment longer, I was able to pry the book open, and in an instant, as the dust flew out, my eye was caught by the leather-bound book laying on top. As I thumbed through it for a moment, unable to read the words carefully scribed onto the page, I descended from its resting place and retreated outside to better understand what I had found. After opening the book once more and letting the light glisten over the ink scribed pages, I began to read the tale that changed my view of this dark property forever. "As we furthered our research, I fear that we have stumbled onto something with grave consequences," its former owner wrote.

As I continued reading, I felt the ever-growing worry he inscribed into the pages as though I were standing right beside him. "My fears have come to fruition, these strange occurrences are becoming more frequent, and we can't control them any longer; we will begin to need more than grace to continue this existence." The page ended with the signature of my dear great-grandfather, Dr. Samuel M. Corbin at the bottom. I turned again, as a cold chill ran down my back while feeling the pages bundle under my fingers and noticed that I was forced to skip dates because they were glued together by some unknown substance, almost as if on purpose.

Time seemed to stand still as the dates on the paper jumped from 26 August 1903 to 17 October 1903 the handwriting of the man who reached out for help in the pages before, transformed into a shaky, barely legible entry that seemed to be written in a rush between moments of turmoil. "Forgive us... Forgive us for what we did, but we did it only to survive... forgive us." The writing ended abruptly and was sealed by a messy signature at the bottom. Still, a mystery as to what secrets are guarded in the journal entries between those short few months but one thing is clear: the good doctor committed some unearthly act on this property years ago that still plagues the existence of this house and all of its belongings. I must find out what my family did...

a few words from

JOHN TARPLEY

What do you love about the genre of horror?

The thing I love most about the horror genre has to be that I can express the darker side of life and humanity through my works and I also get to see how other people express their darkest thoughts, fears, I love that imaginative process.

What is some of your favorite horror literature?

I have enjoy the writings of Edgar Allan Poe, Richard Matheson, Stephen King, H.P Lovecraft and Clive Barker.

What are some of your influences?

I always joke that I take a little bit of knowledge from everyone and add it to my toolbox. I've been so fortunate to have a lot of great friends in this industry who influence me through their works and achievements. I also have my family who have supported these crazy little ideas of mine over the years.

What is your favorite Halloween treat?

I'm not much of a sweets person normally but I do binge on my Halloween candy when I do. I really like the spooky Nerds and loads of sour candy!

You are hosting the perfect Halloween movie marathon. What are the films you choose and why?

Candyman - I still remember seeing this for the first time. It scared me for days afterward. *Phantasm* - The Tall Man, need I say more? My dad introduced me to the series and this would be one I'd have to include for him. *The Strangers* - I love the tension in the movie, and just how almost believable it could be. For some reason this movie really gets to me in a way others don't. *Duel* - that truck was a monster I tell you. The suspense and frightening moments in this movie are great and being a Matheson fan I had to include it. *Pet Sematary* - as excited as I am to see the reboot the original always hold a place in my heart and the desire to have our lost moments back is so great we often don't understand that "sometimes dead is better" *Trick r Treat* - this is just such great Halloween movie I couldn't not include it in the list.

As a designer of horror theatre or experiences, explain your process.

Anytime I set out to create an experience I try to imagine it being as close to real as possible. Experiences these days are really blurring the line between what is real and what isn't, especially with the rise of virtual and augmented realities being used in some of the more immersive attractions. I always strive to create something that sends you home checking the closet and under the bed before finally closing your eyes and I do so by setting an overall tone and atmosphere that can't be found anywhere else.

When is the last time you were genuinely scared by something someone created?
I had the chance to visit some very great haunted attractions this last season (2018) and I'm always the one in the group that has the most fun getting scared. I am constantly reminded that the next scare is right around the corner and it makes me feel great to be a part of such a fantastic community of creative people who also live for this.

Tell us about your contribution to our book. What was the inspiration?
My contribution was originally written as the storyline for a haunted attraction that was to take place on a farm. The guests were going to be able to find out what actually happened between the months of August and October with an overall story arc that continues to bring you back and forth between the frighteningly dark and sinister world of Dr Samuel Corbin and his family and the present day of Great Grandson Adam Corbin. The attraction was set to be held on a large property that housed a large set of woods, open fields and a large carriage house but it was the house that dates back to the late 1790's on the property and when I first saw it I was completely floored by the craftsmanship but it clearly had sat vacant for many years until the current owner began restoring it. You have to walk back to a clearing on the property before the house comes into view but when you see it, the house just draws you in, almost eerie how it makes you feel like you need to know the weathered history that its walls hold.

Describe the perfect Halloween.
The perfect Halloween would be spent trying to get scared at a haunted attraction or event with friends and family or better yet it could be spent trying to scare other people and bring that same amount of excitement I have for the holiday to them.

SCARE CRED: JOHN TARPLEY

John Tarpley, a young professional in the attractions industry, committed to seeing a safe and innovative future. John believes in bringing unbridled passion and extreme levels of ownership to the industry. John has been active in professional attractions management for seven years with skill sets in leadership, employee training and retention, attraction strategies, project management, and experience development.

Random Musings of Monsters and Make-ups

BY JIM UDENBERG

a few words from

JIM UDENBERG

What do you love about the genre of horror?

I always loved the escapism of movies. Horror, gives you the exhilaration of extreme situations in a thrilling safe way. I was always drawn more to the dark and macabre, even at a young age. I prefer fantasy horror over more realistic themes. The world has enough real life horror, give me the supernatural on the silver screen.

What is some of your favorite horror literature?

I grew up much more on films than I did books. I used to say, "I don't have time to read books, I have too many movies to watch." However, I have read quite a bit of Clive Barker's work. I really enjoyed the visceral nature of his writing. It inspired a couple of the drawings I submitted in fact. Beyond that, old EC comics were are big influence on me. I loved the blend of the comic book medium with horror. I will still refer to them from time to time for inspiration for my makeup fx work.

What are some of your influences?

Early on, I was fascinated with the classic Universal Monsters. The first one I ever saw was *Abbot & Costello Meet Frankenstein*. From there I later dove into all the classics. Later on, when the 80's hit hard with the golden age of makeup fx, the works makeup artists Dick Smith, Rick Baker, Rob Bottin, Steve Johnson, KNB Effects and more, are what drove me to pursue a career in makeup effects. In addition, artists such as H.R. Giger, Salvador Dali, and Drew Struzan had a big impact on me.

What is your favorite Halloween treat?

Easy. Candy Corn!

You are hosting the perfect Halloween movie marathon. What are the films you choose and why?

Halloween (for obvious reasons), *The Thing* (one of my all time favorite horror films), *The Shining* (pure genius), *The Exorcist* (still the scariest horror film ever) *IT* (2017) (one of my favorite modern horror films), *Triangle* (a little known low budget gem of a film)

As a designer of horror theatre or experiences, explain your process.

It all starts with the script. I will sit down and thoroughly read the script one time without taking notes. Then, I will read it a second time where I begin to mark and take notes and writing questions. From there I will begin to break down the characters, determining if they should be masks, makeups, dummies etc. From there I will assemble a preliminary budget. Once the green light is lit, I begin the process of making all the pieces needed. Sculpting the masks and prosthetic makeups, making moulds, casting latex and/or silicone. As soon as pieces are ready we begin testing the characters with costumes, masks, & makeup. Refining and improving as we go all the way up to opening day or the first day of filming, or whatever the job needs be it for theater, film, tv, etc. The biggest thrill is the moment you walk your latest creation in. The cast and crew's first reactions are gold!

When is the last time you were genuinely scared by something someone created?

To be honest, I don't scare easily. Jump scares sure, but those are easy to pull off. I guess I would have to say *The Haunting of Hill House* on Netflix. They really created and uncomfortable mood in the show. It didn't necessarily scare me, but I appreciated the creepy mood they created.

Tell us about your contribution to our book. What was the inspiration?

I contributed a few older drawings, as well as some newer character makeups I have done. Most of my early drawings were of events and characters from my favorite movies. But to avoid IP issues, I chose a few of my loose early sketches. They were inspired by things I was watching or reading at the time like the short stories of Clive Barker, and the film *Jacob´s Ladder*, which I consider to be one of the most disturbing films ever made.

Describe the perfect Halloween.

Inviting all my makeup artist friends over for a fun gathering. Seeing all of there amazing creations. And of course, watching as many horror films as possible. However, my favorite thing at Halloween is watching Tim Burton´s *The Nightmare Before Christmas*. There is a long going debate whether that is a Halloween or a Christmas movie. I will ALWAYS defend my position that it is the best Halloween film ever.

SCARE CRED: JIM UDENBERG

A native of northern Minnesota, Jim first became interested in makeup effects at the age of twelve. He began his education at the University of Minnesota in Duluth, training in art, photography and stage makeup before attending makeup school in Orlando. Early student films led to work on shows such as *seaQuest DSV* and *Mortal Kombat*.In 1995 Universal Studios Florida created a new makeup department. Jim was one of four artists hired to start it. Within a year he was chosen to lead the team. During large projects crews grew to over forty artists. In 2004 Jim moved to Norway with his family where he was the head of makeup effects education at the Nordic Institute for Stage and Studio (NISS) for six years. Since 2010, Jim has been focussing solely on his freelance career through his company iMAGiNARiUM FX. 2017 saw the expansion of the iMAGiNARiUM brand to include an entertainment arts center, studio, educational course, and online sales of art and supplies. Learn more at *MakeupFX.no*.

The Visitor

BY KAREN WHITE

October 14, 1980
4:30am
Lake City

I was a freshman at Lake City Community College. Due to circumstances which have nothing to do with this story, I was living away from my parents in a tiny camper. I was sleeping soundly because I had an 8:00am psychology class. I woke up abruptly to strangely hot temperatures. It had to be 85 degrees with the windows open all the way around. I opened the door, sat in the doorway and felt the outside air. It was at least 20 degrees cooler. I thought that was odd. I turned the lights on and looked around. The trophy I'd just won for Poetry Interpretation was on the table. I'd get to brag all about that to Robert when he came over later. I realized in that moment that I was in a perfect place in my life, peaceful. I was in a great theatre department. My best friend Robert had been accepted into the Jacksonville University Theatre Department. He was already cast in their production of The Crucible. I was going to see him the next day. I went back to sleep feeling very happy. I had no idea my life was about to take a tragic turn.

The next morning I went to school, dressing in black as per usual. I was *very* dramatic in those days. I distinctly remember being on my way to class, and being stopped by my mentor Paul Ferguson. He was looking at me with no smile. Paul was almost always smiling. I remember something about there being some bad news. But he seemed want to talk to me privately about it. I was getting concerned. We went to the courtyard next to the Art Department, and sat on one of the benches. He turned to face me and Paul said, "Robert Rivers was killed in an automobile accident last night." Before the reality did it's damage, I first thought about my weird 4:30 am wake up.

The police report stated that the accident occurred at 4:30am. Robert had been headed home from Jacksonville, and had a head-on collision with a semi. There would be no October 14th when I didn't remember. Sure there are other explanations. Maybe The crash woke me? It happened less than five miles away. Sirens? I never heard them. And anyway the emergency vehicles would not have arrived that quickly. I believe Robert knew what the grief would do to me. I believe he woke me up and brought me peace. It was a gift.

Rest In Peace dear friend.
Robert Andrews Rivers
Born: 09/09/1958
Died: 10/14/1980.

BY KAREN WHITE

After spending way too many hours away from her cats, Fran threw her bag and her case files across the front seat of her frozen car and was finally headed home. The reluctant Honda groaned to life, and an audio-patient file immediately picked up on Bluetooth. Fran smacked the STOP button, (Damnit!) before Richard Carter could say another word.....

"Godamnit!"

No more Richard.. Not right now. Today had been a failure. A professional embarrassment. Fran paused, starring past her gloved hands on the steering wheel. Bridgewater State Hospital loomed in front of her like a ton of bad news.

"Damnit!" She felt utterly done.

(Her cats: Parker and Posey had probably already eaten the plants and pissed in her shoes.....)

"God and damnit!"

She threw the car in gear and headed out to the interstate. Fran had tried to be realistic. She knew there were patients who can never, will never be able to function outside of a cell, padded or otherwise. She'd hoped for the padded variety. The patients name on the audio-file had been Richard Carter, a southern charmer, an intelligent, former theology student at Bellevue University. He was also a sociopath, and convicted mass-murderer. Like Ted Buddy, he had the handsome, yet helpless exterior, bringing people in with a winning smile, "Pardon me, I seem to have left my keys in my car."

Unlike Ted Buddy he was very much alive and now due to her failure, the verdict: 8 counts of 1st degree murder. Life sentence, no parole, he would spend the rest of his life at Rhode Island Maximum Security Prison, not Bridgewater State Hospital.

("You tried to help me, ma'am..." his eyes had been dry, warm and empty.)

Women had always been ready to help Richard. He made them feel safe. After all, he was a safe Christian gentleman. A safe future pastor. He was a strong shouldered safe date to take home to meet the parents. Until he decided not to be safe anymore. And those women became fatally unsafe.

Richard had brutally murdered eight women. Eight! His weapon of choice? Whatever was handy. Claw hammers, a tree branch, a bible, (those crime scene photos were the most disturbing....) a knife, broken bottles.....
There was no signature, no display, no messages to ignite the press or law enforcement. Three things happened: In no particular order, He found women, he seduced them, he either deserted them, disappearing with their money and no warning, or he overpowered and murdered them.

Some women, the lucky ones he left behind, were sad when he didn't call them back after a date or after he disappeared, deserting a "girlfriend" of a month or two. Fran interviewed one woman who thought she'd won the fancy preacher lottery after two dates with Carter. Another woman, was setting up a profile on The Knot website and had begun ordering dresses, after his arrest. Carter was a narcissist, he would build women up, flattering their appearance, intelligence, doing chores for them, spending money on them, until they purred and he got bored.

Purred!

(Note to self: I need to get cat food for Parker and Posey. Cat food? Nope, fresh tuna, and God a decent Bordeaux.)

Treating Carter had been the most high profile medical case she'd ever worked on. Successfully having him committed and not incarcerated would have made her career. Despite the genuine loathing she personally had for Carter, he deserved to be in a hospital, where he could be treated and observed.

(Note to self: Fresh tuna, cat litter, maybe catnip, and Bordeaux, and by God there will be chocolate...)

After a quick stop at the Super 8 Grocery, (and liquor store,) Fran was nearly home. She could see Parker and Posey sitting in the window sill, patiently, (Hah! Probably in a heap of her ruined shoes...waiting to judge her...)

Her key squeaked in the lock, (it needed to be replaced...)

"Okay, you little fur people...."

Parker yawned, looking at her judging her disdainfully, Posey was looking over Fran's shoulder at...Richard Carter's sad sympathetic eyes....

"You tried to help me, ma'am"

And Richard Carter claimed life number nine.....

a few words from

KAREN WHITE

What do you love about the genre of horror?

I love the thrill. Being scared in a controlled environment is fun. I also love when directors and authors do something new and different. Like the first demonic possession, the first scary cabin in the woods, or teen at home alone. I like the unexpected.

What is some of your favorite horror literature?

The Shining, The Exorcist, anything by Shirley Jackson or Stephen King. Anyone who knows me knows my love for the original Grimm's collections: evil queens, stepmothers, creepy old ladies living in houses made of candy.

What is your favorite Halloween treat?

Granny Smith Caramel apples, baby! I also love those chewy peanut butter things in wax paper.

You are hosting the perfect Halloween movie marathon. What films do you choose?

If I were hosting a Halloween movie marathon I would turn it into a huge sleepover. I would need a big house and about three days. Big screen TV in each room, the rooms would be themed to a genre and be chronological. Classic monsters, the *Halloween* franchise, *Friday the 13th*, Stephen King, etc. I have a broad interest in film, so I'd want to cater to them all. I like getting people together. I need to do this. Thanks for the idea!

If you could continue any horror story, what would it be?

I want to see more of *It Follows*.

As a designer of horror theatre or experiences, explain your process.

The last role I created was Lady Luck. She was a tough one. I saw her as an evil, ancient goddess type, very regal and fatal. The producers wanted her to be more lecherous and earthly, more "Lady Get Lucky" Hoookay. I modeled her after Alex from *Fatal Attraction* after a couple of drinks. Her sole motivation was to get close and kill.

When is the last time you were genuinely scared by something someone created?

I don't scare easily, but I had nightmares after *It Follows*.

Tell us about your contribution to our book. What was the inspiration?

The inspiration for my short story *8* came from all the boogeymen in our real world. Real people are capable of horrific behavior. My protagonist was too busy thinking of her monster as a case study and not about avoiding being a victim herself. *The Visitor* is a true story. It's about the night my best friend and first love was tragically killed on Highway 441 in Columbia County, Florida.

Describe the perfect Halloween.

The perfect Halloween? A party with all my friends... old and new, with delicious food, great atmosphere, music, karaoke, awesome costumes.

SCARE CRED: KAREN WHITE

Karen White is an authority on villains, crazies, nut bars, and spooky critters. And while she's talking abut herself in third person, she'd like you to know that the first novel she ever read, not on her elementary school reading list, was *Jaws* followed by *The Exorcist*. Not that she should've read those two at age 10, but this is the same kid who had a huge crush on Frank Langella., (arguably the hottest vampire ever...) She is very tight with Cruella Deville, Lady Tremaine, Maleficient, and she's also hung out with Ursula on occasion. And once, when she was really "lucky", she went on a month-long road trip with HHN 21's Icon: Lady Luck. (Those contact lenses were a bitch!) She's married to the Fred Flinstone to her Wima, actor and comic, Kevin White, who knows all about her dark side and loves her all the more for it. And she apparently passed the affinity for the dark and spooky on to her daughter Katie Gile who is OBSESSED with the Universal Studio's classic monsters.

A KRAMPUS

BY NICK WOLFE

I awoke alarmed hearing a shuffle from deep within another part of the house! My heart was beating hard; I waited to hear another noise so that I could decipher its origin and meaning. I heard nothing but the a/c running, so I ventured out of bed and into the hallway. I immediately noticed a dim light coming from the library. The door was open, and as I approached, I heard a page turn and every hair on my body stood on end! Someone was in my house... reading in my library... by candlelight! I held my breath as I slowly looked around the door frame into the room. It gasped just after I did, surprised to see me and blew out the candle!

a few words from

NICK WOLFE

What do you love about the genre of horror?

I love the horror genre for the monsters! Before monsters, it was bugs,sharks,alligators and then dinosaurs but once I was introduced to monsters, that was it.

What is some of your favorite horror literature?

My favorite horror books have to be H.P. Lovecraft at the risk of sounding cliché. His work has a realistic feel to them and that is what I crave the most. Make them feel real!

What are some of your influences?

My influences in art are nature and its golden ratio patterns, textures and color combinations. Some artist who have influenced me are Wayne Barlowe, H.R. Giger, Yasushi Nirasawa and Brom. Since psychedelics are going mainstream, I'll have to mention them too as a great influence in my life as well as my art. I believe they can release you from this construct's confines and show you things that are indescribable!

What is your favorite Halloween treat?

I'd say Snickers.

You are hosting the perfect Halloween movie marathon. What are the films you choose and why?

When I work at Universal Studios, sometimes I'll quote a classic that gets no response. This is when I lecture the room about the greats and encourage the young makeup artists to watch them. These films are ones I've seen a hundred times each and they never get old! The monsters still hold up today and have influenced a generation as they were "ahead of their time". *Alien, Aliens, Dawn of the Dead, Hellraiser, Predator*, and *The Thing* are my top six! The only reason to watch more movies in a row is if you are flying to New Zealand.

If you could continue any horror story, what would it be?

I would love to see a sequel to *The Thing* and learn what happened to Childs and Mac!

As a designer of horror theatre or experiences, explain your process.

My process of design starts with a library of stuff in my head. If I'm designing a face, I have dozens of eyes, noses, mouths, foreheads, etc that I have painted before. I start by choosing the colors then mixing and matching the features according to the form and function of the creature and adding texture, stripes or cracks at the end.

When is the last time you were genuinely scared by something someone created?

I don't get scared of stuff very often but the combination of elements at the Netherworld haunted attraction in Atlanta is the only thing I can even think of! I highly recommend you visit Ben Armstrong and his team!

Tell us about your contribution to our book. What was the inspiration?

My inspiration for this piece came from the model who was a contortionist. I asked her what crazy poses she wouldn't mind holding for a bit. I met her days before the event and took a picture of her from above and sketched out a rough idea back at the hotel. I wanted to go over the top as other body artists were there to showcase as well so I shot a selfie with a flashlight under my chin and took another of my hands for reference, The Krampus in an issue of *Tarot Witch of the Black Rose* also inspired me at the time. Jim Balent is great!

Describe the perfect Halloween.

My perfect Halloween started at the Playboy Mansion when Leonard Pickel invited me to be the lead makeup in his "zombie vampire" house! After the makeup was done, I changed into a vampire costume myself and joined the festivities. I ran into another body painter dressed as Britney Spears who was there to paint the nude models walking around and she told me it was her first time there. I offered her "a tour" and we spent the evening roaming the mansion grounds drinking Crown Royal, eating sushi and exploring the many rooms or areas like the grotto, the blue room,and the zoo. By the time we got to the game room,we were pretty lit and started playing the Playboy pinball machine. When we started playing Hydro-Thunder she started messing with me to make me screw up the game and it went back and forth until we fell out of the game in one of the most passionate kisses of my life! She wound up being my girlfriend for a couple years after that night and we are still great friends today.

SCARE CRED: NICK WOLFE

Nick began his journey into the world of special effects makeup by drawing monsters and superheroes as children. This led to his eventual meteoric rise into the world of face art, body painting, and special effects makeup. He spent the late '90s and early '00s creating makeups for Universal Studios Florida alongside his twin brother Brian. The Wolfe Brothers would receive international attention in 2001 when hired as contributing authors to *Creative Facepainting*, which is widely known as the facepainting bible. In 2004, the brothers founded their own make-up company, Wolfe Brothers Face Art & FX. They would leave in 2008 to tour the world teaching makeup workshops in Europe, Asia, Australia, and across North America. They would also claim the world champion title at the World Body Paint Festival. Although Brian passed away in 2013, Nick continues to generate amazing designs, characters, and advancements to the make-up industry.

247

The Story of Lacy Charm

BY ANDY WRIGHT

Lacy Charm grew up in a torturous hell with a seamstress mother who locked her in a basement and forced her to design and sew dresses for some of the most beautiful, wealthy women in town. The vain Mother was always jealous of the attention Lacy received as a beautiful child. Faking Lacys death was a way to gain attention and rid the Mother of her child's beauty. Keeping Lacy a secret in the small town was difficult, so she burned her face with a hot iron to keep Lacy in fear and from ever leaving the mother's side. Lacy occasionally was able to catch a glimpse of the women's faces as they entered the shop, viewing from behind the walls. Lacy envied the women she designed clothes for. Collecting any items left behind by the beautiful women was Lacy's only way of having a piece of each one of their beauty. Ominous Grim infected Lacy's soul and brought out her dark intentions and lead her to kill her Mother and carve her face off. Keeping her Mother's ear was a reminder of Lacy's screams her mother heard while burning her flesh. Her desire to create the perfect face was fulfilled by her selecting pieces of her victim's faces and sewing them together to help create her new beauty.

OMINOUS DESCENT
HAUNTED ATTRACTION

CHARACTER
LACY CHARM

ANDY WRIGHT

What do you love about the genre of horror?

Mostly how creatively we can bring out things that only exist in our minds and put them in an environment that can be experienced by others.

What are some of your influences?

Dick Smith was my main influence as a kid. What started off terrifying me about the movie *Ghost Story* ended up being the catalyst to me perusing my makeup and FX career. Along the way, I have had the pleasure of working with and learning from many talented artists. One in particular that still influences me today is Jim Udenberg. He was my supervisor at Universal Studios when I started there in 1997. Although he was quite young and new to the field as well, he had a great eye for things and I especially hovered over his shoulder when it came to mold making.

Jordan Patton is another one that caught my eye. He created a whole series of characters called "Dead Necks" that opened up a whole new look to horror comedy. Extremely original creations, the likes I have never seen before. I don't normally geek out over things or am an avid collector or buyer of masks but I do happen to have two of his, "Pumpkin Patch Pete" and "Birthday Boy".

What is your favorite Halloween treat?

As far as candy, peanut Butter Cups. As far as a activity,…I still dress up EVERY YEAR. That in and of itself is a treat.

You are hosting the perfect Halloween movie marathon. What are the films you choose and why?

Nightmare on Elm Street because Freddy redefined the horror icon. *Friday the 13th* because, lets face it, Jason just makes me laugh. *The Changeling* with George C. Scott because, to this day, I get chills talking about it. *Halloween Town* because it captures the lighter and more fun side of Halloween. *Zombieland* because we all like a dark, comedy, horror. *Beetlejuice*,…do I REALLY need a reason? *Young Frankenstein* because of the stellar cast and writing. *The Frighteners* because of the all around fun. *The Lost Boys* because of the classic 80's look of it all.

If you could continue any horror story, what would it be?

I think there is too much continuing. I would rather create a new one, whether it be cheesy or not.

As a designer of horror theatre or experiences, explain your process.

For what I do, everything starts with a solid concept/idea. I used to draw and sketch to get my designs, but any more, over the past many years, I sculpt. I still like to have references as a springboard but primarily I create in 3D.

When is the last time you were genuinely scared by something someone created?

I think it really was the blue lady from *Ghost Story* I had nightmares about here for weeks. It wasn't until my curiosity on how it was created took over that it stopped waking me up at night.

Tell us about your contribution to our book. What was the inspiration?

I got the opportunity to be invited to create "Lacy Charm" for one of the country's leading haunted attractions, Ominous Decent. Eric Dodson, who is one of the key players in the creation of the haunt, approached me with the idea. She has taken the skin off of the faces of beautiful women and put them together into one face that serves to make her the most beautiful she can be.

Describe the perfect Halloween.

I have so many ideas. How long can this be? Transform my whole house and have a crazy awesome party that may or may not involve a murder mystery. Rent out a huge building that has a haunt, huge kids fun activity area, adult party zone, and invite all my family and friends to enjoy it all. It would be totally decked out scenically with different themes in different areas: i.e. Swamp, Castle, Traditional Haunted House, Graveyard, Syfy area, etc. There would be bars and food everywhere, DJ and live bands. Basically an in door/outdoor Halloween style "Burning man".

What I do now: Invite anyone that wants to come and attend my company's annual Halloween party at Pointe Orlando. For the past sixteen plus years, Morphstore.com and Makeup and Creative Arts, LLC has hosted an annual Halloween party at Adobe Gilas. It's open to the public, no cover charges, and it's all about just enjoying Halloween with good people. We have a costume contest, and there are food and drink specials. It's been a great time every year and it keeps getting bigger. You never know what the future will bring and how big it will get.

SCARE CRED: ANDY WRIGHT

Andy is the founder/owner of Makeup and Creative Arts, LLC, which he founded during the tail end of his many years in the theme park industry. MCA was created on the basis of complete concept, design, performance, and integrity. MCA has been at the forefront in designing and creating leading icon characters for major theme parks, commercials, film, and television It also produces a wide range of applications from corrective and daily makeup, to elaborate, multi-piece, overlapping appliances (foam and silicone), full body figures, suits, and an array of props, masks, and prototyping. Along with its growing client base, MCA is the driving force that creates everything for Morphstore.com. With a strong team of in-house artists and a broad range of talented seamstresses, scenic designers, carpenters, and fabricators, MCA uses up to date industry standard materials and digital design that allow the company to walk in both worlds of special FX makeup and atmospheric design.

Learn more at MakeupCA.com.

Special Thanks

I would like to thank the following individuals for without whom this book would not have been possible.

My Family:

My poor Wife who is not a fan of the genre and has endured countless hours of horror.

My Daughters who enjoy a good scary movie from time to time with their Dad.

My Mom – For turning our house into Castle Frankenstein every October.

My Uncle – Who actually built me a "House of Frankenstein" when I was young.

Dustin McNeill – My collaborator in designing the book. His tireless efforts and great kindness brought life to this project. His advice and his friendship mean the world.

David Clevinger – For the first professional haunt job, the education and the countless hours discussing horror and theatre.

Leonard and Jeanne Pickel – Norman says "come up to the house and have some toasted cheese sandwiches. You can meet my Mother… you'll like my Mother. And she'll like you."

I have also had the great opportunity to create some chilling experiences with the following artists. **Mike Aiello, David Hughes, Kim Gromoll, Ray Keim, Mike Wallace, Adrian LePeltier, Skip Sherman, Jason Surrell, Jerry Abercrombie**, and **TJ Mannarino**. Thank you for the morbid and macabre memories. We scared people.

Tom Savini – Barnum, Houdini, Savini - The greatest sinister showman.

Greg Nicotero – Always a friend.

Bob Burns – One of the greatest.

Forest J. Ackerman – *Uncle Forry* – Thank you for ushering in many of us and giving us a way to retain great moments of the monsters.

I HOPE WE DIDN'T SCARE
YOU TOO MUCH...

WE'LL BE LURKING FOR YOU

HAUNTERS TALE
VOLUME: 11

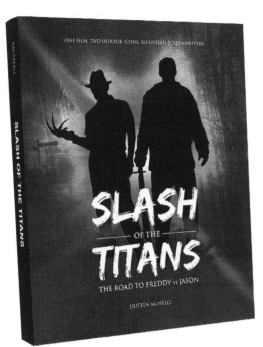

SLASH OF THE TITANS: THE ROAD TO FREDDY VS JASON

PLACE YOUR BETS, WINNER KILLS ALL! Get ready for a revealing look at why it took New Line Cinema nearly ten years and four-million-dollars to find the right screenplay for 2003's *Freddy vs Jason*. Featuring new interviews with the original writers and filmmakers (including Robert Englund and Ken Kirzinger!), *Slash* details the production's troubled history from the surprise ending of *Jason Goes to Hell* all the way to the crossover's red carpet premiere. Read about the many rejected storylines and learn how the project was eventually able to escape from development hell. This is the story of **one film, two horror icons** and **seventeen screenwriters**!

FreddyVSJasonBook.com

PHANTASM EXHUMED: THE UNAUTHORIZED COMPANION

A STORY OF BLOOD, SWEAT, AND SPHERES! Ready your shovels for *Phantasm Exhumed*, the first book on the making of the *Phantasm* franchise. Featuring more than sixty new interviews with cast, crew, effects creators and studio executives, *Exhumed* takes readers behind the scenes of the franchise that catapulted the Tall Man into the annals of horror iconography. Trace *Phantasm*'s history from forerunners *Jim the World's Greatest* and *Kenny & Company* through to *Phantasm: Oblivion* and beyond. Contained within are the classic tales of *Phantasm* lore along with production stories never before told by the filmmakers. Includes 250+ rare photos as well as set journals and introduction by Tall Man Angus Scrimm!

PhantasmExhumed.com

Made in the USA
San Bernardino, CA
15 January 2019